The Past is Ever Present

*A series of significant events
in the life of Thomas Puckle - A Novel*

P. J. Panckhurst

Also by P J Panckhurst
Links in the Chain: Published 2010

ISBN 978-1499753752

Acknowledgements

- Many thanks to all those who helped, encouraged, advised, prompted, or did whatever it took to get this project completed
- Jenna - for her layout and conversion skills
- Deb - for her cover design
- Ron - for his all-round encouragement and patience
- The friends who kept asking when it would be completed thereby encouraging me to finalise it

Special thanks to the other Pam for her meticulous proofreading, her constructive comments and for mentoring me all the way

P. J. P.

Contents

Part 1:
England, 1779

Chapter 1:
Thomas and Alfie

Thomas went back. He had run away many times before but he always went back. Sometimes the stress of his mother and father fighting would get too much for him and he would run away just to try and clear his head and assure himself that there was a better world out there. But he never went far enough to find out and did not get beyond the dirt and filth of the streets into which he had been born. Maybe there was no better place but he found it hard to believe that the whole world would be a replica of his environment. One day he would really leave, he told himself, but he loved his mother and he feared for her safety. That was why he kept going back. He had had enough beatings himself from his father to be afraid of what he might do to her. Sometimes he knew nothing until the next day when he awoke and found himself in the corner, battered and bruised and his mother, own face swollen, tending to him. They would hug each other and say nothing.

This time though, he had been away for two days. He had run away after the latest beating, sleeping in doorways and eating scraps from the street and rubbish bins. He was cold and hungry when he finally arrived back home. He thought of the shed behind the liquor store as home. It was the only place he had ever lived in and the store was where his father bought his booze. That was too handy though. Maybe his father would not be such a drunkard if they lived elsewhere, thought Thomas. He could never understand why his mother put up with it. It wasn't as if his father worked and supported them. Any money he did have he used to buy booze. If he wasn't in Ma Gutsell's liquor store he was in some other gin shop. They all sold the same cheap stuff that caused unwanted misery to many people. Where his mother found the money to put the meagre scraps of food on the table he would never know.

He pushed open the door of the shed. Silence greeted him. The shed was empty, totally empty. Everything had gone: the broken furniture, the filthy blankets they had used as beds, the pots and pans, everything that had made this shed his home. But most disturbing of all, his mother was gone. He gazed around, bewildered, and a dreadful sense of foreboding overtook him. He lowly sank to the floor.

Suddenly a shadow appeared in the doorway. He looked up hoping to see his mother but instead old Ma Gutsell stood there, her long skirts brushing the dirt floor. She and her husband owned the shed and were the ones who supplied his father with the booze.

'C'mon now. Y' gonna 'ave t' leave. Y' can't stay 'ere. We need the room.' She grabbed him by the collar and hauled him roughly to his feet. He pulled himself free.

'What're y' talkin' about? Where's me ma? Where's all our stuff?' The words came out hastily but his mouth was dry and he could not say them properly.

'Don't y' know? Where've y' bin, lad? Y' Ma killed y' Da. It was murder. Murder I say! Murder!' Her voice rose to a screech and Thomas covered his ears with his grubby hands and tried to block out the terrible words.

He could not believe what she was saying. It couldn't be true. It was all his fault. He should never have run away. He feared so much for his mother but never dreamed of her killing his Da.

'Where is she?' he whispered.

'They took 'er away somewhere. Dunno where but I do know she'll be 'angin' tomorrow.'

Thomas felt the room begin to spin. 'Nooooooo!' he moaned and fell in a dead faint at her feet. When he came around he was alone, still on the floor of the empty shed. He did not know how much time had passed and he stayed where he was, hoping that it was all a dream from which he would shortly awaken and his Ma would smile at him as she always did in the mornings, even after her worst beatings.

After a while he rose shakily to his feet. He needed to know more. He didn't think Ma Gutsell would bother telling him but he had to find out where his mother was and try to see her. He went outside, cold and miserable, his body still aching from his beating. He shivered as the wind penetrated his thin coat, and made his way to the street. It was still daylight as he wandered down the road looking for someone who might be able to help him. They all had troubles of their own though and didn't seem to spare a thought for Thomas. Suddenly he heard a shout.

'Tom! Where've y' been?'

He looked up saw and Alfie, the only friend he had in the world. His heart leapt as he crossed the narrow road avoiding the muddy potholes, and almost being knocked over by a beercart drawn by two large shire horses.

'Wotch art, boy!' the driver shouted at him, but Thomas was oblivious to everything except Alfie. He sat down on the edge of the road and Alfie sat beside him.

'I 'eard about what 'appened, Tom. I'm sorry. Watcha gonna do?' he asked.

'Dunno. I ran away again an' came back to this. Musta got too much for her. Do you know what she did?' asked Thomas staring at Alfie, his face beginning to crumble.

'Yeah, a bit.' Alfie paused and then continued. 'Two days ago it 'appened. Think your Da 'ad a go at her an' she up and stabbed 'im. I know 'e was your Da but 'e shouldna treated 'er like

11

'e did. You neither. 'E got what 'e deserved. He'd 'a killed 'er in the end me Ma says.'

Tom shuddered. 'I was always worried about that. Ma Gutsell says that they're gonna 'ang her tomorrer. I 'ave to find where she is. Do you know where they mighta taken 'er?'

'No, but Ma Gutsell should. She's the one who got the coppers. Go an' see her?' suggested Alfie.

Reluctant as he was to see Ma Gutsell again, Thomas agreed. 'She said she didn't know but we might as well ask her again anyway.'

He made no effort to move however and stared blindly at the people passing by, the traffic, the horse-drawn carts and hansom cabs that made their way down the dirty street. The people made no impression on him; nor did the young boys, caps askew and jackets buttoned up, as they swept the horse muck from the middle of the road into the gutter.

'Tom? You orright?' Alfie looked unhappily at his friend. 'We better git goin'. Y' comin' or not?'

'Yeah, 'spose so,' he answered. 'I always hated Ma Gutsell an' don't really want to see 'er again. But it's somewhere to start.'

They made their way back the way they had come and entered the liquor shop. It was crowded with people all in the same dishevelled state that his father had usually been in, drinking the poison that the Gutsells sold as liquor. The noise level from the patrons rose as Thomas and Alfie entered.

'Well, if it ain't the killer's kid. Better watch art boys, 'e might 'ave a knife.'

'Yeah, c'mon boy. Jest try it. Yer Dad was a foin man. There's many 'ere as would like t' get even for 'im.'

'Fine man like 'ell,' retorted Alfie in disgust. ' 'E was a scum bag an' din't deserve to live. You're all as bad as 'e was. Look at y'all. You're drunken sots.'

12

'Now, now. Don't want no more trouble in 'ere.' Ma Gutsell flapped around and tried to shoo the boys out of the door as several of her patrons advanced on them. 'Get art wiv you. Garn, get art! You lotta nuffin' but trouble.'

'What've you done with Tom's stuff?' Alfie asked.

'Eh? Oh, it's bin sold to pay for what I was owed,' Ma Gutsell eyes looked shifty as she answered. 'I ain't gonna be arta pocket for the likes of you.'

'Do you know where they took me Ma?' asked Thomas quietly.

Ma Gutsell stared at him. 'Whatcha wanna know for? Y' can't do nothin' about 'er. She's gonna 'ang tomorrow. Y' could try the jail in Rosamond Street, I s'ppose,' she relented, 'but don't expect it'll 'elp. Now get art. Ye've wasted enough of me time,' she said as pushed them out the door and slammed it shut.

Thomas stared at it ruefully and Alfie aimed a kick at it.

'C'mon Alfie. It won't do no good.' Thomas restrained him.

The two boys started down the road to Rosamond Street when Thomas stopped. 'Alfie, do you think your Ma would let me have some bread? I haven't eaten properly for days an' me head keeps goin' round an' round.'

'You wait right here,' answered Alfie, glad that he could do something positive and he rushed away to see what he could find. Tom's mind was numb. He couldn't think straight. He sat on the edge of a horse trough and waited. Eventually Alfie reappeared and thrust some bread and cheese into his hand.

'The best I could do. Ain't much food at our 'ouse an' me Ma's not very pleased about what's 'appening. We'd better stay away for a bit,' he said. While Thomas ate the food he mulled things over in his mind. 'What're you gonna do when all this is over?' he asked. 'Y' can't help your Ma. Y' know that, don't ya?'

13

'I 'ave t' try, Alfie. She's me Mum 'an I love 'er. I 'ave to do somethin'.' He finished his bread and cheese and stood up. 'C'mon let's go.'

They made their way to Rosamond Street and soon found the jail. It was a small building consisting of one room in the front and a narrow passageway with barred cells on either side leading off it. The sergeant behind the desk looked up as they entered and eyed them suspiciously.

'Well, what is it?' he asked brusquely.

'Please,' ventured Thomas nervously. 'We're looking for me Ma. Is she here?'

'Who's she? We got lots'a women 'ere. Shut up!' he yelled as a clamour started coming from the cells. People were shouting out and Thomas started towards the racket thinking that perhaps his mother was there and had heard him. The sergeant was too quick for him and before he knew it he was tossed out into the street. Alfie followed.

As they picked themselves up, Thomas said, 'I'm goin' back in.'

He re-entered putting his hands up in front of him. 'Please,' he said again. 'I need to know where me Ma is. If she's not 'ere, where could she be?'

'What's 'er name?'

'Mary Puckle'

'You 'ave to be joking,' the sergeant exclaimed. 'She's a murderess. You don't think we'd keep a murderess 'ere, do ya? Not only that, she's bin convicted, so she's not 'ere. No, lad, she's in a place where you don't want t' see 'er. Best not go. Now get orf 'ome.'

'But she's gonna 'ang tomorrow. I can't let that happen. I 'ave t' see her and I 'ave to get the 'angin' stopped! Please,' pleaded Thomas.

14

'Now listen to me, boy. There's nought you can do. She said that she killed 'im, she's 'ad 'er trial an' the verdict's bin given an' that's that! Now be orf,' the sergeant stated, waving them away. 'If you wanna see 'er be at the Square at eleven o'clock in the morning. Then you'll see 'er. Now get a move on or you'll find yourself in trouble too,' he said, as he pushed Thomas towards the door.

Suddenly Thomas shouted at the top of his voice, 'Are you in there, Ma?' There was a lull in the clamour from the cells but no answering voice from his mother. Thomas felt hopeless. 'C'mon, Alfie, it's no use. Let's go.'

It was getting dark as they made their way down the road. Thomas spotted a policeman. 'Sir, please, where do they take the prisoners who are to be 'a-a-anged.' He could hardly say it now.

'Well now lad, it's a 'ell-'ole that you wouldn't wanna see. 'Tis for the damned, for those that done such a wrong there ain't no salvation. It's in the middle of 'Is Majesty's Prison and there ain't no way you can go there. Now be orf,' he said and continued on his beat.

'Tom, leave it. We can't do anymore.' said Alfie. He hesitated. 'I can't take you to my house. Me Ma ain't 'appy about all this. We could sneak into your shed and stay there the night. How's about it? Old Ma Gutsell needn't know and we'd leave early in the morning.'

'Yeah, I suppose. I dunno what else to do. I'm so tired.' Thomas's face showed defeat and his voice quivered.

They crept into the shed and quietly closed the door. 'Are y' 'ungry, Tom?' asked Alfie, ' 'cos I'm starvin'. What say I go an' find some nosh somewhere?'

'Y' mean steal it? What if y' get caught? Y' could 'ang too. It's too risky.'

'I've done it before. I'll be careful. Back in a minute,' and Alfie slipped out the door and took off into the night.

Thomas lay on the floor, cold and shivery but he didn't notice the discomfort. He thought of his mother, what she had done and what was going to happen to her. He did not grieve for his father. He would be no loss to him. He felt the tears well up in his eyes as he thought of his mother though and he could not stop them from overflowing. She would be so scared. He pulled his knees up to his chin and sobbed silently. He did not even hear Alfie return.

'Tom, old man. Ya 'ave t' be strong. Look! I found us some pies. Ye'll feel better after y' get some food inter ya. We'll worry about tomorrer when tomorrer comes.' He took some pies out from under his jacket as Thomas sat up and wiped his face.

'You're a good friend to me Alfie. Where did these come from?' he asked.

'I 'ad t' go a wee way to get 'em. Don't worry about it. No one saw me and no one followed me. Eat 'em up.' Alfie tucked into his pie and eyed Thomas thoughtfully. 'D'ya think it's a good idea to go tomorrer? It'll be awful.'

'How can you ask that? 'Course I 'ave to go. I know it'll be awful but maybe my being there might help 'er some 'ow. Y' don't 'ave t' come.'

'It's not that, 'though me Ma 'ill skin me if she finds art that I went. She's always bin against public 'angin's. Ghouls she calls the people who go to watch. But I want to be there for you, Tom. You're me friend.'

They ate their pies in silence. There was nothing more to be said. Huddling down on the cold floor of the shed together they tried to sleep.

***

The following morning found them in the town square at eleven o'clock along with several hundred other citizens. There was an air of excitement. Many of them had seen a public hanging before and were full of excitement. Thomas had not and because this was his first, and more importantly his mother was the one to be executed, he was full of fear.

The gallows had been erected in the centre of the square and the crowd gathered all around even though the felons had not yet been brought in. People were leaning out of the windows of the surrounding buildings, waving their arms and shouting excitedly in anticipation of the upcoming event. Thomas and Alfie pushed their way to the front and sat on the ground. They could see that there were three nooses. They didn't speak. The noisy rabble around them made hearing difficult anyway. After a few moments the noise rose to a crescendo as people were shouting, 'Here they come!' The boys stood up and Alfie took Thomas's hand.

The crowd parted and a horse-drawn wagon wound its way through and stopped behind the scaffold. Thomas saw his mother in the wooden cage on the back. He felt the tears welling up in his eyes and his body began to shake. The other two prisoners were men. All had their hands tied behind their backs and as they were led up the steps of the scaffold, Thomas's mother tripped. He jerked forward but Alfie held him back. 'No, Tom,' he hissed, 'y' can't help 'er. We shouldn'a come. Let's get outa here.'

'No,' Thomas quickly replied. 'I need to be 'ere for 'er sake as well as mine.'

The three prisoners stood with their hands tied behind them, his mother being the last in the line. The noose was put over the head of the first man. He seemed resigned to his fate and stood impassively as the Sergeant read loudly from his charge sheet.

'Charles Murdoch. You 'ave been tried an' found guilty of the crime of theft and 'ave been sentenced to 'ang.' He paused dramatically. ' 'Ave you anythin' to say?'

The priest on the scaffold with them read rapidly from his Bible as the man called Charles shook his head. The crowd was hushed. A second later the trapdoor beneath him opened and he fell. There was a loud murmur from the crowd.

A noose was placed on the second man and the Sergeant read again from his charge sheet. 'Robert Bell. You 'ave been sentenced to 'ang for the crime of assault. 'Ave you anythin' to say?' This man called out in a loud voice. 'I didn't do it.' The trapdoor opened and he too, fell.

The mob roared and Thomas felt himself tensing up. He kept his head down. He would not look at the men slowly rotating at the end of the ropes. The same procedure followed with his mother. 'Mary Puckle, you 'ave been sentenced to 'ang for murder. 'Ave you anythin' to say?'

Thomas looked up just as his mother saw him. She shouted, 'I did it for you, Thomas!' Then she too fell.

'Ma a a a!' Thomas's voice was drowned by the rising clamour from the crowd and it took him a second or two to realise that their shouts were directed at him.

'Run, Thomas, run,' bellowed Alfie. 'I'll be behind you. Don't stop.'

Thomas turned and started running. He was hampered somewhat by the crowd but panic and fear enabled him to evade the outstretched hands eagerly trying to restrain him. Eventually he found himself beyond the crowd but he kept on running, running, he knew not where but he kept on going. Alfie was nowhere in sight. Eventually he fell to the ground, too exhausted to move. He was on a grassy verge of the road just beyond the town boundary. He lay there gasping in the cool fresh air, the trees overhead offering shaded protection from the hot sun. Finally he fell asleep.

***

It was getting dark when he woke. Maybe it was all a dream, he thought, but the nightmare would not go away. It had happened. His mother had killed his father and had been hanged for her crime. He was on his own. He lay quietly and as his head cleared a little he began to assemble his thoughts.

He was twelve years old. Many boys his age had struck out on their own and were responsible for themselves. When he had had his mother he never would have considered going off. Now that had all changed. He didn't want to think of his mother though, and pushed her to the back of his mind. There would be time to think and grieve for her later. For now, though, he had to think of himself. The crowd had frightened him. He couldn't understand why they were so hostile to him. What had he done? Hopefully they would have dispersed and forgotten all about him by now. He wanted to see Alfie and make sure that he was safe.

A plan formed in his mind. He would go to Alfie's home first and having assured himself that he was well, he would follow a road to somewhere, anywhere. The destination did not matter much.

Chapter 2:
Thomas turns his back

His eyes drifted from the cottage door to the privy and back again. Alfie had to come out sometime. It was getting near bedtime and there was a continuous stream of his younger siblings as they prepared themselves for bed. Finally Alfie appeared. Tom let him go about his business and as he emerged through the privy door he called, 'Pssst! Alfie!'

Alfie jumped with fright and then relaxed when he saw who it was. 'Tom, what on earth are y' doin' 'ere?' he asked.

'Waitin' for you. Your mum is against me so I couldn't knock. Had to make sure you're alright after what 'appened today,' Thomas answered glumly.

'Yeah, I'm fine. Look, come inside. Maybe we can talk Ma around. She knows what happened an' she knows it wasn't your fault. She also knows that I went an' she 'asn't skinned me yet. C'mon. Dad's at work.' Thomas felt uneasy but Alfie insisted.

He led the way inside to where Alfie's mum was ushering the little ones to their beds. Alfie's home-life was such a contrast to Thomas's. Alfie had a father who worked hard to provide for his family. He was a firm but kindly man and his family respected him. His mother tended her brood with all the devotion of a mother hen. They had a real home, with furniture and beds, food which, if not always plentiful, was good and nourishing. Most of all, there was love. All the things Thomas had never had except the love from his mother. Sometimes Alfie's family was short of money, but they managed.

'Hello, Tom. Where've you bin? I'll see to these tykes and then be with you. Alfie, find Tom some food. There's a bit of stew in the pot.'

Alfie raised his eyebrows and smiled at Thomas. 'Told ya,' he mouthed as he busied himself dishing up some stew. Thomas sat down and put his head in his arms. He was very tired.

'Here y' are. Get this into ya. Ma,' he asked as his mother appeared. 'Can Tom stay here tonight? 'E's nowhere t' go. 'E can sleep wiv me an' Billy. Look at 'im. 'E's exhausted.'

His mother was quiet for a few seconds then she spoke. 'You're right, Alfie. Ye've been through too much for a young lad, Tom. You shouldn't 'ave gone to the Square today. Some sights shouldna' be seen. Your ma was a good woman and deserved far better than she got with your Pa.' She busied herself in the kitchen. 'Try not to worry about things tonight. We'll talk about it in the morning. Now eat that up and get yerselves off to bed. Look after him, Alfie.'

Billy was already asleep in the bed that he shared top to tail with Alfie. It was a tight squeeze for the three of them but Thomas didn't care. He didn't want to go to sleep but just to enjoy the warmth and comfort of his surroundings. However he could not fight the overwhelming weariness that overtook him and despite his best efforts, his eyes closed.

*****

'I've made up me mind about what I'm gonna do, Mrs Pyke. I've no one here 'cept Alfie. I'm worried about yesterday's mob. They seem to think that me Ma did what she did because of me. I dunno why.'

'Them mobs get really wound up at 'angings an' such things. They don't care who's right an' who's wrong.' Mrs Pyke muttered. 'They're worse than a pack of wolves.'

'I was always worried about 'er getting killed. Anyway they won't forget me in a hurry and who knows what might happen if I show me face. Best keep well out of the way and head off to the country where no one knows me.'

'Are y' sure that's the best?' Mrs Pyke did not like the thought of him going off on his own but she did not feel any responsibility for him. After all he was twelve years old, and many young people that age took care of themselves.

'Yes. I need to give it a go. I'm worried that that crowd might realise that I'm here and that wouldn't be too good for you either. I'll be alright. When does Alfie get back?' Alfie was beginning an apprenticeship with a shoemaker and although he didn't particularly want to make shoes, he felt proud to have a job particularly when many young ones had nothing. Thomas didn't want to leave before he got back.

'Not 'til tea. If y' really are gonna go, I'll get some things ready for y' t' take. I'll pray everyday for ya, Tom and who knows, you might come back one day.'

***

Alfie and his father accompanied Thomas to the outskirts of the town. It was dark. Thomas was getting good at ignoring the realities of his situation and did not dwell on the fact that shortly he would be taking his leave of Alfie, the only person left that he cared for. He had pushed all thoughts of his mother to the back of his mind and had managed to get through the day without giving in to any feelings of despair.

'Tom, we've to leave y' 'ere,' said Alfie's father. 'Before ya go, I've a few words to say to ya. Ye've done nothin' wrong. Ye must remember that. Your mother's crime weren't your crime in spite of what the mob may 'ave thought.'

'I know,' answered Tom, 'but I'm not going to wait around to talk to them about it.'

Mr Pyke smiled. 'No, of course not. Remember that the night is for sleepin', not for travellin'. Ya don't need to 'ide from people for fear that they might recognise ya. Keep ya 'ead up 'igh. Don't give anyone cause to be suspicious. Stride along the roads full of confidence as if ya owned the world.'

'I'll try and remember what you say. I'll need people to help me so I'll 'ave to look sure of myself. Don' feel it, though.' His shoulders slumped a little.

'I wish I could come with you, Tom,' said Alfie. 'It'd be a real adventure.' He swung the burlap sack from his shoulders and handed it to Tom. ''Ere's your food. Make it last as long as ya can an' please try to get messages back to me. I'm going to miss you so much.'

Tom put his arms around him. 'We'll see each other again, Alfie. You're my best friend. Always remember that, but I 'ave to go. I'll come back one day, I promise.'

He put the bag on his shoulder, picked up his bedroll and turning his back on his old life, headed off down the road. He did not look back. He wouldn't have been able to see anyone anyway, so blinded was he by the tears that filled his eyes.

***

He trudged along in the moonlight, taking care not to trip on the rough ground and finally he came to an old derelict shed. Thinking that it would do nicely for his first night, he flopped down on the dirt floor. It reminded him of his home and he sat up quickly and tried to put all thoughts of that out of his mind. '*Not yet*,' he told himself, '*Time for thoughts later.*'

He had a look in his sack. Mrs Pyke had been very kind and had given him some bread, potato-cakes, cheese and a bottle of home-made lemonade. He knew that they didn't have a lot themselves and he felt extremely grateful. He'd had tea before leaving and for once in his life he did not feel hungry. He put it all back and took out the pocket knife which Alfie had given him. 'You might need to hunt rabbits or fish,' he had said. Thomas clasped it to his chest. He knew what it cost Alfie to part with it. It would be a long time before he saved up two shillings for another one. This was precious. Also in the bag was a tin containing fishing hooks made by Mr Pyke, and some string. If he did succeed in catching something though, he didn't know how he would cook it.

It had been his idea to leave at night, mainly so that no one would see him but also in order to have an early start in the morning. He had a few sips of the delicious lemonade and then curled up in his blanket and settled to sleep, his head resting uncomfortably on his sack. The moon shone through the open door of the shed, comforting him. He knew that the same moon and stars were shining on Alfie and that made him feel closer.

Sleep was a long time coming but eventually he drifted off into a restless slumber, only to awaken some time later gasping, panicking. He couldn't breathe, and clawed frantically at his throat desperately trying to remove the constriction that was choking the life out of him. It took him a few minutes to realise that it was nothing but a dream and he collapsed in a heap, panting for breath. He lay there not moving as grief finally overtook him. He relived his dream and understood the reality of his mother's last minutes of life. He sobbed broken-heartedly and pounded the earthen floor with his fists. When he had no more tears left he lay quietly. Maybe this was the time to confront all the circumstances that had led to his situation. He had to lay his mother to rest. Thomas was only twelve years old but some inner sense told him that if he did not do so, he would always be haunted by the nature of her death. He could control his thoughts during the day but not when he was asleep.

He sat quietly. An owl hooted somewhere in the night. He thought of his mother dead, but this time he was calmer about it, and his heart more settled. She was at peace. She had had no peace while she was alive, and although she had committed a terrible crime, Thomas felt that she would not suffer eternal damnation as the policeman had said. He would not think about the way she died, but more about the fact that she was dead, gone away from all the violence and suffering to a better place. Although he missed her dreadfully and felt so alone, he could not in all honesty wish her back into a world with his father, the man who had caused them both so much misery.

He stood up slowly and went to the door of the shed. The stars were still shining brightly and he focussed on the brightest one. 'I know you're up there, Ma. Be at peace and remember that I love you.'

Chapter 3:
On the Manor Estate

Thomas woke early from an emotionally disturbed sleep. He had lain curled up on the dirty floor of the shed and on awakening felt like burying his head in his arms and staying where he was. The thought of facing the day was almost too much for him. He lay quietly for a while listening to the birds greeting a new dawn and envied them their joy in anticipation of another day.

He finally dragged himself to his feet and looked out the door at the breaking morning. It promised fine weather with clear skies overhead and a slight breeze rippling through the trees.

After a breakfast of cold potato cakes and lemonade, he began his trek. He felt a little more settled and almost began to enjoy himself as he tramped along the road. It was a main road from Athelney, the town that he had just left, and it carried quite a lot of traffic. It was full of ruts and potholes and the carts and wagons lurched dangerously as the horses dragged them along. He remembered what Mr Pyke had told him and after initially walking with his head down, he gained more confidence and began greeting the passers-by with his head high albeit still a little nervously.

He stopped at a bridge and refilled his water bottle from the small stream. As he looked at the fresh flowing water he mentally took his unhappy thoughts and tossed them into the brook. *'There!'* he said emphatically, *'Go and leave me alone.'* He followed the progress of a leaf as it floated downstream and out of sight and imagined that his problems and sadness were floating away with it.

Staring into the waters, he spotted a fish basking in the sun just below the bridge. He didn't need extra food yet, but thought that it might be fun to try to catch one. He needed to practise anyway. He had never fished before and now he felt that there was no point in leaving it until he was starving to learn how to do it. He carefully opened the tin containing his string and hooks. He had five of them, bits of fine wire carefully bent upwards and with a small notch cut near the sharp end and a ring twisted at the other. He attached a piece of string to one of them and leaning over the side of the stone bridge, dangled it in the water above the fish. It scuttled away.

Disappointed, he continued to dangle the hook in the hope that there might be more fish but he didn't see any. After an hour or so he packed up his gear and continued on his way.

This was a totally new environment for Thomas. The traffic on the road thinned out somewhat and as he tramped along he took note of his surroundings. The narrow road was bordered by hedges and thickets behind which were fields of sheep. Further distant were stands of tall trees, oaks, elders and elms, unlike anything that Thomas had seen before.

By sunset he was feeling very weary and looked around to seek a suitable place to shelter for the night. He was well out in the country with farmland all around. He could see a wooded area some distance off and turning down a side lane he made his way towards it. The lane was bordered on either side by neatly trimmed hedgerows and although he could see some small cottages they did not appear to have any outbuildings that he could make use of. He kept on going and eventually found himself on the outskirts of the forest. A cool breeze made him decide to enter it and he kept going until he came across a thicket surrounded by very tall trees. He pushed his way in and it closed behind him. He stomped the grasses and bushes as flat as he could and after eating a little more of his food and water he settled down and attempted to get comfortable.

He heard many strange noises as the forest settled down to its nightly activities. It was a little unnerving for Thomas, who had never been in the woods at any time, let alone at night. He told himself that there was nothing to be frightened of, but then what did he know of stoats and weasels or foxes, wolves and boars? Nothing fortunately, so through exhaustion he slept reasonably well and awoke to the sound of birds calling their morning songs.

He brushed the twigs and leaves off his clothes and gathering up his belongings, wormed his way out of his sanctuary. Standing up, he came face to face with a man and his dog. The man looked just as startled as Thomas. He glowered at Thomas who gaped at him in astonishment.

The man was quite short but powerfully built. He wore a long green jacket with brown flaps over two deep pockets. On his head was a battered old hat and on his feet were boots that came up to his knees. Two leather bags, the straps of which crossed over his chest were slung over his shoulders. Out of one poked a dead rabbit's head and out of the other were two hind feet. He carried a gun over his shoulder and a long beating stick.

'And what might you be doin' 'ere, young lad?' he demanded roughly. 'This is private property, don't you know?'

Thomas stared at him in amazement. 'W-w-where did you come from?' he stammered, trying not to look guilty.

'That ain't none of your business. I wanna know what you're doing here so early in the morning. 'Ave you been poaching?'

Thomas fearfully eyed the shotgun. 'No,' he answered slowly. 'Have you?'

As quick as lightening the man shot out his hand and grabbed Thomas by the collar. The dog growled. 'Now see 'ere, you,' he hissed. 'We won't be 'aving any of your lip. Turn out your bag now. C'mon. 'Urry up.'

Thomas did not like the look of the man nor the dog and just as he was thinking of making a run for it, the man grabbed his bag and emptied the contents on to the ground. He seized the tin and opened it.

'Uh huh! Just as I thought. Bin doin' some fishin'.' He picked out the hooks and looked at them. 'Won't catch much with these but e'en so poachin' is stealin' and stealin' is a jailin' offence. String's wet so it's been in the water.' He shoved them back in the tin. ' 'Ave you anything to say?'

Thomas was dumbfounded, but soon terror overtook him and he turned and bolted. The dog took off after him and in a matter of seconds Thomas was prostrate on the ground and the dog was standing over him. He buried his head under his arms and waited for the shot. Nothing happened. Slowly he lifted his head and watched wide-eyed as the man ate one of his potato cakes.

'Hey, there!' he shouted. 'You leave them alone. They're mine and you're stealing them.' Emboldened he added, 'You could hang for that.'

The man took a step towards him. 'Smart arse, ain't ya? You'd better come along with me. Mr Cotter can sort you out. You're a cheeky young 'ooligan.'

'Who's Mr Cotter?' asked Thomas putting his meagre belongings back in his burlap sack.

'He's the head gamekeeper on this 'ere estate. I'm 'is assistant. We make sure that no one the likes as you goes bagging game or animals off this 'ere land. Belongs to Sir Edric Spicer it does, and he don't like no one poachin' from him. He's very strict about that. C'mon.'

'I wasn't poaching,' Thomas protested. 'I was just sleeping in there. Go on. Have a look. You'll see where it's all been flattened. Go on. You'll see.'

'Don't tell me what to do. 'Course you was sleepin' ya lazy oaf. That's what layabout's do. Still that's trespassin' an' that's almost as bad as stealin'. You come with me and don't try to run. Bongo 'ere will have you down again in a flash.'

He strode off and Thomas was very tempted to make a run for it but he noticed that Bongo kept very close to him and not his master. They walked for about an hour through the forest but neither of them spoke. Terrifying thoughts ran through Thomas's head and he tried not to think of what might become of him after this occurrence. Eventually they came to a track along which they continued for a short distance before coming to signs of habitation. There were a dozen stone cottages grouped together and a mile or so beyond these was an imposing manor house set in park-like grounds.

'Sir Edric's 'ome,' said his escort nodding in the direction of the large house. 'The people in the cottages work for 'im. Lots of other people do too but they don't all live in the village.' He spoke as if trying to impress on Thomas the extent of Sir Edric's power and influence. ' 'Is land extends for miles around. 'E's very rich. Ya don' wanna take 'im lightly, boy. 'E could crush ya jist like that,' and he stamped his foot heavily on the ground.

Thomas stood and looked in awe. The stone manor house was three storeys high. The long, wide driveway wound its way through the garden to the front entrance. Wide steps led up to the heavy wooden door where a huge portico was supported by massive columns. The many symmetrical windows were ornately framed with elaborate surrounds and the huge chimneys with their terracotta smoke pots emerged grandly from the massive roof.

Marty led Thomas along a side path which skirted around the back of the big house to a large cobblestone courtyard. There were many stone buildings there but the biggest of these was the stables. It housed not only the horses for the family's use, but the farm horses as well. Sir Edric was a very keen horseman and as well as the essential horses for farm work he had some very good racing stock. Thomas could tell that he must be very rich.

Beside the stables was a small stone building and this was where Thomas was led. He didn't know what to expect but he tried to be brave. One thing he was very sure of was that he would not allow himself to go to jail or worse, be hanged. He would rather be shot than have that happen. He stood up straight in front of a tall muscular man and endeavoured to look in control of himself. He grasped his hands tightly behind his back to try and keep himself from shaking.

'What have we here, Marty?' the man grunted as he slowly stood up. He was very tall with large gnarly hands which he rubbed together as he stood looking down at Thomas.

'Caught 'im in the forest real early, Mr Cotter,' said Marty. ' 'E had fishing gear in 'is bag. Said that 'e'd been sleeping in the thicket but confessed that 'e did try to catch some fish yesterday. Thought I'd better bring 'im in. 'e was a bit troublesome and tried to run away but Bongo brought 'im down.'

'What's your name, lad?' Mr Cotter asked.

'Thomas... Tom I mean,' he answered thinking that Tom might make him sound older.

'Well Tom. What have you to say for yourself? You'd better make it good.' Mr Cotter sat down again.

Thomas wondered where to start. What did they want to know? He hesitated.

'Come on, boy. Don't muck about. We know what you've been up to! You're a poacher.' Marty was getting impatient and started stomping around.

'Be quiet, Marty. I'll handle this,' Mr Cotter interjected. 'I've heard your side; now you can get on with your work and leave me to deal with Tom. Off you go. Alright, Tom,' he said when Marty had angrily taken himself off. 'Take your time.'

Thomas watched Marty slouch across the yard and gathered his thoughts. He had an idea that Mr Cotter might give him a fair hearing but was sure that Marty didn't like him.

'I don't have anyone. My Ma and Pa both died and I had to move on and look after m'self. I walked from my village of Athelney and slept the first night in an old shed, and the next night in your thicket. So I haven't come far. I had some food with me and there's still some left in my sack. I tried catching some fish even though I didn't need them. It was just for fun, really. That's all there is to it. I wasn't poaching. Marty is a bully.'

Mr Cotter was silent then asked, 'What did they die from? Your parents, what killed them?'

Thomas hesitated. Maybe this man might be a little bit fairer than the man called Marty but he was still in a vulnerable situation. He must be careful. 'They just died,' he answered cautiously. 'I dunno what happened but there was nothing to make me stay.'

'Coppers aren't hunting you, are they boy?'

'No, o' course not. Why would they?' Thomas held his head up but could not look directly at Mr Cotter.

Mr Cotter studied him closely. Thomas was not good at lying and the man knew from his face that there was something that he was keeping from him. However he would not push the issue at this time.

'Well, Tom. I think that you were in the wrong place at the wrong time when Marty found you. If he hadn't you might well have gone on and got into real trouble. You have to make sure that you are not on private land before you fish or snare or net or whatever. If you are on private land that is poaching and is a very serious crime — you could be hanged or deported.'

Tom felt the terror rising again and looked round to find the nearest door. There was only one and he was about to bolt for it when he heard Mr Cotter say, 'I don't think we'll be hanging you but I think we can use you.'

Tom gathered his thoughts and listened. 'We had a young lad just like you working here. He did a lot of chores including cutting firewood for the manor house. Can you imagine how much wood and coal we use keeping that place going? He was chopping a while ago and he chopped his foot. It got infected and he died.' Cotter thought for a bit. 'We can't spare another worker to do his work and we ain't got anyone else. What about it or shall I send you back you came from? Where did you say? Athelney? '

There was no way that Tom wanted to go back. Not yet anyway and despite what Cotter might be thinking, he hadn't done anything wrong. He nodded slowly, trying not to look too eager. This place would be good to hide in for a while.

'Can I have some breakfast before I start? I've some bread in my bag.' He rummaged around and brought out a dry crust. Cotter smiled, took it out of his hand and cast it into a bin. He went to the door and called loudly to a young man who was walking past. 'Mac, take this boy to the kitchen and ask Cook to give him some breakfast. Bring him back here when he's finished. Tom, off you go with Mac. I'll see you again soon.'

Tom had never had such a good breakfast; three plates of oatmeal porridge, four slices of bread fried in bacon fat and a mug of milk.

'You look as though you haven't had a decent meal for a month, lad. What's your name?' asked cook.

'Tom,' he answered. 'I haven't had much to eat for a month although Mrs Pyke did make a pretty good stew.'

'Mrs Pyke?' queried Cook.

'She's my friend's Ma. Lives in my old town.'

'Which is where?'

Tom realised that he had relaxed his guard somewhat and clammed up about his background. He didn't answer but said,'That was very nice, thank you. I had better get back to Mr Cotter. He said that he'd some work for me.'

With that Mac entered the kitchen. 'Ready, Tom. Mr Cotter's waiting. He'll need tea as well,' he told cook. ' I think he's here to stay for a while. C'mon.'

They made their way back to Cotter's room. On his table were some clothes and a pair of boots. He picked them up and tossed them to Thomas. 'They might fit you,' he said. 'Will was about your size. They might be better than the ones you have.'

Thomas looked at them hesitantly. The dead boy's clothes. They appeared to be better than his own but then his were very worn and tatty. There was a jacket, shirt, knee breeches, socks and boots, one of which was damaged. He fingered them cautiously. 'Go on, put them on. We can't hang about here all day. There's work to be done. Mac, when he's changed, take him to the wood pile and get him started. Look out for him today.' Cotter gave his instructions and went off leaving Tom and Mac alone.

'I think he likes you, Tom,' said Mac.

'He seems nicer than that Marty. He would have had me hanged if it'd been left to him. I'll stay out of his way, I think.' Thomas changed his clothes but kept his own boots on. However he did put Will's boots and his own jacket in his bag. Thomas felt that he had done quite well for himself. He had a new home, some new clothes, a full stomach and a job.

By the end of the day he was not feeling quite as pleased. He collapsed into his bed of hay in the loft above the stables and looked at his hands. The skin was peeling from the burst blisters and blood was seeping through the raw flesh. After a little while he climbed down the ladder and gingerly washed them in the water barrel at the end of the building. He wondered how he would be able to hold an axe the next morning.

'You'll have to toughen up, boy.' It was Marty coming up behind him.. Thomas said nothing and dabbed his hands on his trousers to dry.

'Nothing to say, eh,' scoffed Marty. 'We'll see what you're made of. Give it a few weeks and I reckon you'll be outa here. Likes o' you are just wasters. Can't hack a good day's work.'

Thomas spent a restless night in the hay loft. He rolled up in a blanket trying to keep the hay from prickling him but not succeeding very well. It was quite noisy with the horses underneath in their stables blowing and wheezing. He could hear rats and mice scurrying around and got a real fright when the stable cat jumped on him. Nobody had told him that he would be sharing a bed with a mouse catcher. He didn't mind though. The cat purred as it cuddled up to him and its presence was comforting. He decided that he wouldn't worry too much about Marty but would try and stay away from him. He was just a bully. He liked Mr Cotter and Mac and there were other workers and farmhands around. Most of them lived in the village but one or two stayed on the estate. He wasn't sure where Marty lived and didn't really care. He would keep well out of his way.

***

During the next few weeks Thomas continued to chop firewood. His hands hardened and he didn't complain about them, nor did he mention his sore back. He grew stronger. Some days he was taken into the forest with a gang of men and there he learned how to fell trees with axes. He was in awe of the men who could fell a tree, roll it over a pit and with one man standing in the pit and another on the top with his feet firmly planted on two runners, they would saw the log into long planks. It seemed to take them no time at all. They also split logs with axes by using wedges when the grain was perfectly straight.

'Have a go in the pit, Tom. I'll go on top.' Mac was part of the gang today and wanted to test Tom. Tom jumped into the pit with alacrity and took hold of the saw. They started slowly at first to allow Tom to get into the rhythm. Then Mac quickened the pace. Sawdust fell into Tom's eyes and soon he was sawing blind and struggling to keep up with the pace. Just when he thought he would have to let go, Mac called a halt.

'Have a wee spell. You're keeping up pretty well,' he said.

Tom sank to his knees gasping for breath, his arms aching. He could not speak. After a few minutes Mac urged him to take hold of the saw again and soon they were finished. He had no strength left to clamber out of the pit and Mac hauled him out and dumped him on the ground where he lay panting. Just then Marty came along.

'Knew he wouldn't be able stand it,' he sneered.

'Wanna have a go, Marty? C'mon. Show the boy how it's done.' The boss of the gang called over to Ethan, by far the strongest of the group. 'You can partner him.'

'Do you want to be topdog or underdog?' asked Marty.

'I don't mind being under,' replied Ethan and jumped into the hole. Tom sat up. This could be interesting. He had a feeling that Marty was being set up.

They started at a fast pace and it wasn't long before Marty was losing his rhythm and struggling to keep up. His face got red

36

as he sucked in large amounts of air with each pull of the saw. The men gathered around.

'Hang in there, Marty. The lad finished. Can't let him beat you.'

Just then Marty's arms gave out and he toppled head first into the pit. There was a muffled cheer and then the men drifted back to their work. Ethan jumped out and the log remained partially cut, a mocking reminder to Marty that he should have kept his mouth shut. But Tom knew that he wouldn't forget his humiliation and in his own thick-headed way might blame him and seek revenge later.

Chapter 4:
How to ride a horse

The manor house had many rooms. As well as the firewood and coal for the kitchen, Tom had to ensure that there was an adequate supply for all the rooms that had a fireplace. And there were many. He was not allowed into these rooms. In the vast hallways outside the private family and guest suites, were huge trunks with massive lids. He had to keep these topped up with firing and the house staff transferred the logs and coal to the rooms. It was hard work and he was panting by the time he had carted his sixth bag of wood up the back staircase. He sank down on the floor beside the trunk and rested.

'What's your name?' a girl's voice asked him.

He jumped up with a start and felt himself colour with embarrassment.

'T-T-Tom,' he stammered.

'Do you always stutter like that?' she asked.

'N-n-no,' he answered.

'Well, that's twice in two words, so maybe you do,' she replied and skipped off down the hallway. Thomas stared after her. She was about his age and he assumed she was a daughter of the household. He carried three more loads up the stairs but did not see her again.

'What's her name, Mac?' he asked later when they were eating their evening meal.

'Now don't you go getting any silly ideas,' Mac replied. 'She's well above your station, lad and likely to stay there.'

Thomas flushed. 'I wasn't thinking anything. I just asked her name, that's all. I'm not stupid.'

' 'Course you ain't, lad. Just be careful.'

He did think about her though as he lay in his hay bed. Her name was Charlotte and he wondered what it was that allowed her to be born into such wealth and he into such poverty. It could easily have been the other way round. He tried to imagine himself living in the big house, waited on hand and foot by people ready to obey any command, able to have anything he wanted, riding horses, hunting and fishing on the estate. Would he really want that? It sounded pretty good but he sensed that the girl was not even as free as he was. His life had been hard but he was now his own person. He could do what he liked and he only had himself to worry about and nobody to answer to, except Mr Cotter of course.

He saw Charlotte a few times in the garden but he knew that he wasn't allowed to talk to her. Sometimes she would come to where he was chopping the wood and watch him. It made him very nervous and he told her to go away.

She laughed at him. 'I don't have to do anything I don't want to do and I certainly don't have to take any notice of you. Anyway I'm just watching.'

'Well, don't talk to me,' Tom said stiffly.

'You started it,' she replied huffily, and after a few more minutes she departed.

One day when she was watching and would not leave, he planted his axe in the chopping block, grabbed his jacket and walked off.

'Where do you think you're going, boy?' It was Marty. It seemed to Thomas that he was always around when he felt at a disadvantage, as he did now. 'Skiving, eh!'

'Shut-up, Marty. You're not my boss,' he answered.

Marty made to cuff him but suddenly noticed Charlotte watching him. He froze. 'What's bin going on 'ere? Wait 'til Sir Edric 'ears of this. You little upstart. You're for the chop now.' He rubbed his hands in glee. 'Gotcha this time.'

'Don't be so daft, y' big nutter. I didn't do nothin' and you know it.' Thomas turned around but Charlotte had disappeared. He went back to his chopping but was fearful of the cock an' bull story Marty would dream up. However he was totally unprepared when Mr Cotter informed him that Sir Edric wanted to see him. He felt panic rising in his chest. Who would believe his word as opposed to Marty's?

'I didn't do anything, sir,' he pleaded with Mr Cotter. 'I only spoke with Miss Charlotte to tell her to go away. If Marty says anything else he's lying.'

'I'll come with you,' answered Mr Cotter. 'Now wash yourself up a bit and don't forget to take your cap off when you meet Sir Edric.'

Thomas had never been beyond the hallways and his knees were shaking as he stood outside the big oak door to Sir Edric's library. He remembered Marty's words, ' 'E could crush ya, just like that.' Cotter tried to reassure him that if he had done nothing wrong, all would be well but he was not convinced and followed him into the room with much trepidation. He stepped inside and looked around, unable to believe his eyes. His mouth fell open as he gazed around him. He had never seen any like it in his life and did not know that such opulence existed. From the carpeted floor to the ornately decorated ceiling, the beautiful furniture and the well-stocked bookshelves... he was spellbound.

'Thomas,' hissed Mr Cotter.

Thomas started. He pulled himself together and moved up to the desk behind which sat Sir Edric. He was a fine looking man and Thomas felt dreadfully inferior in many ways.

'Put your head up boy, so I can see your face,' Sir Edric commanded. Instantly Thomas recalled the words of Mr Pyke. *'Keep your head up high, lad. You've done nothing wrong.'* He stood up straight and looked up.

'Marty Dewson tells me that you have been fraternising with my daughter,' Sir Edric said.

Thomas looked askance at Mr Cotter. 'He means being friendly with her,' he explained.

'I wasn't, sir. Really I wasn't, but she comes to see me when I'm doing my work and won't go away when I tell her to. Honest, sir, I know she's a well-bred lady and I'm nothing to the likes of her.'

'Marty says that there's more to it than that. He said that you meet her quite often.' Sir Edric stood up and walked around the desk to Thomas.

'He's lying, sir,' responded Thomas, desperately. 'Marty doesn't like me and he'd like me to get into trouble.'

'Why would he want to see you in trouble?' Sir Edric looked at Mr Cotter.

Cotter shrugged. 'Sir, ever since Tom came here Marty has scoffed at him or made fun of him. The men see that and they like Thomas and stick up for him. As a consequence Marty is often on the butt end of their jokes. The men won't be bullied, but Tom is just a kid and therefore fair game to Marty.' Sir Edric returned to his chair while Mr Cotter finished his explanation.

'Well, Thomas, I've spoken with my daughter and although I might not believe either you or Marty, I do believe her when she tells me that she's been watching you chop wood. Nothing else. I've told her to stay away from you and there's no need for me to tell you to stay away from her, is there?'

'N-n-no, sir,' stammered Thomas thinking that his knees were going to give way but somehow he held himself upright.

'Now, Cotter. Would you please tell Marty to see me as soon as he comes back. Thank you both, ...and Thomas, Mr Cotter tells me that you're a good worker. Keep it up. You may go now.'

'Yes, sir. Thank you, sir,' said Thomas and with a sigh of relief, he stumbled from the room.

'He's a good lad, sir,' ventured Mr Cotter when he had gone. 'I'm sure he has a history of some sort but I don't know what it is yet. I do trust him though.'

'Don't be too trusting of someone you don't know,' Sir Edric advised. 'He might let you down some day.'

Thomas never found out what passed between Sir Edric and Marty but he knew that it wouldn't be good for him, and he would have to be more careful than ever.

***

Some weeks later, Mr Cotter called to him across the courtyard. 'Tom! I need you.' Tom wandered over to him. 'You're to go out with Marty today. He needs to check out the stream up at the head of the lake. Outlet must be blocked. You can help him free it.'

Thomas' heart missed a beat. So far, since the episode with Sir Edric, he had managed to keep out of Marty's way, but to spend a whole day with him alone! He would have to be on his guard.

'We'll have to find you a horse,' Cotter continued. 'It's quite a step to the lake. We've a gentle mare that should be good for you. Come and we'll get you acquainted with her.'

'I think I know the one. A small grey that makes a heck of a noise when I'm trying to get to sleep. We get on well. I'd like to ride her.' Thomas had never ridden a horse before but he had watched others do it and he didn't think it could be too hard. Mr

Cotter showed him how to put the halter on and they led the docile creature out into the yard.

'Stand on the barrel and put your leg over her back,' Cotter instructed.

'Does she have a name?' asked Thomas as he did as he was told.

'Yep, it's 'Sweet Pea' 'cos she's as sweet as a pea can be. You won't have any trouble from her. Let's go into the paddock and you can have a trot around.' He led Sweet Pea by the halter whilst Thomas gripped the reins tightly. He felt himself slipping sideways.

'Grip her round her middle with yours legs, Tom. That'll help balance you.' Thomas steadied. Once in the paddock Cotter let go of the halter and Thomas was on his own. He walked Sweet Pea slowly around the paddock and back to Mr Cotter as Marty arrived.

'It'll take us all day to get to the 'ead o' the lake at that pace,' he mumbled. 'We'll have t' go faster than that or we'll be sleepin' up there.'

'Cut it out, Marty. Give him a chance. Now Tom, squeeze with your legs and gently kick your feet. She'll go a bit faster. That's it. Sit up straight. That's right. Don't lean over her neck or she'll think you want to go faster still. That's good. Now just gently pull back on the reins and loosen your legs when you want to stop. Right. Now sit still. There, that's all there is to it... to riding Sweet Pea anyway. You'll be fine. Watch out for him Marty. I'll see you both when you get back,' and with that Mr Cotter strode away.

'C'mon then, slow coach, we'd better make a start. Follow me.' said Marty and mounted his own horse. He had a saddle to which there were tied numerous bags and tools including an axe which Thomas presumed was to be used to help clear the blockage. Thomas didn't know where they were going and trailed along behind. They rode in silence. Thomas might have enjoyed it if he hadn't been so anxious about Marty. He was sure something would happen today and he didn't like the look of that axe.

'Mind if I walk for a little way, Marty? ' he called. 'I'm a bit sore.'

They had been on the track for over an hour and although the going was easy, it was a new experience for Thomas. Marty waved his hand and kept on going. Thomas was not sure if that was a 'yes' or a 'no' but he knew that he had to get off his horse for a stretch. He gently pulled on the reins and slid to the ground. He was hungry and thirsty but Marty had the food, or so he hoped. He plodded on and rounded a bend. Marty was nowhere in sight. The track kept going so he followed it until he came to a small river. He couldn't tell if Marty had crossed it or not. He yelled,

'Marte-e-e!' There was silence apart from the noises of the forest. He called again. 'C'mon man, where are you?'

Just then Marty appeared from the bushes on the far side of the river.

'If you can't keep up you deserve to get lost. Now get on your nag and get movin',' he yelled as led his own horse out of the bushes and mounted it. Thomas mounted Sweet Pea and splashed his way across. He kept close to Marty and was relieved when they finally reached the lake. It wasn't a very big lake but it was well stocked with fish. Sir Edric was very keen on his fishing and it was up to Mr Cotter and Marty to ensure that there was a ready supply and that the lake was always in good order. Hence their mission today to restore its natural flow.

They wound their way around it and finally came to a rocky creek.

'This is it. It feeds the lake and isn't flowing very well so it must be blocked further up. We'll eat first and then take a look,' said Marty as he tossed Thomas a packet containing bread, and a bottle of water. Thomas nodded and began to eat. He was ravenous and devoured the food very quickly. Marty took his time.

'If you've finished eatin' you can get on up there and see what you can find, but don't touch anythin'.' He waved his hand up the creek and Thomas thankfully started along the shingly shoreline. The less time he spent in Marty's company the better. He followed a slight bend in the stream and before long came to the blockage. Trees had fallen in a storm and had created a log-jam which captured other branches as they flowed along. Water had spilled over the banks and flooded the land. It was boggy and Thomas wondered how they would even get near the jam to release it. He was reflecting on this when Marty appeared.

'Now, boy! What do you think I've just done down there?' he asked.

'I dunno. Had your lunch, I 'spose.'

'Don't be dumb,' snarled Marty. 'If yer must know I tied the 'orses well back from the water. These trees have to go somewhere when we release 'em and we wouldn't want the horses swept int' the lake now, would we?'

Thomas could see the wisdom in this but didn't acknowledge it. He had an idea about how to clear the log-jam but didn't think that Marty would receive his suggestion kindly, so he waited for him to come up with his own idea.

'I think you should clamber out ont' the trees an' tie a rope on t' one of 'em. Then we might be able to dislodge it,' suggested Marty.

Thomas stared at him. 'You must be mad. The whole lot could go at any time with me standing on it. I'm not going to do it.

You can do it if you want, but I'm not.' He stood his ground as Marty advanced on him.

'I 'spose you have a better idea,' he sneered.

'Might have made sense if you'd brought a large grab hook,' retorted Thomas. 'Then we could have flung it across and had the horses pull it free. Wouldn't need to get too close that way.'

'Real smarty, ain't ya? Why don't ya go down and bring back the 'orses and gear. Make yerself useful.'

Glad to be doing something instead of arguing, Thomas headed back to where he had last seen the horses. They were not there. He looked around to see if he could locate where Marty had tied them. There was forest all around and he could not see them.

'Stupid Marty. What's he done with them?'

He stood on the bank of the creek whistling and hoping to get answering whinnies in return. Suddenly there was a terrifying roar and water rushed round the bend sweeping trees and branches along with it. Thomas reacted, but not quickly enough. He was swept off his feet and pushed into the centre of the swirling mass. He couldn't swim and felt himself beginning to panic as he went under the surface and popped up gasping and choking. He tried to grab a branch and just as he succeeded in getting a grip there was a blinding pain in his head. He fought to keep conscious but slowly the world turned black and he released his hold on the branch and floated with the debris into the middle of the lake.

Chapter 5:
Sam and Jenny

'I could do with a nice fish for me dinner. Gettin' a bit sick o' baked hedgehogs and toasted snails. What about it?' The woman looked at the man as he laid out the lengths of wood in a round tent-shaped pile. He didn't answer but continued his work. Inside the pile, oak logs had been cut and stacked in a cross-hatch pattern. He wondered if it had been a mistake to bring her into the forest with him. He was used to the life of a charcoal burner but although her life hadn't been a bed of roses, this existence was tougher and lonelier. He liked having her around though and she did help pass the long dark nights.

He watched as she laid earth and bracken on the pile and beat it with a paddle to flatten it and make a seal.

'It would make a nice change,' she smiled at him. 'I'd cook it nicely.'

He laughed at that and looked over to their home on the edge of the clearing. Some home... a framework of poles covered with sacks and turf. It was typical of a charcoal burner's hut but was quite cosy inside. A raised narrow bed occupied one side while a small table and two stools lined up along the other.

She cooked on an open fire outside. There was no point in building a permanent structure. They never remained in one place long enough to warrant it but moved on to wherever the wood was ready for cutting. The winter would be on them soon and the forest was no place to be camping in when the cruel cold weather descended. They would seek other employment until the cold season passed and then return to make charcoal again. It was getting harder to sell it now that furnaces were making coke but it was still worth the effort. He could see it coming to an end soon though.

These thoughts flashed through his mind in an instant and he saw that she was still waiting for an answer.

'We'd better finish this first and then we'll see. If we get it all ready and the weather is right tomorrow morning we'll light it.'

'You don't like poaching do you, Sam?' Jenny commented as she made her way around the pile, slapping more earth on the sides to ensure that there were no gaps.

'Do you like me going on to someone's land and stealing their fish and animals? That's what it is. Stealing, and the penalties if you get caught are harsh. And so they should be! If I got caught, I'd be hauled up before the local magistrate and I could be hanged or transported to heaven knows where. I'd be a convict and you'd never see me again. All for a bloody fish.'

He walked around the pile making sure that the airways around the bottom were clear. He would love a fish for his dinner too but he had been poaching several times and had had some near misses with the gamekeepers. They had unnerved him. The gamekeepers thought they were pretty special and lauded it over the locals. Mr Cotter wasn't so bad but that Marty Dewson, now he was a bad one. The keepers had a continuous battle with poachers, with the poachers often winning and getting away with their bag. Even rabbits were 'out of bounds' so to speak, if they were on private property. The gamekeepers could come into their homes and look for signs of poaching and woe betide the family if any was found. At least he could burn the evidence in his charcoal fire.

'Don't be like that, Sam. Of course I don't want that to happen. But we're fast running out of food. We've a few potatoes left, some flour for damper but nothing much of any substance.

Wee bit of porridge maybe? Just forget I asked. We could go into the town but it takes time and we have to be here tomorrow for the fire. Pity we don't have a stream through here, might have caught one there.'

'OK.' Sam said resignedly. 'I'll go down to Sir Edric's lake and hope like hell that there aren't any gamekeepers around. Will that keep ya happy?' Sam wanted to please her but it was risky. He knew that many men poached and that they only did it to feed their families. The fish in the lake were for Sir Edric and his cronies to provide a day of sport. They had plenty of food anyway and it was not critical for them. For the poachers though it often stood between them and starvation. Sam and Jenny finished off the pile and made ready to go.

'I'll come too,' said Jenny running to get her shawl.

'No you won't,' countered Sam. 'No point in two of us running a risk.'

'Don't be silly. I can be a lookout. Anyway you know you want me to,' she smiled sweetly at him.

He was silent for a moment and then scooped her into his arms and kissed her fiercely. 'I love you, Jenny Crean. You're to stay well back in the forest and if anything happens you're to come straight back here and wait. If I don't turn up, so be it.' He released her and grabbing his sack, set off for the lake with Jenny trotting alongside to keep up. It was getting dark but that was all to the good.

Having ensconced Jenny in the trees, he approached the lake with caution. All was quiet.

He made his way carefully round the shore until he came to a slight bank. He lay on his front and dropped his line into the water. He waited. Nothing. He tried again and again and again. Time passed and just as he was losing patience he felt a tug on the line. Very carefully he drew it in and there was his fish. He felt a

49

surge of exhilaration slightly marred by a twinge of guilt. It was easier to catch fish in the daylight but much riskier.

He put it in his bag and started back around the lake. One would be enough. *'Something has stirred the lake up a bit. All them trees along the shore must have something to do with it. Wonder if they would be alright for charcoal?'* He muttered to himself as he went closer to investigate. The moon came out from behind a cloud as he examined the logs and branches. A movement caught his eye and he froze. There it was again followed by a deep groan. He put down his bag and carefully moved closer. Suddenly he realised what he was looking at and rushed to the water's edge.

'My God,' he exclaimed to himself. *'It's a young lad, not dead yet but pretty close I'd say.'* He dragged Thomas out from the tangled mess and laid him on the bank. He must get Jenny. She would know what to do.

***

Marty took his time returning to report the mishap. He collected the horses and after staring at the lake for a while, mounted and leading Sweet Pea, slowly made his way home. He was a bit worried about what Sir Edric would say but he would have to be told. It was nightfall when he finally arrived at the village and he went straight to Cotter's cottage. He knew he would be there. He tied the horses up and knocked on the door. The older Cotter boy opened it.

'It's Mister Dewson, Da',' he shouted into the house.

'Then let him in, boy. Don't keep him standin' in the cold.'

Marty entered the humble dwelling and closed the door. It was very warm and cosy inside and the Cotters had just finished their evening meal.

'How was your day, Marty. Get the job done?' asked Cotter.

'Well, yes. The stream is flowing freely again but I'm afraid that there was an accident and young Tom is dead.' Marty turned his hat in his hands and looked at the floor. There was silence. Even all the children were quiet.

'What on earth happened, Marty? Sit down man, sit down.' He got up and went to the cupboard where he kept a bottle of brandy. Sir Edric gave him a bottle every year. He kept it for emergencies. He poured a glass and handed it to Marty.

'I tried to stop 'im but 'e's a 'eadstrong young lad and never liked takin' orders from me anyway. 'E rushed right up to the log-jam afore I'd even decided what to do. I yelled 'im to get back but 'e wouldn't. I was worried that if it went 'e would go with it. That's what 'appened. 'E climbed on it and shouted for a rope but 'e must'a dislodged a branch and away it went, takin' 'im too. I searched for 'im but there was no sign. 'E's probably at the bottom of the lake. I know we didn't get on but 'e were a good worker.' Marty sipped his drink and continued, 'I 'spose I'd better go an' tell Sir Edric.'

'I'll come with you. You've done your best. It wasn't your fault.' Cotter donned his jacket and hat and made for the door. He nodded to his wife. 'Be back soon. C'mon Marty.'

Sir Edric was at home. 'Unusual for you to visit at this hour, Cotter. Couldn't it wait until morning?'

'No, Sir. It couldn't.' He explained what had happened as Sir Edric listened carefully.

'I wondered if I could take a few men and have another look for him in the morning. He might have surfaced.' Marty said nothing.

'Then someone else will find him,' reasoned Sir Edric. 'No point in taking men away from important work to look for a dead boy. We'll spread the word that he's missing and then if someone finds him they'll know who he is. Thank you for telling me and

Marty, you should look after your workers better than that. You were the boss on that job. The accident should never have happened.' Marty clenched his teeth but did not respond.

Cotter had to be content with that but the early morning saw him and Mac riding off in the direction of the lake. They returned several hours later without having sighted Thomas.

***

This was not surprising because the evening before, Sam and Jenny had managed to carry him all the way back to their hut. They stripped off his wet clothes and wrapped him in as many blankets as they had. Sam lit the fire outside and soon had hot water boiling in the billy. Jenny gently washed Thomas's face and cradled him in her arms. She crooned to him as she rocked him and felt him stirring. His eyes flew open.

'Ma? Is that you,' he whispered.

Jenny smiled. 'No, m' darlin'. I ain't but I will be if you want me to. Go to sleep now.' Thomas' eyes closed and she laid him back down and went outside. Sam was forlornly poking the fires as sparks spiralled their way upwards to join the stars in the heavens.

'What are we going to do with him, Jenny? There's a doctor in the town. We could put him on the dray and take him there.'

'We can't afford to pay a doctor and anyway he'll need looking after so we'd have to bring him back here. Let's see what he's like in the morning. You watch over him while I cook our fish.' Jenny mixed some flour and water to form a dough which she wrapped in large green leaves. These she placed on the hot coals of the fire to cook while she poached the fish. Soon all was ready and after setting aside some of the fish and fish stock for the boy they ate their meal.

'Think the weather will be or'right tomorrow for the burn-off?' she asked.

'Hope so. We need to be here for that so we can't take the boy to town anyway.'

'I can look after him. He's badly bruised and half drowned but nothing appears to be broken. Has had a real bash on the head though and I think that's most of the problem. Jolting him around on a dray won't do him any good. He's best just left peaceful and quiet.'

'Let's go to bed. Tomorrow is a whole new day.' Sam put another log on the fire to try and keep it going. As Thomas had their bed they lay huddled together on the cold floor with one blanket between them. Sam had a feeling that it could be a long night.

***

Thomas had a very restless night. His body started to burn with fever and his eyes were glassy. Jenny tried to feed him the fish and stock but he vomited it up. She was scared that he would choke so she plied him with water instead. He was delirious and totally unaware of his surroundings. She tended to him all day whilst Sam took care of the fire that would make the charcoal.

He lit it by dropping burning charcoal down the hole in the top of the pile. Quickly he covered this hole with a large piece of turf. Once the fire started to burn it was important that he controlled the airflow by blocking off the holes around the base or alternatively freeing them up just enough to keep the fire from burning too fiercely. It was a skilled business and Sam was good at it. The process would take three days and then once the fire was out it would take another two days to cool down.

He drank some water from the jug. It was hot work. Jenny emerged from the hut and joined him. 'I think you've made more progress than I have today. The boy has a fever no doubt from lying in the water and getting so chilled. Probably pneumonia. I wonder who he is and where he came from?'

Sam put his mug down. 'I'll make some enquiries when I take the charcoal to town. That'll be a week away though and I guess he'll either be recovered or dead by then.' Jenny shuddered and turned away.

The good weather continued for the burning and on the third day, Thomas' fever broke. Jenny was sitting beside him as he opened his eyes. He moved his head and the pain made him gasp. She took his hand and spoke. 'You've a bad gash on the back of your head. Lie still and the pain won't be so bad.' She plied him with more water.

'Where am I?' he asked.

'We found you tangled up in some trees in the lake and brought you back to our camp. We're charcoal burners. You're very lucky that we happened to be down by the lake and saw you in the water. Now see if you can have a bit more sleep. I'll just be outside.' She covered him gently and stood looking at him silently as he closed his eyes. He brought back so many emotions in her and she struggled to hold back her tears. Eventually she went outside to tell Sam that he was awake.

'Who is he?' he wanted to know.

'I haven't asked him that yet. He's sleeping again but we'll soon find out.'

Thomas slept uneasily until the next morning. Jenny made him some porridge and propped him up as best she could. He didn't have the strength to hold the spoon, so she fed him. When he had had enough she spoke to him.

'What's your name?' she asked.

He thought for a bit. 'Thomas. Tom.' he answered.

'Well, Thomas or Tom, you have been a very sick young man. Do you remember what happened to you? We found you in a lake. How did you get there?' She gently mopped his brow. He did not answer straight-away and lay with his eyes closed. That way his head didn't hurt so much. She thought that he had dropped off to sleep again when he suddenly sat upright.

'That Marty,' he said as he grabbed his head and winced in pain. 'I remember. He tried to kill me.' Jenny laid him down again and saw the fear in his eyes. She took his hand.

'Well, he very nearly succeeded,' she said. 'But you're safe here with us. We won't let anything happen to you.' She went to the door and called to Sam. 'Come in here, Sam. You might want to hear this. Tom, this is my husband, Sam. I'm Jenny. You might try and tell us what happened. Take your time.'

Thomas tried to assemble his thoughts but he was very confused and wasn't making much sense.

'Let's leave it just now. You can tell us later,' Sam suggested.

As they sat on a log by the fire Sam ventured, 'There's a gamekeeper over at Sir Edric Spicer's place called Marty Dewson. I wonder if Tom was poaching and found him. Wouldn't put it past him to try and kill the boy. I've heard that he's a nasty bit of work. I've also heard that he poaches from Sir Edric as well but he's too clever to get caught. Wonder if it's that Marty.' Sam was thoughtful.

'If it is and he did try to kill Tom, he mustn't know that he's still alive. He might have another go. We'll know soon enough when Tom can talk about it.'

Jenny stood up wearily and began poking the fire. She realised how tired she was. 'I'll watch the fire. Do you think that you might be able to snare a rabbit? We need some decent food for Tom. Please.'

'You're missing Will aren't you? I think this boy reminds you of him, doesn't he?' Sam put his arms around her and held her close.

'I kept pretending that he was Will. Did you notice his clothes?' she whispered. 'They were very much like Will's, but I suppose that all country lads dress in a similar fashion. I am so glad that this boy didn't die. I wouldn't want his mother to go through what we went through.' She hesitated. 'He thought that I was his mother,' she added quietly.

Suddenly she jumped up and ran to the hut as a terrible strangulated scream came from Thomas. He was sitting up gasping and pulling at his throat, unable to breathe. Jenny held his hands until he calmed down.

'Sorry,' he moaned. 'I keep having this nightmare.'

'Do you want to talk about it?' Jenny asked.

'No,' said Thomas. Sam came to the doorway.

'Who is Marty, Tom?' he asked quietly.

'He's the gamekeeper at the manor. Mr Cotter is the head keeper and Marty works under him.'

'Why do you think he tried to kill you? Were you poaching by any chance?'

'No! 'Course I wasn't. I worked at the Manor. I was at the lake to help him. He never did like me. Not since he found me. Mr Cotter did like me and that annoyed Marty.' Tom was getting tired and he closed his eyes.

'We'll talk some more when you are rested.' They left him and Sam reluctantly went hunting while Jenny watched the both fires. After supper, they talked again.

'Where did Marty find you?'

'I'm not saying. He took me to Mr Cotter who gave me some clothes.' He stopped and looked around the hut. 'Where are they? They belonged to a boy who died. They are the only clothes I have now and there's somethin' precious in the pocket.'

'Tom, I've washed your clothes and they aren't dry yet. Is this what was in the pocket?' She handed him a pocket knife. He took it gratefully.

'A friend gave it to me,' he said as he felt tears welling up in his eyes.

'Tom, do you remember how Marty tried to kill you?'

It was not clear in his mind but he told his story as best he could remember. He didn't want to think too much about it. It was too terrifying. And what did it matter now anyway? He knew that Marty hated him and he had had the feeling that he would try something that awful day.

'Won't they have missed you at the Manor?' Sam suggested.

'Depends what Marty told them. He'll have made up a good story. I'm not going back,' he said adamantly. 'If he finds out that I survived he might have another go.' Tom lay back. He was tired.

'The charcoal's cooling,' Sam said. 'Tomorrow I'll sort it and the next day take it into the town. I'll ask there if anyone is missing from the manor. I won't let on that you're here and you can stay as long as you like. There is one thing that you should know though.' He hesitated, looking at Jenny, then spoke quietly. 'Will was our son.'

Thomas stared at him. He thought about the boot with the cut in it and the ultimate result of that injury. He held out his hand to Jenny. 'I'm very sorry about Will. It must have been hard for you to look after me. I probably bring back a lot of memories.'

'Will was a good lad and we miss him terribly. Our memories of him are happy ones. I think you're probably a good lad, too.'

***

Sam carefully drove his old horse and dray with its load of charcoal to the furnaces outside the town where it would be used to smelt iron ore. Because it burned at a very high temperature it was a perfect fuel for the huge smelters. He was pleased with the results of the last few weeks. Now he headed off to buy some provisions and to try and find out about Thomas. He didn't know how he was going to go about asking his questions. He had to keep Thomas's whereabouts a secret.

What he didn't know was that the town was Thomas's home town, Athelney. Not that it mattered. The townsfolk had forgotten all about the Puckles and Sam didn't know Thomas's surname anyway.

Carrying out his mission turned out to be a lot easier than he had anticipated. The first thing he saw was a notice nailed to a post. He tapped a man on the shoulder. He was finely dressed and Sam thought that he might be able to read.

' 'Scuse me, Sir. What does that notice say? I can't read and I thought that you might be able to help.'

'It's about a boy who's missing from the Manor. Probably drowned in the estate lake, so the story goes. Everyone knows about it.'

'Well, I don't. What happened?' he asked quickly. 'I work in the forest so it might be good to have a bit of background in case I see him.'

'Well, yes I suppose that's right. His name was Thomas Puckle. Actually he used to live in the town. His mother was hanged for killing his father and the townsfolk thought that he might have had something to do with it so he ran away. Nobody knew where he was until this notice appeared. Anyway apparently he worked at the Manor and while he was out with one of the gamekeepers he disobeyed him and climbed onto a log-jam. It gave way and washed him down the river and into the lake. The gamekeeper couldn't find his body so they've put these notices up in case somebody does.'

'Well thank you for all of that. I'll keep a lookout,' and with that Sam wandered thoughtfully back to where he had left his horse and dray. He purchased some more requirements and headed home.

Chapter 6:
Almost caught

Sam made his way to the Cotter home in the Manor Village. It was dark and no one saw him. He knocked on the door and waited. After a few minutes it was opened by Cotter himself.

'Yes, what is it?' he asked.

'I need to talk with you in private, sir. My name is Sam Crean. I'm Will Crean's father and this is important.'

'Will's father, eh! Just a minute.' Cotter grabbed his coat and went to the gate with Sam. 'I remember you now. What's this about Will, poor lad?'

'It's nothing about Will. It's about another lad called Tom Puckle. You know him, I understand. Presumed drowned a few weeks ago.'

'Yes, that's right. He disobeyed Marty Dewson and paid with his life. I was really sorry about it. He was a good lad. Wasn't usually disobedient. I don't know why he was this time.' Cotter rubbed his chin thoughtfully.

'He wasn't,' answered Sam. 'He tells me a different story from the one Marty told you.'

Cotter stared at him. 'What are you talking about? Do you mean he's still alive? What do you know of this?' he demanded.

'More than you obviously,' and Sam told him the whole story as related by Thomas.

'I don't believe it. Why would Marty do that? I'm glad Tom is alive but I can't believe that Marty would try to kill him. Where is he? I'd like to talk with him.'

'I'm not going to tell you that and anyway he won't be there for very long. When he's a little stronger we're leaving and taking him with us. He's scared of Marty and thinks that he'll have another go at him if he knows that he's still alive. You mustn't tell him. We could've taken Tom away and you'd never have known but he said that because you and Mac had always been good to him, he wanted you to know that he was still alive. So here I am and now you know. Best you keep an eye on that Marty. He might succeed next time with someone else. Anyway, I must be off,' and Sam made to move on.

'Wait!' Cotter restrained him. 'I really would like to see Tom. I won't tell Marty. I'm not that silly, but I'd like to talk with Tom, say goodbye... I don't know. I just don't want to forget about him.'

Sam thought about it. 'Or'right. Let him get a little stronger and I'll bring him to the head of the lake at dawn a week from today. He can explain what happened and then maybe you'll believe him. Don't let Marty follow you though.'

'I won't. He's not usually up that early anyway. I appreciate this. Thank you. Tell Tom not to worry.' He shook hands with Sam and made his way back home.

***

True to his word, Sam and Jenny took Tom to the lake. It was cold and misty and as they waited for Cotter they huddled together on the dray. It was loaded with all their worldly goods for as soon as their business was completed, they intended to leave the district.

They heard a horse coming through the forest and Cotter drew up alongside.

'Thank you, Sam. Thought that this might help a bit,' he greeted them and threw a sack containing some mutton on to the dray. 'Tom, it's good to see you lad. I'd like to talk with you in

61

private. Do you mind? We won't go out of your sight, Sam,' he added as Sam started to protest.

The two of them walked some distance away. 'Tom, I know everything. I know about your mother and why you ran away and now I know your story about Marty and I believe it. We have no proof, so I can't do anything about him. I've told Mac that you're alive and also about Marty. I thought that he needed to know and he can watch his behaviour too and tell me if he thinks that there's cause to worry. Something wrong with that man. Sam reckons that he's a poacher too so we'll wait for him to make a mistake. Maybe we can get him then and send him packing.'

'As long as he doesn't come my way I don't care. I've had enough of him. One day I might be big enough to tackle him but right now I want to stay out of his way,' said Tom.

'You'll be alright with the Creans. They're good people and they'll watch out for you.'

'I can look after myself. It's just that Marty who scares me.'

'I've something for you. You were a good worker at the Manor. Here's five shillings to help you on your way.' Cotter handed the money over to Tom who could not believe his eyes. It was more money than he had ever had before. 'I've got your sack and tin as well,' added Cotter. 'They're on my horse. You've got a lot of good things going for you, Tom. Just have confidence in yourself and what you can do. Learn a lot from Sam and Jenny. They are good people.' They wandered back to the others and Cotter gave Tom his bag. It was a little heavier than it had been but he failed to notice. His eyes misted as it brought back memories of the Pykes and their kindness and of course, Alfie. As Cotter rode off, they all settled themselves on the dray and headed off in the opposite direction without looking back.

***

Cotter and Marty went about their business but Cotter was very vigilant. He and Mac watched Marty and Marty's friends as well. If Marty was a poacher then it was possible that his friends were also.

Marty didn't poach because he needed the food. Heaven knows many people were forced into poaching because of poor wages and a man needed to provide for his family. There was no one else to help. Some did it for the excitement, particularly young ones – those with no responsibilities. Marty didn't have a family to care for, so his poaching was not caused through necessity nor for excitement but through greed. He poached game and sold it on the black market. Most of his deals were organised in the pubs and taverns and Mac took to frequenting the pubs a little more than usual and kept an ear open for anything that might indicate that Marty was up to no good.

'I think there might be something brewing in two nights time,' Mac reported to Cotter. 'I can't be certain that it's true but I overheard Marty and two others talking in the 'Fighting Cock' last night. One of Marty's mates had had too much grog and started talking too loud like. Marty tried to shut him up and finally dragged him outside and biffed him a few times. Left him lying there in the mud. After the others had all gone I chucked a bucket of water over him an' he came 'round. Marty might've been dumb to do that 'cos when this fella did come 'round, he started ranting and swearing and ready to tell everything. Just to get back at Marty.'

'So what do we know?' Cotter asked patiently.

'Well, they ain't gonna poach from us, that's the first thing,' explained Mac. 'Second thing is, it's pheasants they want. They're gonna go up to Fullerton's Field up on the Fuller estate. There will be six of them I think, an' they'll meet by the bridge on the Attlesford road at eleven o'clock on Thursday night.'

'That's a long way. Why do they want to go that far? There are plenty of pheasants down here.'

'Yeah, I know. Maybe it's quieter up there. If they mean to shoot the birds it's less likely that they'll be disturbed,' Mac replied.

'We'll see about that. This poaching is getting out of hand. You never know if they really will use guns to shoots the birds or are arming themselves in case the gamekeepers disturb them. We'll disturb them alright. Now I want you to go up to the Fuller Estate,' Mr Cotter instructed. 'Tell Sir Hugo what is supposed to happen. Tell him that I'll bring six men and if he can do the same we'll meet him at the bridge at nine-thirty. That'll give us time to hide ourselves and wait for the poachers.'

'Right,' said Mac. He added thoughtfully. 'I wonder why they want to use guns. That's running a real risk. At night pheasants fly into the hedgerows or lower branches of the trees to keep out of the way of foxes. It's easy to blind them with a lamp and then grab them. Little noise that way as well. Poachers know the law. If they've got guns or dogs or nets they'll be deported. Still, gotta catch 'em first.'

'I should think that they would bag more by using their guns even if it is riskier,' Cotter answered. 'Now I want to have a word with Sir Edric to let him know what's going on.'

***

It was bitterly cold when Cotter and his companions arrived at Attlesford Bridge and met up with Sir Hugo and his men. The moon was high and there was a real chill in the air.

'Gonna be a beaut frost tonight,' ventured Sir Hugo as he shook Cotter's hand. 'How do you reckon we should handle this?'

'Well, sir, we think that this crowd will have guns to shoot the birds but we don't know how many they have. Maybe just

Marty has one. Who knows? I'm armed but my men are not.' Cotter showed Sir Hugo his weapon.

'Well, I'm armed too,' Sir Hugo replied, 'and my men aren't. So we only have two guns between us. Let's hope we don't have to use them.'

'Fuller's Field is where it's supposed to happen,' explained Cotter. 'I think we should surround it and lay low to let them enter. Once they're in there, we've got 'em. How does that sound/'

'It's as good a plan as any. John, George and Harry – you take all these horses up to the top paddock and make sure that they can't get out. Take their bridles off and then they'll look at home in case these johnnies see them. Come back and join us. All you others spread yourselves around the boundary and hide in the hedgerows. Be careful. With this moon you might be spotted. When you hear the signal from me surround the poachers. Don't let any get away. You might have to use force and remember that some of them may be armed. Off you go.'

Sir Hugo followed his men into the paddock and ensured that the gate was shut. There were some sheep in there and he wondered if they were also on the poacher's list.

All was quiet and very cold. He hoped Cotter was right. He didn't know Cotter but had heard good things about him. He'd also heard rumours about a boy who had gone missing when out with Marty Dewson. Now there was a no-gooder if ever there was one. Why Sir Edric had employed him he would never know. His mind drifted as the time passed very slowly and he drew his cloak closer around his body to keep out the damp. He could not see his men and realised that they had secreted themselves very well.

The still night air was broken as the gate creaked and the sheep scattered to the far side of the field. Shadowy figures crept silently through and the gate creaked as it was pushed shut. The shadows spread themselves across the paddock to a clump of trees and scrub in the middle. A light shone dimly from a lantern, then another and another, all shining into the clump.

Sir Hugo bided his time until he could be certain that the poachers had some pheasants in their bag.

'Now!' he shouted and raced towards the copse. There was panic among the felons as they dropped their booty and tried to make their escape. Men came from all directions and scuffles broke out but the poachers were outnumbered. There was a shot and a yelp. Sir Hugo knew that he had not fired his gun. He did so now, into the air and shouted. 'Stay where you are. Joe! Grab one of these lanterns and let's see what we have here.'

It had all happened so quickly. Joe shone the lantern on the men lying incumbent on the damp grass.

'Well, what a scummy looking lot.' Sir Hugo pushed at one man with his foot. 'Which of you is Marty Dewson?'

'He ain't here.' Cotter came forward. 'None of these thieves is Marty and none of them has a gun either. Looks like Marty might have shot one of his own men and he's managed to scarper. Look around you lads,' he ordered. 'He might be still here but I doubt it. He would have to get out the gate. There's no way through the hedgerows.'

'That gate creaks. We would've heard it,' reasoned Mac.

'Maybe not in the confusion,' countered Cotter.

They melted into the darkness as Cotter asked Sir Hugo, 'What do you want to do with these rogues?'

'I'm injured,' one of the poachers whinged. 'Been shot in me leg. Can't walk,'

'It's just a nick. You'll have far worse than that if you don't shut up. I'll take them to my place and lock 'em up for the night,' Sir Hugo told Cotter. 'Tomorrow I'll take 'em into town and let the authorities handle 'em. Magistrate might be lenient but I doubt it.

There was a gun involved even if these men weren't the ones who pulled the trigger. I wish we'd caught Marty. I don't like the thought of him being on the loose.' Sir Hugo issued orders and soon the poachers were trussed up and were soon on their way to be locked up. Cotter and his men waited for the searchers to return from their fruitless quest for Marty and then they too, headed for home.

'That Marty has a charmed life,' he said to Mac as they rode along.

'I don't think he'll hang around here now,' Mac answered. 'He'll go off and make trouble somewhere else.'

Part 2:
1786

Chapter 7:
Curiosity killed the cat (1786)

Thomas had changed a lot since he had escaped death at the hands of Marty Dewson. He was no longer an immature youth but a well-built young man of almost twenty years and in the intervening time had learned a lot from the Creans and the folk in the village where they lived. They had settled in a village called Gunnislake in the heart of the Tamar Valley in Cornwall with Jenny opening a small bakery and Sam doing various jobs around the district. He could turn his hand to anything from laying hedges to making besom brooms. He helped thatch roofs and built dry stone walls and everything in between.

Thomas had been fascinated with the village smithy. He loved the whole atmosphere and was thrilled by the heat from the coal and charcoal fire, the noise of the metal on the anvil as the smithy beat iron into shape and then the hiss as the hot object was plunged into a bucket of cold water. A smithy could do anything but usually repaired farm implements or shod horses as a priority. When not busy with these he would make gate hinges or pokers or hooks and trivets for the open fires.

When Thomas first arrived, he was allowed to pump the leather bellows to feed oxygen into the fire to keep the temperature high but he was so interested in all other aspects of blacksmithing that Jack, the blacksmith, undertook to teach him all he knew.

Thomas was a favourite with the villagers. He was polite and trustworthy and very popular. He had a lot of friends and liked to swim with them in the river or in the pond behind the village. After his episode with Marty and the log dam he was very afraid of water but hadn't liked to confess this to his friends who swam frequently. As Gunnislake was situated on the banks of the Tamar River there were many opportunities for them to swim and eventually he plucked up courage and copied what they did. In the end he taught himself to swim.

However, he liked his own company and whenever he could, he ventured into the countryside on his own. He usually took his dog, Bouncer, and his old burlap sack containing his food, a canvas shelter and a tinderbox. The latter had been put in his bag by Mr Cotter when he had come to say goodbye at the lake all those years ago. It had contained flint, fire steel and dry tinder in the way of some fibre and Thomas made sure that it was always ready for use. His precious pocket knife was always to hand in his pocket.

If he was intending to camp somewhere over night he always told Jenny and took a bit of food with him. He enjoyed doing that and it was on one of his solo trips that he saw Marty. His heart sank. Fortunately Marty did not see him. Seven years had passed since their last encounter but Thomas knew that Marty would never forget him any more than he would forget Marty. It disturbed him to see his old foe in the neighbourhood. Sam had found out about the rout at Fuller's Field and how Marty had escaped. Everyone thought that he would have taken himself a long way off, but after seven years he might well have thought that folks would have forgotten him and that it would be safe to come back. All the other men involved in the poaching had been deported to the colonies with punishments ranging from seven to fourteen years with hard labour. The fact that they had wives and children made no difference. They were associated with Marty who had a gun and that had counted against them so their sentences were harsh. They knew that they would never see their families again and that the home-life for their wives and children would be worse than ever with a man to support them.

Thomas felt sorry for these men. It was their poor circumstances that had led them to commit their crime in the first place. They were enticed by Marty who wanted the pheasants for selling and he had promised the men a small share of the proceeds. His motive was greed, theirs was need.

All this passed through Thomas's mind as he watched Marty ride along the path through the forest. He lay low to the ground and kept his hand on Bouncer. Only when Marty was out of view did he let him go.

'C'mon boy. Let's go,' he said as he shouldered his sack. Bouncer on the other hand had other ideas and bounded down the lane after Marty. Thomas whistled to him but he took no notice.

'Darn,' he thought and started to follow. *'Better not let Marty see me. He thinks I'm dead.'* He rounded a bend in the path but there was no sign of either Bouncer or Marty. He wondered about the wisdom of carrying on along the track that Marty had ridden down. He had no desire to inadvertently bump into him but he needed to find Bouncer. He continued on his way, now and again whistling for Bouncer. A man on a horse could travel much faster than a man on foot and he knew that Marty would soon out-distance him if he kept moving. He stopped being concerned that he might be seen by him. He just wanted to find Bouncer. He walked for an hour or so trying not to worry and remembering that sometimes in the past Bouncer had found his own way home. Maybe that's where he had gone now and was eagerly scoffing his dinner with no thought for his master. Thomas didn't really think that would have happened though.

As they were on public land, there was always the possibility that he had been picked up by a stranger and taken somewhere. Thomas hoped that that possibility hadn't occurred. Dogs that were stolen were often used for dog fighting. Thomas had seen dog fights in the past and they were far from pleasant. He avoided them if he could and made sure that his dog was safe. But unfortunately Bouncer didn't always comply with his master's wishes.

He came to a clearing by a stream and decided to make his camp there. It was getting cold and damp and he was hungry. He would go back home tomorrow and if Bouncer wasn't there he would recommence his search. He took the light canvas out of his sack and slung it over a tree. That would give him adequate shelter for the night. Next he gathered dry pieces of twigs and with his tinder, soon had a fire going. He searched around for more wood and amassed a stock pile that would keep him warm all night. His supper consisted of meat balls cooked by Jenny and a loaf of bread. He heated the meatballs on a stick over the fire and apart from the fact that Bouncer was missing he felt quite content.

It was dawn when he awoke and he decided to continue searching a little longer. On the other side of the clearing the path meandered through a forested area. He couldn't be sure, but he thought that he was heading south. He kept on going and when he emerged from the trees he was on an open area leading to a clifftop. Seagulls wheeled and screamed overhead and he realised that he had reached the sea. Wandering over to the edge of the cliff he dropped to his knees and peered over. Two men were on the beach below and while he watched them he wondered what they were up to? Thomas knew that smuggling was rife along the coast but he didn't think that this looked like a suitable beach although he didn't know anything about smuggling. It seemed to be too rocky but it did appear to have some good caves. He watched as the men entered one of them and after a few minutes they emerged carrying a large box. This they deposited beside a row boat which was drawn up on the sands. They repeated this action many times until there was a stack of boxes and bags lined up beside the boat. Thomas wished that he had an eye piece so that he could get a better look. The men loaded everything into the boat and with a heave, launched the craft into the surf. They jumped in and were soon rowing swiftly round the point towards a small fishing village a mile or two down the coast.

Thomas was curious. *'They're up to something mischievous and I'm going to find out what.'* he murmured to himself. Jumping up, he followed the track along the cliff top, most of the time keeping the row boat in view but losing it when the track meandered inland. It was not long before he entered the village and it was easy to find his way down to the harbour. It was very picturesque with its fishing boats bobbing gently in the water or drawn up on the shingle. The village itself was fairly typical of fishing villages in Cornwall. The cove was bounded on both side by sloping hills dotted here and there with cottages and farm buildings. Close to the harbour were three fish processing factories. Many of the men who were not occupied in fishing itself were employed in these factories, washing, cleaning and salting the fish. Women and children were also included in this. The main fish was pilchards and these were salted and cured before the oil was pressed from them using large screw presses. They were then packed into barrels and sent by dray to the towns.

The narrow road which ran from the harbour and up the hill was bounded on both sides with thatched roofed stone cottages. In the centre was the pub, 'The Pilchard's Inn'. Smoke from the fires in the cottages penetrated Thomas's senses as he made his way down to the sea wall.

Thoughts ran through his mind. *'Why had the men rowed all that way when they could have loaded a dray and brought the* stuff along the cliff path?' he wondered. 'Why were these boats not out fishing?' It was a beautiful day, the sky was clear and although he didn't know anything about sea fishing, to him the conditions looked perfect.

He sat on the seawall as close to the boat of interest as he dared. As he watched the men unload it others came to give them a hand and soon everything was on a wagon and being trundled up the hill and out of town.

' 'Nother lot coming in t'night. Plenty of room for it now we've got that out.' Thomas pricked his ears as one of the men spoke softly.

'Yeah. We shouldn't 'ave left it so long but the time 'ad to be right. We'll get rid of the next lot quickly though.'

Thomas tossed stones into the water and appeared to be taking no notice of what was going on around him but his heart was racing with excitement. 'They must be smugglers after all,' he told himself. Probably most of the village was involved. A plan began to form in his mind. He did not stop to think of the risks but knew that he would have to be careful. May be it was just as well that Bouncer was not with him although he still wanted to know where he was.

He left the seawall and walked through the village, being careful not to look too suspicious. He didn't want people to notice him or remember him. But one person did notice him and certainly remembered him from another time.

Marty was sitting in the tavern beside the window discussing nefarious activities with two other men. The reason the fishermen had not put their boats to sea was because a big smuggling operation had been planned for that night and all hands would be required. Consequently the inn was fairly full. Beside Marty was Bouncer, tied to a chair leg to stop him wandering into the street.

74

'The boat should arrive off shore 'round midnight and we'll follow the usual plan,' Marty elaborated. 'We'll hide ourselves on the cliff top an' wait for the signal t' say that it's arrived safely. One long flash, one short and another long. After 'alf a minute it'll be repeated. OK. When that 'appens we'll signal 'em back with the same so's they know all's well at our end. No signals, no delivery! After I've given the owl's call to alert the rest of our lot, we'll go down to the beach and meet the rowboat. Joe'll stay on top as lookout. They'll send in one, or maybe two boats at a time just in case there's a problem. Don't wanna lose all their men and boats all at once, do they?'

'Who's on t'night?' one of the men, John, asked. He was a tall thin man, aged around thirty years with a rugged complexion. He was also a fisherman but could be relied on in the smuggling activities. He didn't particularly like Marty. Nobody did much but they liked the money that his activities brought them. A hard core of smugglers was assisted by local inhabitants and how many were required on the night depended on the amount of goods being smuggled. There were smuggling gangs operating all along the south coast and the authorities were very aware of them. In some places it was open warfare with both sides being armed. The smugglers usually outnumbered the law and got away with huge amounts of contraband. Marty was getting quite rich with his enterprise.

'Tonight's important,' he said. 'All the men'll be involved. Should be mainly brandy and geneva and tea, maybe a few other bits and pieces. Most of it will 'ave to be carted off tonight so we'll need ev'ryone and their drays. Lunnen agents are waiting for it. The rest can be stored in the cave until tomorrow. Those doin' the transportin' will meet up at Highcliff House as usual. The rest of us'll gather at the top of the cliff at, say, thirty minutes before midnight. We don't wanna t' be too early in case we get spotted.'

He supped at his ale slowly. 'There will be thirty odd of us up top. Should be enough to get the stuff off-loaded and take it through the tunnel. The men at the other end will load their drays as it comes through and 'ead out with it.'

He casually glanced out of the window and observed a young man walking in a leisurely fashion down the street. He watched him for a moment before recognition slowly dawned. A vision came rushing into his mind, a pile of logs rushing down the river and a young boy being swept out into the lake.

'Robbie. That young fellow out there... I want you to follow 'im, see where 'e goes. Does 'e live around 'ere? Do either of you know 'im?'

'Never seen 'im afore. How long do you want me to tail 'im for? 'E might be 'eading for Lunnin an' I don't wanna go that far.'

Robbie was a bit slow in the head and sometimes Marty got really exasperated with him. He didn't know why he bothered to include him in the smuggling operation. There were plenty of villagers only too happy to supplement their wages by assisting in a little smuggling. It was good money, better for Marty than the rest of them of course, but they didn't complain too much. The tea was purchased in France by agents there for seven pence per pound, smuggled across the Channel, carted to London and sold for five shillings per pound. Marty paid his part-time smugglers sixpence a night but his drivers who ran the greatest risk could earn three shillings a night. The people of the villages they passed through at night could have alerted the law but usually they didn't. They too, benefited from the smuggling. They were fully rewarded with cheap contraband for keeping their mouths shut. What they didn't see, they didn't know about.

> *'Five and twenty ponies*
> *Trotting through the dark.*

Brandy for the Parson,
'Baccy for the clerk,
Laces for a lady, letters for a spy
And watch the wall, my darling, while the
Gentlemen go by!'
- Rudyard Kipling

Marty's mind came back to Robbie and the task he had set for him. All he needed to know was if Tom left the district or if he was going to hang around and be nosey. There was a lot at stake tonight. This was to be one of the bigger operations that he had organised and he couldn't afford to have an outsider like Tom wandering around making a nuisance of himself.

'Just find out if 'e leaves the town or 'angs out somewhere. Come back to me 'ere. Now get going or you'll lose 'im. And don't let 'im see you.' He sat silently for a while after Robbie had taken off and then beckoned to the barmaid. 'Got a few minutes for me, darlin'? I need something to take me mind off me problems.' He pulled her roughly onto his knee and kissed her firmly. She squirmed as he held her fast and finally freeing her arm, she slapped him over the face. John roared with laughter.

'Let that be a lesson, ya dirty old man,' he said grinning a toothless grin. 'Not all the maids luv ya.'

'This one will,' he replied as he stood up. 'C'mon, ya wench,' he growled and moving quickly, he grabbed her and threw her over his shoulder. Grunting with the effort he headed for the stairs. The other patrons looked on with interest but no one interfered. She beat him about the head and shoulders but he was too strong. Wait till her brother found out about this, she thought, he'd kill Marty. Meanwhile, Marty himself had a fight on his hands. He opened the door of the nearest bedroom and, kicking it shut behind him, he threw her on the bed.

'Now my little cat, you'll pay for that. No sorry wench does that to Marty and gets away with it.' He began unbuckling his belt.

Jumping off the bed and looking around quickly, Joan saw a water jug on the washstand. She grabbed it and quickly sloshed the contents over Marty. He was drenched and gasping, he made a lunge at her across the bed. Still grasping the water jug, she smashed it over his head and rushed for the door. Grabbing her skirts high, she bolted down the stairs and out the door cheered on by the patrons in the tavern. Marty, in a blind fury and forgetting where he was, chased after her. It was a big mistake. This was not his town and although he organised the smuggling and paid the people who helped him, these citizens were not his people. They looked after one another and although they did nothing to help Joan, they followed her down the road to 'keep an eye on things.'

Quite a crowd had gathered by the time Joan reached her home. Marty was slowing down, sensing that this might not have been a good move on his part. He needed these people, particularly tonight. Not much point in upsetting them. As he hesitated, the door was flung open and a young man appeared. He was about twenty five years of age, a fine specimen of a man with dark skin and bulging muscles. His only clothing was a pair of baggy trousers which were held up by a wide leather belt, and a pair of brown leather boots. His hair was black and tied back with a red scarf. Joan was in the doorway behind him.

'That's him, William.' She pointed at Marty who had by this time come to a halt in the middle of the road.

'You ain't gonna let 'im get away with it, are ya, William?' shouted one of the bystanders. 'He'd a 'ad 'er if she weren't so quick.'

'C'mon, Marty. You was pretty brave when 'twas just the maid. Not so tough now, eh?'

William stepped out into the road. 'Shaddup all of you. None of you helped 'er. I'm 'shamed of all of you. And you our friends. We look after each other, remember. Protect us from scumbags like this. I didn't think you'd do this, Marty. You gotta keep on the right side of us. 'Aint no smuggling operation without us. Let this help you remember that,' and he punched his right fist squarely on Marty's left jaw.

Marty fell to the ground and put his hands up. William hauled him to his feet and aimed another blow but Marty ducked his head and butted William in the middle of his stomach. It was like butting a brick wall and he straightened up, somewhat dazed. William hit him again and he fell in the dirt.

'Get up,' he commanded and hauled Marty over to Joan. 'Say you're sorry you touched her and you'll never do it again for if you do, so help me, I'll kill you.'

The crowd was quiet, listening for Marty to answer. The apology was almost inaudible but they cheered anyway. They had never seen Marty humbled before. They didn't like him; he was a bully and a coward. However they were all in the smuggling racket together, even William, and to an extent, they relied on each other. That's what made it so successful.

Marty stiffened his shoulders and started back to the tavern.

'Watcha all starin' at. Never seen a fight before? I didn't wanna hurt him 'cos we need him tonight. 'Ain't you got better things to do?' and he stormed off, leaving them smirking. William did not hear this. He shoved Joan inside and shut the door.

'Where would I be without you, William?' she asked as he freshened up at the sink.

'I always said I'd take care of you. Ma and Pa ain't around no more to do it. Sure you didn't 'tice 'im e'en just a little bit?' He looked at her hard. She was an attractive girl with long brown hair, a healthy complexion no doubt brought about by the vigorous south coast weather. She was four years younger than William but he had always protected her, more so since their parents died in that terrible storm ten years ago. 'Men like 'im don't need a second chance.'

"Course I didn't. There's plenty of nice lads around without me having to look at someone like Marty. He was in the pub and just called me over.' Joan felt quite indignant that William should even think such a thing.

'Just be careful, that's all,' said William as he gave her a hug. 'As soon as we have a bit more money I'll get shot of Marty. There'll be no more smuggling for me.'

Chapter 8:
Friends when you need them

Robbie followed Thomas out of the town and up the hill to the track that led to the cliff top. Thomas took his time and was in no hurry. It was mid-afternoon and he had time to fill in before the night's activities began. He didn't know what time that would be, but expected it to be after darkness had fallen. He didn't notice Robbie who, for all his faults, managed to keep out of sight. Arriving at the edge of the cliff he looked over. He had a good view of the cove. Rocks were strewn out into the sea and at one end they stretched up the beach to the foot of the cliff. All was deserted. Quickly making up his mind, he hiked to the far end of the cliff where he could see a pathway leading down to the beach. It was very steep and he descended carefully, finally arriving at the entrance to the cave. Looking all around and satisfying himself that there was no one about, he entered.

The entrance was fairly narrow but once inside he noticed that it widened considerably and was quite dark. He took off his burlap sack and extracted his tinder box and a small lantern. He was very proud of the lantern which he had made himself. It was a small four-sided metal box with an opening door on one of the sides. In this door a glass window had been inserted. Through the pointed top of the box was a metal loop which allowed it to be held or hung up. Inside was a small holder for a tallow candle. The whole of the box was hatched with slits to let the air circulate.

It was only a matter of minutes before Thomas had a light emitting from it and he looked around the cave. It was about thirty feet wide and narrowed towards the back. Walking to the rear, he realised that there was no end, that the cave funnelled into a narrow tunnel that sloped slowly upwards. It had a sandy floor. Holding his lantern high, Thomas felt his way along the rock walls. He noticed that ledges had been carved into the walls and small lamps anchored on to them. He continued until he could go no further. His way was blocked by a huge wooden door. Feeling around for a handle he found a large iron ring. He turned it but it didn't budge. He tried again, turning and pulling and yanking, and finally giving up, he sat down in the sand and leaned his back against it. Rummaging in his sack he took out some bread and began to eat.

'This must be where they bring their stuff. They'll unload the boats on the beach and then carry it through here to whatever is on the other side. Wonder what is on the other side of this door?' he mused as he packed up his bag. He headed back out to the daylight and as he exited the cave he failed to notice a man atop the cliff who disappeared as soon as Thomas made his appearance. He clambered up the path and looking around spotted a very large homestead built quite a long way back but in the same direction that the tunnel ran. He wondered why he had not spotted it before. The landscape was quite sparse with huge rocks and boulders dotted here and there but there were trees around the house and out buildings. That must be part of the smuggling operation, he thought. He looked at his closer surroundings and selected a large rock surrounded by scrub in which to hide. He would have a long wait.

Meanwhile Robbie hurried back to the tavern and found Marty drowning his sorrows in a tankard of ale. He related Tom's movements and when he got to the part about him entering the cave Marty exclaimed, 'Right! That's it! 'E'll pay for that. Where is 'e now?'

'Dunno,' answered Robbie.

'Whaddya mean you dunno?'

'I left when 'e started back up the path. Didn't want 'im to see me, did I? What 'arm can 'e do? 'E don't know about us,' Robbie reasoned.

' 'E could be off getting the law by now. 'E's a stranger around these parts and won't have the loyalty the rest of us have got. Don' feel right. E'en if 'e don't know about tonight 'e could mess it up if 'e brings the law.' Marty's head hurt and he couldn't think straight. 'Shaddup, dog,' he said as he kicked Bouncer under the table. 'I can't think with you whinging.'

'Why would 'e do that?' asked John. 'It's just a cave with a tunnel. Why would 'e be suspicious? There are a lot of caves like that around here.'

'Because 'e's that sort of nosey-parker. I know 'im and 'ave a score to settle with 'im.'

'Ain't too late to call it off. If there ain't no signal there ain't no delivery,' said John.

Marty thought for a moment. 'No, we'll carry on. You both go to the cliff now. If there's any sign of anything dangerous you come back Robbie, and John, you stay watchin'. Now get goin'.'

As they started back to carry out their assignment Robbie commented, ''E's in a right mood.'

'Yeah. William 'it 'im for trying to 'ave 'is sister. Made a fool of 'im and 'e don't like that,' John exclaimed.

All was quiet on the cliff and they settled themselves down to wait. What for, they weren't sure. However, after a little while Thomas stood up and walked around his rock before settling back into the scrub.

'Didya see that?' whispered Robbie.

'Yeah. 'e's still 'ere. That'll make Marty real 'appy. You better go and tell 'im. I'll stay.'

***

It was a perfect night for the smugglers, calm with neither wind nor moon. Thomas was very restless after his hours of inactivity and he moved his arms and legs to keep his blood flowing. He was cold and hungry and wondered about the wisdom of spying on this operation. It wasn't as if he was going to do anything. He didn't know how many people would be involved but thought that even if there were just two it would be two too many for him. He daren't go down to the beach but would keep himself secreted behind his rock until all the smugglers had passed by and then he would watch them by leaning over the cliff. When they had finished their labours he would head off, find somewhere to camp for the night and in the morning, if he hurried, he would be home before Jenny and Sam had started their day's work. It was a simple adventure in his eyes. What could go wrong?

Consequently, he was amazed at the numbers of the smugglers when they started arriving. He watched from behind his rock and saw them hide themselves amongst the brush and settle down to wait. Suddenly he saw Marty. It was dark and there were many moving shadows but he was sure that it was him: medium height, strong build and drooping shoulders. Yes. It was him alright and Thomas found his heart pounding in his chest. Was this man to haunt him all his life? He squeezed himself even further into his hideout, endeavouring to make himself as invisible as possible.

All was quiet. Thomas almost kidded himself that they had all gone home when suddenly there was movement all around.

'That's the signal, John,' whispered Marty. He went to the edge of the cliff and held up his spout lamp. Pointing it out to sea he gave the return signal: one long flash, one short and then another long. After half a minute he repeated it. Thomas peeked out from his hiding place just as Marty let out his owl's call to alert his co-smugglers. They emerged from their cover and made their way quietly down the track. Thomas waited. When he thought that they had all gone he crept out of his hideout and over to the cliff top. He could not see far out but knew that the lugger must be out there somewhere.

Suddenly he froze. Something was digging into his back and a voice hissed in his ear, 'If you don't want a bullet in y' back, y' better get down there too. Move it.'

Thomas slowly got to his feet. Of all the stupid idiotic predicaments to get himself into. He wondered if he could take this man on but then saw another one behind him. God, what a mess! He stumbled towards the start of the track but being dark, he couldn't see the pathway clearly and kept falling. He felt himself being pushed out of the way by one of his captors who snapped, 'Follow me,' and he led the way down with Thomas behind being prodded all the way.

'Over there,' he was ordered and pushed to the rocks at the bottom of the cliff. 'Tie 'im up, Robbie. Make sure the knots are tight. Don't want 'im gettin' free. Marty wants a word with 'im.'

In no time at all Thomas was securely tied to a metal stake in the rocks. He felt panic rising as he struggled to break free. It was hopeless.

'Save ya strength boy. Ya might need it later when Marty gets a 'old of ya. I don't think he likes ya much. What ya do t' 'im?'

'Nothing,' answered Thomas, struggling furiously at his bonds.

'Ain't no use doin' that. Ya'll just exhaust y'self.' Robbie went over to have a word with Marty who was gazing out to sea through his spyglass. 'Boy's over there. 'E ain't goin' far.'

'E'll keep. I think the boats are coming. I'll deal with 'im later,' replied Marty as he compressed the glass and put it in his pocket. ' 'Ere's the first boat.'

Several men ran into the water and steadied the heavily laden tub boat as it grounded in the sand. The four oarsmen jumped out and began manhandling the oak barrels which were tied to a rail that encircled the boat and were now floating in the water.

'No problems?' asked Marty as he went to help.

'No, didn't have to sink 'em. Weren't none of them law boats about. We've a better chance of gettin' shipwrecked on these 'ere rocks than being caught by 'em.'

Marty knew that it wasn't always as easy as the man made out. He had been on operations when the revenue boats had turned up and the barrels which were tied to a rope encircling the boat were cut free. They were attached to each other and, perfectly weighted with stones, they sank beneath the surface and floated out of sight ready to be retrieved later. That was dangerous in itself if the revenue men awaited their return.

He gave his energies to the job in hand and as fast as one boat was emptied another one appeared. Men laboured furiously to roll the barrels and carry the chests into the tunnel and through the door at the end. Barrels and tea chests started to stockpile on the beach.

'John, get a few men from the 'ouse to come down and lend a 'and or we'll be 'ere all night,' instructed Marty.

'Right, boss,' John replied as he rolled a barrel through the entrance of the cave and along the tunnel. The lamps had all been lit and dark shadows loomed on the walls as he passed them and reached the door. It was wide open and John could see that everyone was busy. He thought that Marty should have had more men but he was too mean to pay more people than he had to.

'We'll be all night, alright,' he thought. He singled out four men and dispatched them to the beach. Then he took stock of his surroundings.

The tunnel door opened into a huge barn which was now being rapidly filled with boxes and barrels. As fast as they could, other men were trundling them out to the courtyard where they were loaded on to an assortment of carts and drays. There were men and horses everywhere.Several were ready to go and clattered out of the courtyard with two men up top, a driver and a watchman, who carried a shotgun. The work continued as John hurried back down the tunnel passing more men including William and Robbie, who were arguing as they leaned into their barrels.

'Ain't none of your business, so best stay out of it,' John heard Robbie say in response to something that William had said. He idly wondered what it was about but soon forgot when he reached the beach and collected another barrel.

Thomas was amazed at the amount of stuff being landed and temporarily forgot about his predicament. Each man seemed to know his job and Marty was keeping an eye on things. He appeared to have forgotten about Thomas. Finally the last boat landed and as it was being unloaded Marty took one of the oarsmen aside. Thomas could not hear what they were saying but from the gesticulations and loud voices he assumed that they were having an argument. The oarsman kept looking at Thomas and appeared to be quite angry.

Suddenly Robbie appeared and crouched down beside Thomas. 'Ya better 'ope that Marty loses that argument 'though I don't think it'll do ya much good,' he whispered in his ear.

'What's it about?' Thomas whispered back.

'Ya'll find out soon enough.' Robbie answered.

Thomas was full of apprehension. He felt so cold and had lost all feeling in his feet and hands. His mind was numb and he was finding it hard to comprehend all that was happening. He looked up at the starry sky and singled out the largest star.

'I've been daft again, Ma,' he whispered. 'Are you with me on this one?' A warm breeze wafted past him in the cold night air and he felt comforted. He suddenly became aware that there were very few people left on the beach and all the plunder had gone through the tunnel. The oarsman jumped into his boat and shouted to Marty, 'I ain't no murderer. You do your own dirty work.'

Marty ignored Thomas and stormed off through the tunnel. He was very angry and wasn't used to his wishes being ignored. The last of the goods were being cleared from the courtyard and most of the men had gone home. The final horses and drays were loaded and soon there were only John, William and Marty left.

'What were you and Robbie arguing about?' John asked William as they moved away from Marty, who was checking his ledgers.

'That boy out there. There's something funny going on. What's he to Marty? Robbie tells me that he heard him arguing with the boatman and getting really het up. Wanted them to take him out to sea and dump him. I'm trying to think of a plan to get him out of this mess. I'm no killer and I ain't gonna let the likes of Marty near the lad,' said William.

'He had us follow him 'ere today and report back. Suppose it's my fault that 'e caught him.' John was a good man and looked worried about how things had turned out.

'No, it ain't. The kid don't seem very smart else 'e wouldnt'a got 'isself in this situation. Chances are 'e'd always have been caught with the number of people we 'ad 'ere tonight. Someone would 'ave spotted 'im. Keep Marty busy for a while and then call by my cottage when you're finished 'ere.' With that,

William, with one eye on Marty, vanished back down the tunnel towards the beach. As he passed the lamps, he extinguished them one by one hoping to slow Marty down when he had finished his paperwork and went after Thomas. He rushed out into the night and clambered over the rocks to get to him.

'C'mon, lad. There's no time for sleeping,' he whispered. But Thomas was not asleep. He was nearly unconscious with cold and fear. William shook him and he struggled to regain his senses. Taking out his knife William slashed the bonds which bound Thomas to the stake. 'We've gotta 'urry. Marty could be 'ere any minute. Can you stand?' He helped Thomas to his feet but his legs and feet had lost all feeling and he flopped to the sand.

''Ain't nothing for it but t' carry you,' and William hoisted Thomas over his broad shoulders and headed up the path. He hoped John was still keeping Marty occupied. He was puffing by the time he got to the top of the cliff and when he lowered Thomas to the ground, he panted, 'Be a help if you could walk a bit... or even run would be better,' he added.

'I'll try,' answered Thomas and slowly, with William's help, he regained his feet and took a few tentative steps. 'I'll loosen up. Where are we going?'

'My place, but we 'ave to get there and 'ide you afore Marty comes. 'E'll be suspicious of me. We can't go near the big 'ouse so we'll have to detour. Quickly now, you'll have to move faster.'

'Can you please get my sack from behind that rock?' Thomas asked. 'It means a lot to me and I'd hate to lose it.'

'OK, but you start movin' in that direction and maybe your legs'll start t' wake up.'

The feeling was coming back into Thomas's limbs when William caught up to him and they moved as fast as they could with William leading the way. Reaching the top of the track leading down to the village, they stopped. William pointed down to the left.

'We'll have to go that way... behind the cottages. If we go down the main street someone might see us. Best nobody knows about you yet anyways. I don't think that they'd tell Marty but most of the men who were working tonight won't even know about you and might let somethin' slip if they see a stranger at this time of night. C'mon,' he commanded and led the way down. Ten minutes later they were slipping into the scullery through the back door of William's cottage. He lit the lamp and pulled the window coverings. Then dragging the table to the centre of the room he clambered onto it. Thomas watched and suddenly realised that there was a manhole into the roof.

'Up you go, lad and don't make a sound no matter what ya see or 'ear. 'Ang on a minute.' William disappeared and returned in a minute with a blanket and pillow. 'What's your name by the way?'

'Tom,'

'Sleep well then, Tom. 'Ere's a piece of bread. No time for anythin' else. We'll talk tomorrow.' He replaced the cover after Thomas had climbed through and sat down at the table to wait. He was sure that Marty would come.

Thomas wrapped himself up in the blanket and looked around wondering where he could get comfortable. He wished he could light his lamp but he wouldn't want a light to show through the cracks in the ceiling. He finally flopped down near the manhole and rested his head on the pillow. He was very tired. He ate his bread and settled down to wait.

'Who were you talking to?'

William jumped as Joan came through her bedroom door behind him.'I'm not going to tell you at the moment, but I think Marty'll be 'ere any minute and if you aren't 'ere, you can't tell him anythin'. You'd better go back to bed and I'll tell you all about it later.'

Joan was not at all keen to see Marty particularly as she was in her nightshift. She disappeared into her bedroom and closed the door. William sat quietly. There was a light knocking at the front door and John stood on the doorstep.

'I forgot about you, John. Come in. D'ya know where Marty is?'

'No. but 'e'll have found out by now that you rescued the boy. You did, I suppose?' he asked.

'Yes,' William answered and pointed up to the manhole.

'I left the barn through the doors, not through the tunnel. Marty would too, because he locks the door from the barn side. Then 'e'd 'ave to go back along the top and down the path t' get t' 'im.'

'I never thought about the lockin' up,' said William as he poured John a mug of ale. 'I put out all the lamps 'oping to slow 'im up. Never mind. 'E might not even come. 'E might do nothing. 'E might just go back t' the pub an' leave the boy on the beach. 'E was in a bad way and would've died by morning. I don't know what this is all about but I'm not leavin' 'im in Marty's clutches.'

'Me neither. I'll help in any way I can. What're ya plannin'?' asked John.

'I ain't got a plan yet but it can't be too 'ard. We just have to get 'im 'ome with 'is own people and our job's done.' William was interrupted by a loud banging on the door. 'Sounds like this is our man.' He opened the door to an irate Marty who had a pile of rope in his hand. Not only that, he had Bouncer by his side.

'Where's that boy?' he demanded.

'Come in, Marty. John's 'ere too. This is all most unexpected. What's the problem? Ya better leave that dog outside. I don't like dogs in my house.'

'Don't be smart with me, boy. Ya know what this is about. The boy on the beach has gone an' I don't think 'e got away on his own. Someone cut 'is ropes an' I think it was you.' Marty pushed his way in dragging Bouncer, who was on the end of a lead. He threw the ropes on the floor.

'Marty, from what I could see, your prisoner was just a boy. What did 'e do to make ya wanna to kill 'im? You could end up swingin' yourself if ya do manage kill 'im. No one around 'ere will protect you. They don't like you much.'

'Don't know why not. I pay 'em well and you too. So what 'ave you done with the boy? If you don't tell me it'll be the last time you smuggle for me. You too John.'

'I'd rather sleep easy in me bed with a clear conscience than 'and the lad over to you,' was John's reply.

'Clear conscience be damned! You're a smuggler! 'Ow could ya have a clear conscience?'

'Smugglin's one thing to my way of thinkin'. That's really just a matter of wits. But murder! That doesn't come into my way of my thinking. You're a no gooder, Marty Dewson, and there's no way I'd give you the boy even if I did have 'im,' said John adamantly.

Meanwhile as this conversation was going on, Bouncer was becoming very agitated. He whined and strained at his lead and tried to get away from Marty who lashed out with his foot and kicked him. Bouncer immediately turned and bared his teeth with a throaty growl. Jumping back, Marty released the lead. William grabbed it.

'Here boy. Whassa matter? Do ya want off? Let's see what ya do?' He released Bouncer who immediately ran around the room sniffing the floor as he did so. Marty backed away as he turned, but it was not Marty who interested him. He stopped under the manhole and barked madly.

92

'Ha!' exclaimed Marty. 'So you 'ave somethin' up there.'

'What's up there's my business an' I suggest ya get on ya way now. I've nought more t' say t' ya.' William opened the door as Bouncer barked at the ceiling.

Without a word Marty stormed out.

'What's eatin' that dog?' John said, getting up from his chair. 'Come 'ere, boy.'

'I think I know,' said William, as he locked the front door. He pushed the table over to the middle of the room and climbed up. Opening the cover he exposed Thomas who immediately wormed his way through and onto the table.

'Bouncer! I've missed you so much.' He put his arms around the dog as Bouncer barked and whined and licked his face.

'So 'e's your dog, is 'e?' asked William

'Yep! I lost him when he followed Marty along a track. I'm so happy to have him back.' Thomas was ecstatic.

'Well I think 'e's 'appy to have you back too,' said William. 'Now, John what're we going to do?'

'I think we should ask Tom what this is all about and 'ow he came to be watchin' us on the beach. Looks like we've lost a bit of earnings 'cos of him and I'd like to know that it was worth it,' was John's answer.

Chapter 9:
A new experience

Thomas lay quietly up in the loft as Joan busied herself in the small scullery making the porridge for their breakfast. William sat at the table in the kitchen with Bouncer beside him. He had not dressed completely, but wore his long shirt and stockings.

"E'll have to stay 'ere for a while unless we smuggle 'im out at night. After what 'e's told us about Marty's other attempt on 'is life, I think it's best that 'e stays up there for a few days and then we'll see what 'appens next. Marty can't stay around 'ere forever. I know 'e goes over to Guernsey and Calais to organise goods and 'as other ports over this side that do just what we do. Or did do. Suppose that's all come to an end for me and John.'

'You don't seem too upset about it,' ventured Joan.

'I'm not. I never did like Marty an' did it for the money an' the excitement. Never did I do it to 'elp 'im.' William climbed on the table and opened the hatch. 'C'mon down, lad. 'Ave some breakfast and then you'd better go back up. I'll look after Bouncer today.'

Thomas needed no second bidding and was soon tucking into a huge bowl of porridge followed by four slices of toast and a mug a tea. He sat back feeling replete.

'Thanks, Joan. That was just what I needed. I feel a new man. I owe you and John a huge debt, William, and I'd like to repay you in some way but can't think how at the moment. I haven't any money but I can work. One thing worries me though and that is what Jenny and Sam will be thinking. I have to get home and let them know that I'm alright. I'm more than two days late so I need to be on my way. I can come back though and work for you maybe,' he said as he tried to assemble his thoughts.

'Don't be so daft, lad. Do ya think we rescued ya at great cost t' ourselves just t' let you outa the front door and down the track to 'ome. Whaddya think Marty's doin'? I'll wager 'e's put the word 'round already. 'E'll 'ave made up some story about you, 'ow ya owe him money, or ya betrayed 'im or disgraced 'is daughter or somethin' like that. 'E'll be offerin' a reward for ya and there's plenty who'd take it. I'll stake my life on that.'

There was a knock at the back door and Thomas shot onto the table and through into the roofspace. William quickly replaced the man cover and Joan opened the door when all was ready.

It was John.

'This weather's appalling,' he observed. 'I 'ope you weren't thinkin' of takin' ya boat out t'day. Wouldn't be worth it anyways as the fish will be well under if they've got any sense. That sea's really rough.' He hung his wet waterproof jacket in the back porch and placed his boots neatly underneath.

Joan poured him a mug of tea while William related the conversation he had had with Thomas at breakfast. John agreed that it was too risky until Marty had left, but understood his concern about Sam and Jenny.

'I'll go and see them,' he offered. 'Michael Chudderley will lend me 'is 'orse so it shouldn't take too long. I'll tell 'em to expect 'im back when he turns up. Marty has put up five shillings to anyone who can tell 'im where Tom is. But 'e knows 'e's 'ere alroight. 'E's not that stupid and 'e'll have men watchin'.'

'It's all so mad. The kid ain't 'armed Marty ever. It's just that Marty took a dislike to 'im. Unless there's something that Tom ain't tellin' us. Maybe 'e saw Marty stashing some loot somewhere and Marty's scared 'e'll get it afore 'e does. Or maybe 'e thinks Tom knows somethin' 'e shouldn't, and may use it against 'im unthinkin' like.' William's imagination was working fast. 'How about this... maybe Marty had something to do with Tom's father's death and Tom saw 'im?'

'William, don't be stupid,' said Joan. 'He's just an ordinary young man whose had a lot of bad luck. I don't mind if he stays here. I'll look after him. That's good of you to offer to go, John. Make sure you're not followed. The last thing we want is for Marty to get wind of where he lives.'

***

John's mission was accomplished successfully and Thomas began to relax. He liked William and Joan but was mindful that his presence in their house could perhaps pose a threat from Marty. The storm that had struck the day after the smuggling operation lasted several days and kept the fishermen in port. They were soon tired of being land bound and spent their days at the pub but they knew that the dangers of sailing in a storm such as this were very real. Thomas was also getting tired of being in the cottage all day and night and one morning he finally asked William if he had a plan.

'I'll tell you later Tom. I'm off to the pub. John will be there an' 'opefully Marty'll be gone. We can work out the best thing to do.' He took his coat off the hook, put on his boots and went off.

'Can't be too hard, can it? I just want to get home,' Thomas said to Joan. 'You would too if you were in my situation, wouldn't you?'

'I wouldn't be so daft as to get myself in your situation in the first place,' she said. 'Spying on the smugglers was stupid. A lot of smugglers are really awful people. Most are ordinary individuals like William and John who want to make a few extra shillings or hopefully pounds, but others are totally ruthless and will do anything to avoid getting caught. You might not think it, but you were probably lucky coming up against Marty's group.'

'Why do you say that?' asked Thomas.

'Because of William and John, silly. They're good men and wouldn't let Marty harm you. Some of the others wouldn't care what happened to you if they thought that your freedom meant that you might rat on them.' Joan busied herself tidying the cottage before she too went to her work at the pub. Marty no longer tried to approach her but she stayed as far away from him as possible. Thomas was left alone but not for long. William and John returned.

'Lad, we 'ave a plan. The weather's supposed to clear tomorrow an' the boats'll be going out. Tonight we'll smuggle ya onto my boat, and you can 'ide there overnight. It's called the 'Fortune' so I 'ope it brings you good fortune. Then tomorrow as soon as it's clear we'll sail ya 'round the bluff to a little bay further along the coast where you'll be met by Michael Chudderley who'll set ya on the right path for 'ome. 'Ow does that sound?'

'Anything, as long as I'm on the move. But it does sound like putting you all to a lot of trouble. I could just sneak out of here at night and walk home. No one would see me.' That sounded the simplest plan to Thomas but he knew that he'd probably get lost again. Anyway William was the boss. He was the man of the house. Thomas thought that it could be quite exciting though as he'd never been on a boat before.

Nightfall came and Thomas was led by a roundabout route through the darkness to the wharves where many of the fishing boats were tied up. A lot were also drawn high up the beach and when high tide came they would float at their moorings. It was bitterly cold and still raining but William assured him that the weather would have cleared by morning.

The boats were rocking violently at the wharf as the swells caused by the high winds swept in from the open sea. Thomas

97

hoped that the men were right in predicting that the storm would abate by morning. Although it had been a very sad event, he took comfort in the fact that William's parents had been drowned in a storm such as this and as a result William was not one to take chances.

Luckily the *Fortune* was not one of those tied to the wharf or Thomas would have had a particularly uncomfortable night. William's boat was drawn up onto the beach and they clambered aboard hoping that all the good folk were in their beds and none were stupid enough to spend an uncomfortable night on their own boat and notice what they were doing. The *Fortune* was typical of the Polperro boats; around twenty-six feet long with a deep draught of six feet and a gaff rig on a pole mast stepped on the keel. They were known as Polperro gaffers. There was no decking except for a small wooden covering in the bow.

'Under ya go,' whispered William. 'It won't be too comfortable though but it's the best I can do. I'll throw this old piece of canvas over the top to cover ya. It'll keep some of the weather out as well as keeping ya hidden. So don't come out, no matter what ya 'ear. OK?' He handed Thomas a water bottle and some food, put the canvas over him and was gone.

The space in the bow of the boat was reasonably roomy but hard and very cold. He was glad that William had lent him a fisherman's knitfrock. It was a long jersey and although it was tightly fitting on William, it was a little too large for Thomas. It was designed to keep the sailor's back warm and knitted from unwashed sheep's wool. Thomas thought that he smelled like a sheep but that was preferable to getting colder than he already was.

With the cold night air, the howling wind, the waves rushing up the shingle beach and the shishing backwash, sleep was impossible. Thomas thought about his life so far. He had had many adventures, not all of his own making and he wondered if it was time for him to settle down. Many of his friends were married or had an 'intended' but somehow he didn't think that he was ready for that.

'What do you think, Ma?' he thought. *'I still miss you a lot and wish I had you to talk to. Jenny's nice but she's not you. Maybe I should go and see what Alfie is up to. If it wasn't for Marty maybe I could stay here and be a fisherman too.'* His mind continued to drift and the hours slowly passed. He wished that he had Bouncer with him but William had thought that it would be too risky. He might bark or jump out and draw attention to the boat. That would never do.

He suddenly sensed that the wind was lessening in strength and although he knew that he shouldn't do it, he put his head out and realised that the rain was also letting up. He suddenly began to feel more confident about the morning's voyage.

He must have dozed off because he awoke very abruptly to the noise of someone in the boat.

'It's just me, Tom.' William's voice was most welcome. 'John's with me. Don't come out.'

Thomas was aware that dawn was breaking and the air was calm... no wind and no rain. Bouncer nosed his way into Thomas's hideout and licked his face. He then lay down quietly beside him and awaited events. The boat was rocking gently as the men stowed their gear and made ready for sea. There was no one else about as they launched the boat and headed straight out.

'Ya can come out now, lad. It's safe enough. There's no one about. It's a good day for fishing so they'll all be out soon.'

Thomas dragged himself out and looked around. The wind filled the sails and the sea was choppy and his stomach felt a little squirmy. He tried not to take any notice but soon he was heaving over the side, much to the glee of William and John.

'You'd never make a fisherman,' mused John. 'The sooner we get you back on land the better.'

They headed west keeping the coast on their left and after some time rounded a bluff and nosed into a small uninhabited bay. They dropped the sail and threw the anchor overboard. The boat rocked gently in shallow waters and William brought out some food.

'We'll wait 'ere until Michael shows up. 'Ope this weather 'olds. We should get in a good day's fishing if it does.' Time passed slowly and suddenly there was a shout from further up the beach.

'Looks like this is it,' said John as he stood up.

Thomas was suddenly lost for words. What could he say to these men who because of him, had lost part of their precious income, had rescued him, housed him and now had helped him to evade Marty.

He stood up and realised that he still had William's jersey on. He undid the buttons down the side and took it off.

'Here you are, William. Thank you both for all that you've done for me. I'll repay you some day, I promise.'

'Try an' keep outa trouble, Tom. We might not be 'round next time,' William laughed. 'Now off you go and good luck!'

Michael stood waiting patiently on the shingly beach and Bouncer sniffed all around him then sat quietly at his feet.

'Looks as though he likes you,' said Thomas as he shook hands with him. He turned and watched as William manoeuvred his boat and with a final wave headed out to sea.

'My horse is up the top. You'll have to ride back o' me 'til we reach the road to your home.'

'Must say I'm pleased to be back on land. This is good of you. I don't know my way around this area and could easily have got lost.'

An hour later the track opened out on to the road to Gunnislake and Thomas dismounted.

'Thank you so much, Michael. I'll be fine from here.' He waited until Michael turned his horse and galloped off before he started on the last leg of his journey.

***

Thomas resumed his work at the blacksmith's after he arrived back home. He loved everything about the smithy but he realised that it was not something that he would always want to do, not in Gunnislake anyway. Having been away for that week on the coast made him realise that there were a lot of other experiences he would like to have. The more he thought about it the more he thought that he would like to move on. He was a free man and if he moved much further away he would, hopefully, never encounter Marty again. The thought of Marty cast a long shadow over him and the only way for him to be free was to go somewhere where Marty was unlikely to be. A long way away. Maybe he could try a large town or a city. He knew that there was a place called Plymouth on the south coast. It was a port from where a lot of the sailing ships left from to go over the sea to other countries. There could be a lot of work there. But it was not all that far away and might still in Marty's territory.

'*London!*' he suddenly thought as he hit the red hot hinge with his hammer. '*London would be ideal. Plenty of people to get lost among and should be plenty of work.*'

He told Jenny and Sam of his idea.

'I wouldn't go immediately,' he said hastily, when he saw the look on Jenny's face. 'I'd need to save some money and I'd like to buy a horse. London's a long way and if I had a horse I could easily come back and visit.'

'You're right there, Tom. It is a long way. I doubt that you'd get back here very often. You'll meet some young miss and settle down and that will be the end of it.' Sam smiled at him. 'You're a grown man now. You have to make your own decisions and do what your heart tells you.'

'Tom seems to be one that trouble seeks out. I'll always worry about him, particularly if he is on his own.' Jenny turned to him. 'We'll always help you to do whatever you want. You are a fine young man. Everything that we wanted Will to be.' They were silent for a moment then she added, 'If you must go, so be it.'

'Thank you Jenny. It helps to have your blessing. I won't leave for a few weeks though. I'll see Albert Evans about a horse. He seems to have plenty at his place and if I get it soon I can practise riding it. I haven't really ridden since that awful time with Marty. I shoe horses a lot so I'm familiar with them. I can get work along the way too.'

Things went according to Thomas' plan and in a few weeks he was on his way.

Part 3:
1787 -1795

Chapter 10:
Hannah (1787 - 1795)

Hannah carried the two buckets of water from the stream and tipped them into the large tub which was situated in the shed near the small farmhouse. The tub was set into a brick surround with a fire roaring underneath. The water was heating nicely. *'Two more buckets should do it,'* she thought as she replaced the round wooden lid. It was the day of the week that she hated most. Washday! Always by the end of that day she was wet through, thoroughly exhausted and ready to drop. It was the same every week. She had started filling the tub at five o'clock in the morning and when it was full she left it to heat while she got breakfast. Sometimes her brothers would fill it for her the night before but they had come in late from their toil and she had told them not to worry. Now she wondered about her consideration for them.

She washed for her father and three brothers who worked all day in the fields either under the blazing sun or the bleak cold winter skies. The two older boys were adults and had been awarded some strips of land outside the town but with the Land Enclosure Act they now had their land beside their father's instead of spread all over the place. They all worked it together and all lived in the old farmhouse. Her mother had died four years previously and Hannah had automatically taken over the running of the household. Her father, Simon, had made it quite clear that he would not take another wife and she could have a home with him as long as she wanted it. She was twenty-two years old, had admirable qualities and was very efficient in the running of the house. Many a young man in the district would have asked for her hand in marriage if she had given them any encouragement. But she was not in any hurry and knew she was needed at home. Some of her friends thought that she was being left on the shelf and would remain a spinster for the rest of her life. Most of them were married and had little ones but she could not see the point of exchanging one life of hard work with her father and brothers for another life of hard work for a husband she did not love. She had made up her mind that she would only marry someone she loved, as her mother had done. Her parents had had a very happy relationship and Hannah knew that some of her friends were not experiencing that with the men they had chosen. No! She would stay where she was until someone she truly loved came along.

Hannah was housekeeper and maid of all things to all of them and although she loved them all dearly she wished that the older ones would find wives to take care of them, but they seemed in no hurry to depart the family nest and set up their own homes either.

When the last of the garments had been washed and strung up to dry and the tub emptied bucket by bucket, Hannah heaved a sigh and wearily made her way into the kitchen to make a cup of tea with the hot water from the kettle hanging over the open fire. Flopping into a chair and resting her feet on the pouffe she regarded her surroundings fondly. The kitchen was a relatively bare room with a scullery off to the left. A table and four chairs stood in the corner and a settee was along one wall. A large cupboard made by her father lined another wall and the chair she was presently seated in and one other were placed at a distance from the fire so as not to impede her movements while she was cooking.

A large pot hung from the bar across the fire and standing up tiredly she peered in, fervently hoping that there was enough food in it for their dinner. Kerrin, her eldest brother, had shot two rabbits the day before and she had immediately made them into a rich stew with plenty of vegetables. If she added a few more vegetables there should be sufficient for all of them. They had meat occasionally because they had a few sheep, a pig and some hens. They also had a milking cow. So with the vegetables that grew in the garden they were considered to be reasonably well off.

She continued with her household chores, finally bringing in her partially dry laundry and leaving it in the shed to be completed on the morrow. The men came in from the field and after a wash in the water barrel at the end of the house, sat down for their meal. Hannah had provided bread and cheese for their lunch but they were very hungry when they came in and grateful for their food. 'You've done well, lass,' said her father. 'Did your washing dry?'

'No, I'll have to put it out again tomorrow. 'Tis such an effort,' she answered as she gathered up the plates and took them into the scullery. She washed them in a bowl filled with hot water from the kettle. She would scour out the stew pot tomorrow. She was far too tired now.

She lay in her bed in the tiny moonlit bedroom and tried to sleep. Her mind and body were exhausted. She heard her men folk getting themselves ready for bed and rolled over to face the wall. The household settled down and she finally drifted off into a disturbed sleep. It was very windy and the banging of the shed door woke her. She sat up quickly and looked out the little window. The moon was still shining but partially hidden by cloud so she could not be sure of what she was seeing. She thought she saw a man entering the barn but just then the moon passed fully behind a cloud and the yard was in darkness.

'That's strange,' she thought as she lay back down. She wondered if she should wake her brothers but decided that she was probably imagining things and they needed their sleep without her annoying them with her silly notions. They had never really been bothered by intruders in the past but you could never take chances. She sat up again quickly when she heard a whistle. No mistaking anything this time. She jumped out of bed and rushed into the bedroom which all her brothers shared. Snoring reverberated from every bed.

'Kerrin, wake up. I'm sure there's someone in the barn,' she urged. She shook him violently.

'Whaddya doing,' he said as he struggled into consciousness. She told him of the man she thought she had seen and the whistle that she had definitely heard. By this time all the men were awake and complaining of the disturbance.

'Alright,' she said. 'If you won't go and have a look, I will!'

'Don't be silly. Ain't women's work. Andy, you go,' said Kerrin.

'Nope,' Andy answered. 'You're the oldest. You go.'

'This is silly. He could have robbed us by now and be well away,' protested Hannah.

'Ain't much to steal in the barn, is there?' Davie was the youngest.

''Course there is, stupid. There's the cart, and farm tools and hay and animal feed and the horse gear. But if you're going to stay here, I'll go,' and with that she hurried to her bedroom to get her cloak. She wrapped it closely around her and crept to the back door. The boys were already there and making their way into the yard.

'You stay here,' said Davie quietly. 'This is men's work.'

Hannah smiled at him and whispered, 'Be careful.' She watched, as, keeping to the shadows, they slipped over to the barn.

107

'Look at that,' Kerrin whispered pointing to the door. The wooden plank that normally held the doors closed together was lying on the ground and the door was shut fast, secured from the inside.

'Now, what?' asked Davie.

'There must be someone in there.' Kerrin bashed on the door. 'Come on out if you dare. There are three of us here,' he yelled as he picked up a long stick from the wood pile.

Immediately there was furious barking inside and someone fumbled at the big doors. They heard a voice say, 'Be quiet, Bouncer,' and the doors were gingerly pushed open. Kerrin held up his stick but reeled backwards as a big black dog came bounding at him knocking him over. The other boys rushed to his aid as a voice yelled 'Bouncer' and then another body joined the melee. They scrabbled around in the dirt grunting and groaning and snarling until suddenly a gunshot reverberated through the cold night air and the struggles ceased. However the moans continued as the combatants parted company. One moved aside and dragged the dog with him.

'Whadya think you boys are doing?' roared the man with the gun.

'It's ok Father. I think it is, anyway. Did you shoot anyone?' Davie crawled over beside him rubbing his head as he went.

'Of course I didn't. I'm not that bad a shot. I pointed it in the air. What a hullabaloo.' He directed the gun at Thomas and Bouncer as he went over to Kerrin and Andy who were lying on the ground. Blood was pouring from Andy's nose and Kerrin was just coming round. Hannah knelt beside them. She swung around to Thomas and uttered through clenched teeth, 'How dare you come on our property and beat up my brothers?'

'I didn't even hit them,' he protested. 'I was trying to get my dog and they banged heads. Anyway they shouldn'ta rushed Bouncer,' he added.

'Your Bouncer rushed Kerrin first and anyway what're you doing here in our barn? Papa could have shot you and asked questions later.' Hannah helped Andy to his feet. Tears were streaming out of his eyes as he said, 'I think he broke my bloody nose.'

'I tell you I didn't,' Thomas shouted.

'Be quiet all of you. Now come inside and we'll hear what this young man's excuse is. If it ain't good enough and we've caught him red handed, he'll pay the penalty.' Thomas froze. He had a fair idea what the penalty would be. Why was he always getting into these situations?

'Sir, I haven't stolen anything. Have a look in my bag. I'll get it,' and he turned to go back into the barn.

'Stay right there!' roared Simon. 'Davie, you go in and get his bag. Light the lantern. Hannah, take Kerrin and Andy inside the house and tend to them. Young man, there's a dog kennel over there. Put your dog in it and remember that I'm watching you and I have the gun.'

'I'm not gonna run. I wouldn't leave my horse behind anyway,' Thomas said as he urged Bouncer to the kennel and shut him in. *This man must be of some importance to have a gun,* he thought to himself as he returned.

'What horse?' frowned Simon.

'This one,' said Davie as he led Thomas's nag out of the barn.

'Well, bless me. Are you a highwayman?'

'Not likely,' shrieked Thomas. 'No highwayman would have a horse that old. He'd never get away.'

109

'What's in his bag, Davie?' asked Simon. 'If there is one thing belonging to me, this young man will hang.'

Thomas began to shake. He knew that there was nothing in it, but this man seemed keen to hang him. Or was he just trying to scare him? More likely that was it.

'Sir, I only needed shelter for the night. I've been making my way from Gunnislake to London and been on the road six months or more working as I go. I do jobs here and there in return for shelter and food. I got caught out and didn't get things sorted before dark. I was going to camp under a bush but then saw your place and thought that it would be warmer in the barn.'

'Where's this Gunnislake?' asked Simon.

'A long way south of here. Down in the Tamar Valley in Cornwall. I lived there, but decided that as I was young and single I would move on and see what the rest of the country is like.' Thomas was quite proud of this. Most countrymen and women did not venture far from their birthplaces and generations of families lived in the same valleys and dales for hundreds of years.

'Well, let's go inside where it's warmer and talk,' said Simon and putting his gun down, he led the way inside.

It was warm in the kitchen where Hannah had stoked up the fire and was making a hot drink. She glared at Thomas as he followed her father through the door. He stood awkwardly until Simon told him to sit on the stool just inside the door.

'What a peculiar young man,' she thought. *'He could've run away. Papa would never have shot him but there he is standing like an oaf waiting for the noose!'*

'Right,' said Simon as he took the tea Hannah handed him. 'You'd better repeat your story.'

'What makes you think we should believe you?' asked Kerrin when Thomas had finished.

'Because it's true,' retorted Thomas. He remembered fronting up to Mr Cotter with Marty and trying to explain his situation, and again with Sir Edric. He always seemed be answering to someone and this irritated him. The sooner he got away from here the better.

'If you'll just let me get my stuff and animals I'll be on my way. I won't trouble you anymore. Just let me go.'

'What a wimp,' thought Hannah. 'The boys would have fought their way out of a situation like this. They wouldn't just stand there and wait for something to happen. They would make it happen.'

'You can sleep in the barn tonight but be off first thing in the morning. I don't know whether to believe you or not but I never want to see you again. Get yourself well away from here. I don't trust men who just appear in the middle of the night. That's my last word,' said Simon, 'so get going.'

***

As Thomas lay in the hay with Bouncer by his side he thought about the events of the night. Had he been lucky or was the man testing him? He didn't want to move on too far just yet and had been told that there was a village a few miles away. He didn't have to do what the man said. He could please himself and with that thought in his head he went to sleep.

Chapter 11:
Turnpikes and Pikemen

It was dark and raining as Thomas left the farmyard. The road to the village was not a major road and was narrow and muddy. As he rounded a bend, he spotted a turnpike at the intersection of three roads. The man who occupied the dwelling beside it welcomed him and invited him to share a pot of tea. Thomas accepted with alacrity. He was cold and hungry.

'You're more hospitable than the folks in the farmhouse I've just left,' he dramatised. 'They thought I was a robber and I just escaped with my life.'

'People around 'ere work hard for what they 'ave and don't want any of it taken away, not even by me,' the pikeman answered. He put some more turf on the little fire in the small grate and the smell of peat permeated the cold air. Thomas looked around. It was an interesting building, not very big and the small room they were presently sheltering in was attached to a cottage which was inhabited by the man, his wife and two small children. From this room where he was warming himself, the man emerged when a traveller appeared at the turnpike. A sign was attached to the wall above the door leading into the building. It detailed the fees for the turnpike.

Pedestrian travellers were exempt from tolls as were soldiers and mail coaches. Other charges were based on the size of the carriage or wagon and the number of horses pulling it: one shilling for a coach and four, sixpence for a coach and pair and fourpence for a coach and one. Higher rates were charged for wagons and carts with wheel rims less than three inches in width as these were deemed to cause more road wear whilst wider ones would act as rollers and not damage the road as much. One horse and rider would pay one and a half pennies. A fee of ten pence per score was charged for oxen and cows, and five pence per score for a drove of sheep, calves and swine.

As Thomas could not read it made no difference to him. He would take the man at his word and pay what he was told. Often however, because many travellers could not read, a pikeman charged what he liked, usually more depending on what he thought the circumstances of the travellers might be. He used the extra amount to supplement his meagre income of ten shillings and sixpence per week from, which he had to pay for the oil to light the lamps on the pike each night.

'From what I've seen, people often object to paying the toll,' said Thomas. 'Have you felt their anger?'

'Have I ever! Feared for me loif at times, I 'ave. I'm jist trying to do me job. Collectin' the money's important. Pays for the upkeeps of the roads, it does, 'though ya wouldn't think so t' see some of 'em.'

'Have to agree there,' said Thomas. 'But I've travelled on a lot of them and have to say that yours are no worse than many others.'

'Wot 'appens is this,' explained the pikeman. 'Some of the locals who 'ave money sets up a trust called a Turnpike Trust an' they buys a length of road an' then they sets up a turnpike every five miles or so to get some of their money back an' they pay roadspeople to keep it in good repair. Idea's good but it don't always work though.'

He slurped from his mug of tea as Thomas asked, 'Why not? Sounds simple enough.'

'Cos first, the road repairers don't do their job properly an' don't spend the money where 'tis meant to be spent an' that's on the roads, an' second, people don't like payin'. With turnpikes 'bout every five miles it's a stop-start affair for 'em. Always diggin' in their pockets an' some get real angry 'bout it. I'm just doin' me job though but they don't like it.'

'Well, if they want to get on with their journey they have to pay and that's all there is to it,' said honest Thomas.

'Don't you believe that young man,' responded the pikeman. 'They just go through the fields an' dodge us.'

'Really!' exclaimed Thomas. 'How do they get a coach over the fields? Passengers wouldn't like that much.'

'I don't mean the coaches.' The pikeman was scornful in his reply. 'I mean riders and flocks and herds.'

'What do the farmers say? Bet they're not happy about that.'

''Course they ain't 'appy. But they're used t' people cuttin' 'cross fields an' 'though they grumble and talk 'bout trespass, they don't do nothing 'bout it 'cos it's bin the custom for people to do that. Wagons go around the side roads where there ain't always turnpikes an' we miss out on their money. Those roads are worse'n these though so they get an awful ride. An' the mobs! They're somethin' else.' The man threw his hands up in despair just as as a loud cry was heard from the pike.

'Pike! Gate! Hallo! Anybody there?'

'Comin', comin!' he muttered as he rushed out into the rain and mud to collect his one and a half penny from the rider waiting to be let through. Having paid, the pikeman turned the pike and the rider spurred his horse and took off.

Thomas watched from the doorway. 'Can't be much fun on a day like this,' he said.

'It all adds up,' the man muttered as, turning his back on Thomas, he put the money away in a tin box chained to the wall, and locked it.

114

'Looks pretty secure but also very visible,' commented Thomas.

'Yeah. But remember travellers don' usually come in 'ere. I just felt sorry for ya.'

Thomas laughed. 'My good luck. But even I could take that box from you.'

'Just you try it. I'm stronger than ya think. I've taken others on who've tried to relieve me of me takin's. Give it a go an' see what 'appens.'

'No. You don't need to worry. I'm honest and God-fearing. I don't have much but what I do have is my own. Even that old nag out there and m' faithful Bouncer here. Probably my most valued possessions. Now I must be off. Thank you. Here's my one and halfpenny to keep your... What on earth is that?' Thomas rushed to the door in time to see a rider take the pike with a flying leap and disappear down the road and out of sight.

'Nothin' I can do 'bout folks like that. They're a pain in the arse but they get away with it. I can't chase 'em 'cos I can't leave me post. Someone further down the road might get 'im, though.'

Chapter 12:
A foot in the door

Thomas had been in the town of Penshurst for two weeks when he saw Hannah. He was working at the blacksmith's, having been befriended by him. He fortuitously had too much work and no competent help and accepted Thomas's offer to work for a bed and a small remuneration. The blacksmith had a loft where Thomas slept each night and his pay was just enough to buy food for himself and Bouncer. His horse was in a paddock on the outskirts of the town and for a few pence each week the owner looked after him and attended to his needs. All was well in Thomas's world. Until he set eyes Hannah, that is.

He was standing at the door of the forge getting some fresh air and quenching his thirst when he glanced down the road and saw a woman alighting from a wagon. She looked a little familiar but he did not realise that it was Hannah until he saw Kerrin helping her down. He watched as she gathered her basket from the back of the wagon and hurried down the street her long skirt swirling about her legs. He thought about hurrying after her but James, the smithy interrupted his thoughts.

'Better get back to work, lad. There's much to do an' we can't stand around gawkin' all day.'

Thomas turned away, his thoughts in turmoil. What was different about her today that made him notice her? He found it difficult to concentrate on his work.

'If you hit that any harder you'll ruin it,' James observed. 'What's the matter with you?'

'Nothing,' Thomas answered as he brought his mind back to the job in hand. 'I haven't had my lunch yet. Do you mind if I nip down to the baker's and get a loaf? I'll only be a minute.'

'Or'right. Only a minute, mind ya.'

Thomas threw off his apron and walked out into the sunlight. Hannah was nowhere to be seen. He walked to the bakery all the time watching for her, gazing down alleyways, peering into shops, looking down side streets. He was so preoccupied that when a heavy hand descended on his shoulder he jumped and spun around, his fists clenched.

'I thought my father told you to get outa here! You ain't welcome. He won't be happy to know you're still skulkin' around.' Kerrin's hand tightened on Thomas's shoulder and he could feel the strength of the man's grip.

Thomas was so relieved to see that it wasn't Marty he almost shook his hand. Then he realised that Kerrin's face was not at all friendly and he responded. 'I'm sure as hell not skulking and you can tell your father that I'm not leaving town just because he says so. I haven't done anything wrong and if he says I have he's lying.' Thomas shook himself free and stood as tall as he could. Even so, Kerrin was taller and broader.

'I don't care what you think. Just don't bad mouth our father. Stay outa our way and the further away the better. I can settle this here, if you want.' Kerrin bunched his fists ready to fight. A crowd was gathering and Thomas, realising that he would be out-muscled, turned away. He continued to the bakery, bought his loaf and returned to his work.

Kerrin was there talking to James. He turned around when Thomas stopped in the doorway,

'Watch this criminal. He'll rob ya blind,' he said to James.

'What on earth are you talking about?' exclaimed James. 'The lad works for me. He's one of the best I've had.'

117

'He's being stupid. An oaf,' said Thomas angrily. 'He thought I was going to rob them when I sought shelter in his father's barn. Why would I settle down for the night if I was going to rob them? It's crazy.'

'I don't trust you and if I were you, James, I'd be very wary of 'im. Send 'im packing.' With that Kerrin stalked out the door.

'I don't know anything about you lad, but you're a good worker. Don't let me down otherwise you will be down the road.'

'I'm as honest as the day is long,' said Thomas. 'You have nothing to fear from me.'

***

'Saw that rogue Tom in town today,' Kerrin said he as reached for a piece of bread to mop up the gravy on his plate.

'You didn't tell me,' interjected Hannah.

'So you know who I mean. I wasn't going to mention it even, but thinkin' about it, you should all know that he's still around. Just let me know if he ever bothers you, Hannah.'

'Don't be daft. He's no robber. Too much of a wimp. Why should he bother me?' Hannah gathered up the plates and took them to the scullery.

'What do you think, Dad? Is he a wimp?' Andy looked askance at his father.

'I know no more 'bout him than you do. We can't force him to leave. What was he doing, Kerrin?' Simon asked.

Kerrin related the episode in the town, neglecting to tell them of his role in it. He did however say that he thought that James Blackler must be losing his wits to employ him.

'But James didn't have the experience that we had,' suggested Simon. 'He'll be on his guard now that you have warned him and so will Tom. He doesn't need to stay. If he wanted to he could up and off and make trouble elsewhere. If he's innocent he has nothing to worry about.'

***

Thomas lay on his straw palliasse with Bouncer by his side. He had never felt like this before. 'What do you think, old boy?' he asked Bouncer as he stroked his head. 'Do you think she's pretty?' He thought about how she had looked when he first met her. No wonder he hadn't taken any notice. It was the middle of a windy night, he recalled, and she had appeared after her brothers in her nightshift and cloak with her hair blowing everywhere. How could he have not thought that she was pretty then, even when he was fearing for his life? Even later in the dim light of the cottage she had hardly been discernible. Today had been a beautiful sunny day, and Hannah had been dressed in a lovely pale blue gown with her long hair kept under the control of a matching bonnet. She looked very different this time and Thomas was spellbound. He had to see her again. But how? He couldn't just appear at her door. He would soon be driven off by all those men in her household. Anyway, would she really want to see him? She had been just as hostile as her brothers that night. She might even tell her brothers if he seemed to be making a nuisance of himself. Then there would be trouble. Did he want to see her so much?

Suddenly he felt very lonely. He was a man on his own. No family, apart from Jenny and Sam, no woman, no home, no money, no friends. Nothing except Bouncer and an old horse.

'I haven't amounted to much, have I, Ma? I wanted you to be proud of me. But what've I done? Nothing. I seem to get into trouble wherever I go. I wish you were here. I could talk to you about Hannah. What should I do? Forget about her or risk getting beaten up? And what if she doesn't want me? She might have someone else in her life.'

He lay quietly and mulled things over in his mind. Eventually he fell into a fitful sleep only to awake sometime later, clawing at the horrible constriction of his throat that he still experienced at times, with Bouncer fervently licking his face.

***

Thomas had not yet thought about how he could arrange to meet Hannah but had decided that for his own peace of mind he must. He went about his work at the blacksmith's as industriously as ever but his mind was no longer on the job in hand. He kept wandering to the door in the hope that he might espy her again, but he didn't.

He formed a plan, but doubted that it would work. However it was the only one that he could think of and as he did not work on Sunday mornings he took that opportunity to put his plan into action. As a precaution, he left Bouncer behind and taking his horse, he headed for the Fenwick farm. It was very early and he thought that he might have to wait there a little while. He had no way of knowing the time but he was patient and was prepared to wait for as long as it took.

'I'd better not take Snag too close,' he said to himself and with that, he dismounted and led his horse off the road to a small copse. He tied her securely to a tree and then, keeping close to the hedgerow, he made his way to the bushes at the side of the cottage. Making himself as comfortable as possible, he settled down to wait. He could see the back door from which a shingle path led to the outbuildings. Hannah would have to come out sooner or later. He remembered waiting for Alfie to come out of his house all those years ago. He could afford to be patient this time. He had all day.

He fell into a doze and was startled awake by someone riding into the yard. He peered out from his bushes and was astounded to see Andy leading Snag into the barn and locking her in.

He fell back into his position and wondered what to do. He didn't want to lose his horse and apart from that it was a long walk home. He waited. After a few minutes Simon and Kerrin came out and disappeared into the barn. As they came out Simon remarked, 'It's surely his horse. What was it doin' tied up in the copse? He must be around here somewhere. But why? That's what I'd like to know.'

'Either he still wants to pinch our stuff, an' I can't think why, or he's after our Hannah,' Kerrin said earnestly.

Simon stopped in his tracks. 'What on earth makes you think that?' he asked.

'Well she's a good lookin' woman an' any man would want her. She can housekeep better'n most. If she weren't me sister I'd marry her. Seems to me that's more likely than him wanting to steal our stuff. Why ours, an' what would he take it away in? Can't carry it all, can 'e?' reasoned Kerrin.

'Maybe he'd load it on the wagon. That's the most sensible thing, don't you think? It's what I'd do,' answered Simon.

'Then he'd have to get rid of the gear and the wagon. Folks around here would recognise it and know it was ours. No! I think it's Hannah. We'll have to be vigilant.'

'You were the one who thought he was a robber. Now you've changed your mind. Why?' Simon was puzzled.

'Had time to think about it. I think that *if* he was a robber he would be after jewellery and small stuff from the house that he can stash in his bag. Not stuff from the barn. Maybe he wants to get to know us better so that he can rob the house.'

'Kerrin. You aren't thinking straight. One minute he's not a robber but just wants our Hannah. Now he wants to rob the house. Or do you think he wants to do all those things? Now come on. We have to get moving. We'll be late.' Simon headed for the house while Kerrin lingered in the yard. He looked around and was about to walk off when he spotted a movement in the bushes.

'Hey!' he yelled as he realised that someone was hiding there. He took off after Thomas, who was fast but did not know the area of the farm. He worried that he would get boxed in so he made for the road. Cutting across a paddock he hurdled a gate and raced up the road. Kerrin gave up and went back to the cottage.

'It was that little wimp. I can't believe that he'd have the gall to come back here,' he said angrily. 'If I catch up with him I'll let him have it. Anyway we have his horse so that will slow him up a bit.'

'You can't keep it,' Hannah exclaimed. 'He just needs to tell the constable and if he finds it in our barn we'll all be in trouble. Stealing's a hanging offence. You're going to have to get it back to him.'

'If he wants it, he can come and get it. I'll just say we found it tied up in our copse, which we did, and we didn't know who it belonged to. Now we'd better get going or we'll be late. Andy, have you harnessed up the wagon yet?'

'Not yet, but it'll only take a second,' he answered. 'Come out when you're ready,'

Thomas watched from the safety of the hedgerow and saw the wagon leave the farm. He noted that the whole family were in it and as soon as they were out of sight he hurried back to the barn to retrieve his horse. To his dismay the barn was locked. He walked right around it but it was quite secure. His first impulse was to break the door down but he realised that that would make him a true felon and would land him in a heap of trouble. With great reluctance he started the long walk home.

***

Thomas laboured hard at the blacksmiths and by the end of the day he was very tired. But he had decided in his mind what to do next.

'James,' he asked cautiously. 'Would it be possible for me to borrow your horse, please?'

'Why? Where's yours? Not gone lame, has it?' James teased.

'No no. Nothing like that. It's up at the Fenwick farm and I want to go and get it back.'

'What's it doing up there?' James wanted to know. Thomas wondered how much to tell him. He hesitated.

'C'mon lad. I know Kerrin doesn't like you so how come your horse is there?' insisted James.

'I left it tied up in a copse and they found it and took it to their barn. I tried to get it back after they left but they locked it in so I couldn't.' Thomas couldn't believe what he was saying and James couldn't either. It sounded so stupid.

'I've never heard such nonsense. Why didn't you just tell them it was yours?'

Thomas felt uncomfortable. 'They warned me never to go to their place again. In fact they told me to get out of town. They're really hostile to me. You know that much but that's only half of it,' Thomas explained.

'Then why on earth go there in the first place?' James was puzzled and Thomas looked really uncomfortable.

He thought about it and finally mumbled, 'I wanted to see Hannah.'

James stared at him and then he laughed. 'Well my boy, we've all done something stupid over a lass at some time. You're no different.' He chuckled away merrily and Thomas flushed.

'I'll tell you what I'll do to help you,' he added. 'You can take my horse as long as you don't lose him, but to help you worm your way in, I'll give you something to take back to the Fenwick's. They left some hinges to be repaired. They might think its funny that you're delivering them, but it'll give you an excuse to knock on their door. I don't think they'll knock your block off if you have a genuine excuse.'

'It seems like a good idea,' said Thomas. 'I just hope it works.'

***

The sun was going down as he arrived at the Fenwick farm. He dismounted at the back door and held the reins of James's horse tightly in his hand. It was his getaway horse if need be.

He rapped loudly on the door and nervously waited. Eventually he heard a scraping sound on the other side and the door was opened. It was Davie.

'What're you doing here?' he demanded.

'I'm delivering some hinges that James repaired for your father, and while I'm here, I'll collect my horse. I think you have it here.' Thomas tried to feel confident as Davie stared at him without comment. Then, slamming the door, Davie went back to the living room.

'It's that Tom fellow with some hinges and he wants his horse. Pity Kerrin and Andy aren't here. They'd soon sort him out,' he stormed at his father. Hannah jumped up.

'I'll deal with this.' His father rose to his feet and went to the door.

'What is it, young man?' he asked Thomas.

'I have your hinges, sir, and I'd like to collect my horse while I am here, if you please,' he said simply.

'Tom, are you sure there ain't somethin' else to all o' this? You were here the other day, weren't you? That's how your horse got to be here.'

Hannah appeared at her father's shoulder and Thomas gave a start to see her there. His heart began pounding and his face flushed. Simon watched him closely. Could Kerrin be right? Was it Hannah that he had come to see after all?

Thomas looked around swiftly but could see no sign of Kerrin, so replied, 'I did come the other day, sir, but things got muddled up and because Kerrin doesn't like me, he jumped to the wrong conclusion and thought I was here to rob you. I'm not, sir. Never was and never will be. I'm not that sort of person.'

'Then why did you come?' Simon asked.

'Honestly, the first time was to sleep in your barn and the second...,' he paused not knowing whether to go on or not.

'C'mon, lad, what was the second,' persisted Simon.

'To see Hannah.' He flushed. 'That is the honest truth.'

'Don't believe him Dad, and Kerrin wouldn't either if he was here,' interjected Davie.

Simon swung around to face Davie. 'Well he ain't and anyway I'm the head of this household, not Kerrin. I say what happens and doesn't happen an' you should remember that, my boy.'

'But Dad...'

'There ain't no buts, Davie. Now go and git Tom's horse and wait outside. You, Tom, come in here. Come on.' he repeated as Thomas hesitated and looked at Hannah. She looked uncomfortable but her father didn't notice. He pushed past her and into the living room. Thomas and Hannah followed.

'Sit down,' Simon motioned to Tom. 'Now that Davie is not about, we can talk. What's this about Hannah? Why do ya wanna see her?'

Thomas felt really embarrassed at his direct questions, but knew that if he didn't answer he would be lost. 'I think she's very pretty,' he mumbled, 'and I'd like to get to know her, sir, if that's alright with you?'

'And what about me?' interjected Hannah. 'I should have some say in who wants to get to know me and I certainly don't want to know a would-be robber.'

'Hannah! Be quiet! Men have to discuss these things. You should go and join your brother outside and leave it to us.' Simon rose from his seat as he spoke.

'No! It's my life you're talking about. Kerrin isn't here to stick up for me so I have to do it myself.' Hannah was adamant.

'Sir, I wouldn't want to upset Hannah. I'm not what you think. I'm a simple fellow really and I wish I could prove it to you.'

'Simple is right,' retorted Hannah. 'You must be to keep coming back. Kerrin would knock your head off if he was here.'

'Hannah! Stop this. I've said before that I make the decisions about this household and I'll make this one. Now settle down.'

'You make me consort with this person and I'll not be part of your household at all. Mama always said that I should know my own mind and I'm surprised that you're even thinking about allowing this man to 'get to know' me. He's a nobody and we know that he is violent. Look at the way he attacked the boys the first time he came here.' Hannah was very indignant.

'Sir, Hannah is wrong in her impression of me. I am not like that but she must be in agreement with this. I can't possibly force my attentions on her. I would never do that. But my heart tells me that it will never rest until I have at least tried to convey my feelings.' Thomas was becoming quite poetic, but that did not make any difference to Hannah who still looked appalled at the whole situation. 'I might not look much and I've no possessions to offer Hannah, but I'm respectable and I'm not in any trouble. I'd take care of her,' Thomas continued.

'You're never going to get the chance, and that's that!' stormed Hannah.

Simon held up his hand. 'Hannah, please! Tom, now is not the time. I think you should leave. Kerrin will be back soon and it's best that you're not here when he comes.'

Thomas looked as though he was about to say something but changed his mind. He stood up and turned to the door.

'Don't get your hopes up Tom, but I'll get in touch with you one way or the other.'

***

'There's something not quite right about that young man and I intend to find out what it is before I make my decision.' Simon had thought about it overnight and he looked closely at Hannah as he said it.

'Papa, you can't still be thinking about that man. This is my life and future that you are playing with.' Hannah jumped up from the breakfast table. 'Forget it!'

'Hannah I won't encourage him if I don't think he is worthy of you, you must realise that. You are the most precious thing I have now your mother has gone. but no man is perfect and Tom might not be either.'

***

Simon sat in the alehouse awaiting Thomas's appearance. He was not a hard man. His beloved wife had softened his heart on many occasions and he missed her dearly, especially at times such this when her wise counsel would have been invaluable. He loved his daughter, there was no doubt about that, and in many ways she was like her mother, attractive, strong-willed and independent. He knew that she would not marry Tom if she didn't want to, and he wouldn't have wanted her to but the young man intrigued him. He wanted to know more about him. He remembered his own courtship of his wife. He had nothing to

127

offer except a promise of life-long love. He had not failed in that respect and they had been very happy until the day she died. Love had been enough. He looked up as Thomas rushed in to the alehouse.

'Sorry I'm late, Mr Fenwick,' he said breathlessly as he sat down.

'Don't worry about that, boy,' Simon responded. 'Would you like an ale?'

'I'll get it,' Thomas answered and a few minutes later he slid into his seat opposite Simon and put his drink on the table.

'Now sir, where do you want me to start? You want to know about me?'

'Start when you were born. If you're after my Hannah, I want to know all about you,' said Simon.

Thomas hesitated. Would Mr Fenwick know if he was lying even by omission. He could never lie to Hannah so if he didn't tell the truth now, Mr Fenwick might eventually find out and that could be worse. He might never trust him. So, very nervously, he commenced to tell Simon all about his life. He didn't leave anything out and when he had finished Simon was silent.

'Mr Fenwick, are you alright?' he asked anxiously.

'Yes, yes of course. I'm just thinking about what you've told me. It's unbelievable,' Simon said.

'But it's true, sir. You have to believe me.'

'Oh I do believe you. At least I think I do. I just find it hard to believe that all this has happened to one so young. How old are you?'

'I'm not sure. Probably early twenties I should think. We didn't worry about birthdays when I was a boy. Getting through each day was enough. We didn't have special days.' Thomas paused. 'Now you know my story, does it make any difference? I would never harm Hannah, ever.'

128

'And what about Hannah? She may well resist,' Simon said thoughtfully.

'You said that you made the decisions in your family,' Thomas ventured.

'Aye, I did say it. But do you really think that I would make her go with a lad she didna want?'

'Nooo. I wouldn't if she was my daughter. I have nothing to offer her yet but I do love her. I know I do and if I have a chance I'll make her love me too.' Thomas stood up.

'Sit down young fellow. Your story is amazing and I'm impressed that you've not turned bad with all the adversity you've had in your life. Maybe I'll give you a chance and hopefully Hannah will meet you.' He thought awhile, 'There's a town fair in the Market Square on Saturday. I'll make sure she's there. I'll have a world with the boys too and make sure that they don't interfere. It is up to you to change her impression of you. Just tell her what you have told me.'

'What, all of it?' queried Thomas. 'I'd rather not – not yet anyway, particularly about my mother.'

'If what you say is true you have nothing to hide and she needs to know anyway. Hannah is very wise and she might think that some of the things you did were unwise but on the other hand she might think you were very brave. Try her out.' Simon stood up. 'I must get going. It's up to you.'

***

Thomas arose early and headed for the river. He had found a secluded spot where, each evening, he swam and tried to wash the grime from the days activities from his body. He was unusual in doing this. Most men didn't care and didn't wash from one week to the next. But he liked to be clean and especially he wanted to be nice for Hannah. He jumped in and using a piece of soap given to him by James's wife he washed his hair. Bouncer loved this activity too and needed no urging to jump into the water with Thomas. They romped around for a little while and then Thomas said 'You love this too, don't you, boy? But come on. We have much better things to do.'

He headed for the bank and climbed out, dried himself on a scrap of cloth and put his almost clean clothes back on. He felt great. Suddenly his stomach contracted when he remembered that today was the most important day in his life and he had not thought about what he would say to Hannah. But then maybe he shouldn't plan what to say. Just let it happen.

He wandered down to the Market Square where the fair was to be held. Every week there was a market where the local folk sold their surplus produce. But this fair was much bigger and could only be held with the permission of the local squire. Because of this, it was only held twice a year but it attracted people from all over the district. The stalls selling anything from pickled onions, honey, herbs, grains, eggs, milk and cheese spilled out of the square and into the streets. The square itself was divided up into areas where sheep, cattle, horses, pigs and hens could be displayed and sold.

In addition to all of this, entertainers created a fun atmosphere. They usually set up in an adjoining paddock and charged a few pence for people to watch. They included musical groups, dance troupes, jugglers, acrobats, puppets and marionettes.

He looked around the gathering crowd and spotted Kerrin with a young lass on his arm. *'Mmmm! Maybe he has a heart after all,'* he thought. *'Hard to imagine it though.'*

He wandered casually around talking with people he knew but all the time keeping an eye open for Hannah. He came across a crowd surrounding a man standing on a ladder.

'C'mon up folks,' the man shouted. 'This is where to get it! Merrywether's All Purpose Cure. From dandruff on your top to bunions on your bottom... ooops... I mean feet, an' ev'rywhere in between. Cure all your ailments with Merrywethers! Fix your stomach, gallbladder, kidneys an' whatever else ails ya.' He held up a bottle. 'Only one shillin' per bottle. Fix ev'rythin' wot's wrong wiv ya. Give it a go!'

'Ya reckon it's good do ya?' a voice shouted.

Thomas looked around and suddenly noticed a man pushing through the crowd and up towards the caller. He looked closely and saw a small man, solidly built with a pale complexion. He also noticed that he had a wooden leg and a crutch under one arm.

'I bought ya stuff an' look at me. Take a look ev'ryone. Did it fix me leg? Not on ya Nellie. An' now I only got one. T'other got chopped orf t' save me loif. Do y' reckon y' should buy it?'

The crowd pushed forward shouting at the unfortunate man up the ladder.

'Wot,' he shouted back. 'One complaint not cured 'mong millions! Ya ain't gonna listen to him are ya? Wot abart all o' those wot got cured?'

'Well where are they?' someone yelled from the back.

The crowd surged and Thomas was horrified to see Hannah being pushed along with them. He charged into the melee and elbowed his way to her side.

'Hannah,' he hissed as he grabbed her arm. 'Let's get outa here.' He pulled her to his side and put one arm around her shoulder and with the other, forced his way through the crowd. He took her over to a seat and sat her down not taking his arm away from her shoulder. After a few minutes she stood up and made to move away.

'Thankyou for that. It was a bit frightening, but I'm alright now,' she said, eyeing the crowd as two policemen moved in to stop any trouble. Thomas pulled her back down onto the seat.

'Hannah, I need to talk with you. Your father has given me his permission to meet you and I want you to listen to what I have to say. You can then decide if you want to see more of me or not and if you don't, I'll leave Penshurst immediately although it would break my heart to have to do so. You'll never see me again.' He gazed earnestly into her eyes, silently pleading that she would let him speak.

Hannah looked at him thoughtfully. 'Very well then,' she said, 'although Papa has no right to start making arrangements for me. Mama would never have allowed him to if she was here. I suppose talking to you can't hurt but don't get too confident that I will get interested in you.'

'Hannah, what I said at your house the other night was all true. I was not there to rob you. I have much to say to you but maybe not here. There's too much going on with all these people here. I know! Let's buy some buns and lemonade and go down to the river where it's quiet. Don't look at me like that,' he added as she raised her eyebrows at him. 'I promise I'll not touch you, just talk.'

'Well alright. Maybe for a little while,' she said standing up. He took her by the arm and the softness of her flesh under his hand made his heart pound. They made their purchases, which used up all of Thomas's money. He really had nothing to offer her.

They left the fair and although they did not know it Kerrin's eyes followed them as they went. But he did not intervene. His father had told him that if he did so he would knock his block off and although Kerrin was a big fellow, father was father and nobody disobeyed him. He spotted Davie in the crowd and beckoned him over. He might get away with it.

132

'Hannah has just left with that oaf. Follow 'em and don't do nought and don't be seen. Just watch wot 'appens. 'An don't tell father either, or we'll both be in trouble!'

Davie didn't ask questions but followed Thomas and Hannah to the river all the time keeping well out of sight. He watched from behind some undergrowth as they sat down on the bank and started to eat their lunch.

'I'm going to start at the beginning, or what I think is the beginning, and you can ask any questions you like. I'll be truthful,' Thomas assured her. He started with the death of his mother, his friendship with Alfie, Mr Cotter and Mac, his experiences with Marty, his new parents, Sam and Jenny, smuggling and William, John and Joan, finally ending up in Simon's barn.

'That's the truth of it. Please believe it. I know it sounds far-fetched but it is the truth,' he pleaded.

Hannah was silent. He looked at her closely and was amazed to see a tear appear in the corner of her eye and slide slowly down her cheek.

'Please don't be upset,' he implored. 'I didn't mean for that. I just wanted to tell you about my life so that you can make up your mind about me. Don't be sad about it. Many good, happy things have happened to me too. I've met some wonderful people and I have met you. Just to do that has made it worthwhile.'

She smiled up at him. 'But your mother,' she whispered, 'and your childhood. It's so sad. My life was so happy until my mother died. She and father were very happy. My brothers loved her very much too. There was no violence in our household, just love and fun. So different from yours. How did you bear it?'

'Because I loved my mother and she loved me. We looked after each other. We should have left and I would have taken care of her but it was difficult and I was young. I never thought of her killing him though. I should have done it myself but then I would

133

have been hanged. Anyway it doesn't matter now. My life is what it is now and I offer it to you, Hannah. I love you dearly and want to spend the rest of my life with you. I have nothing to offer except my life and my love, one mad dog and an old nag.'

'Mmmm. Doesn't seem much of a bargain.' She paused. 'I've heard all you've told me, Tom, but I don't really know you. I don't even know if I like you. I'll give you a chance. Just don't let's rush things. I need to get to know you better. I don't know if I can love you and I certainly wouldn't want to out of pity. If you love me as you say you do, you won't rush me.'

'Of course I won't. Just to hear you say all that makes me very happy.' Thomas jumped up and pulled her to her feet. 'I won't rush you but I've wanted to kiss you ever since I saw you in town that day,' he said quietly and took her in his arms. She did not protest but tilted her face up to meet his lips. They did not notice Davie slip out of the bushes and run back to the fair. He found Kerrin and told him briefly what he had seen.

'Did you hear what they said,' he asked impatiently.

'No, I was too far away but it all looked pretty cosy to me. Now I'm off to enjoy myself. You do what you like,' and he sauntered off to find some amusement.

Chapter 13:
Happiness

Thomas had never felt so happy. It was six months since he had found the love of his life and he was never going to let her go. He did everything correctly, did nothing that would cause her father concern and tried to get on with her brothers. With Andy and Davie it was not too difficult but Kerrin still did not like him.

'I don't know what it is about your brother,' he said to Hannah one evening as they sat beside the creek. 'He still doesn't like me. I worked with him in the barn today and he hardly spoke at all. Does he still have a problem with me or is his love-life going astray?'

'You should ask him. I think he's trying to make up his mind about marrying Molly. She's really nice but Kerrin has always been a bit of a lad and it would be a big step for him. I don't think it's you he is preoccupied with. You could try and talk to him about it. He might open up a bit.'

'You're very wise, Hannah,' he said as he pecked her on the cheek. 'Maybe I'm afraid of him.'

Hannah whooped with laughter. 'I used to think you were a wimp,' she smiled. 'I remember thinking that the boys would have fought their way out after that barn episode but you seemed happy to take your punishment.'

'You might remember that I did fight them all but that wasn't my choice. They pounced on me. After that experience there was no way I would tackle them all again.'

'No, I suppose not. Anyway I don't think you're a wimp any more. You got past my father and that's saying something for your bravery.'

'I haven't asked him if I can marry you yet. It might be a little different when I do,' he said adventurously.

'When will you do that?' she answered quietly.

Thomas stared at her. 'When do you want me to?' he asked tentatively.

'As soon as you want too,' she replied taking his face in his hands and gently kissing him. He felt totally overwhelmed. She did want to marry him, he thought in awe. He grabbed her to him and passionately kissed her back.

'You have made me so happy,' he murmured. 'I'll ask him now. Nothing like the present.'

He jumped up and rushed along the banks of the stream dragging Hannah by the hand and, in his haste, tripped on a tree root. They both tumbled headfirst into the water. It was not deep and they came up coughing and spluttering and covered in weed and mud.

Hannah started laughing and began splashing water over him. He reciprocated and soon a full blown water fight was in progress.

'Wimp am I? You'll soon find out! Take this.' They didn't notice Simon standing on the bank until he yelled out, 'Hannah, that's no way for a lady to behave.'

'Since when have I been a lady?' she responded as she made her way to the edge of the stream and held out her hand to him. He pulled her out and they turned to watch Thomas clamber up the bank. He sat dripping water and eyed Simon.

'Just the man I need to see,' he said with a big smile. 'I would like to marry your Hannah and make her my Hannah, if that's alright with you.' He took her hand. 'She wants to marry me, too.'

'Wondered when you would get around to it, young fellow,' Simon answered. 'I thought you might, so I've given it some thought. Have had the worry of Kerrin on me mind though an' I hope you are not in the same situation that he is.'

'What's that?' Hannah asked.

'He's got that young wench Molly with child and I say he has to make an honest woman of 'er. I've 'ad 'er father down here rantin' and ravin' at me. Anyone would think it was my fault. You ain't in that condition, are you Hannah?'

'Of course not,' she answered indignantly. 'How could Kerrin be so stupid. Be nice to have a baby in the family though. It'll make you a grandpa!'

'I don't want to be a grandpa, at least not under those conditions. Would want it done proper.'

'It'll be done proper. Kerrin will make a good father. He has you to model himself on. Now do we have a yes or a no?'

'Eh? Oh, yes I suppose. Don't let me down lad and let Kerrin get married first otherwise won't be no room in the 'ouse for you.' He kissed his daughter, shook hands with Thomas and went back inside to his fireside.

'Hannah, I have to get some money before we get married. I've saved a little bit but I'll have to see James about paying me decent wages. If I'm to marry you I need to be able to support you,' Thomas said, his teeth chattering.

'If we don't change our clothes we will catch our death and there won't be a wedding. Come into the house an' I'll find you some dry clothes.'

***

'James, I want to get married,' Thomas said to the blacksmith the next morning.

'Don't tell me lad,' he answered. 'You're asking the wrong father. I ain't got any daughters an' I doubt my sons would be interested.'

'Don't be daft, James. I want to marry Hannah!'

'Well, ask her then,' he said trying to make is as difficult as possible for Thomas.

'I have and I've asked her father too, and both have said yes.' Thomas tried to explain.

'Wot! You asked her father to marry you. That ain't right, Tom. You shouldn'ta done that.'

'James, don't be an idiot. Anyway I'm getting married and I need some money. Can you give me some more work an' pay me proper wages? If you can't I'll have to look somewhere else for work. I can't get married on nothing.'

'Of course you can't. You are the best worker I've ever 'ad an' I won't let you go. Let's see now. How does one shilling a day sound and you keep living in the loft until you marry. You can't have Hannah living in the loft 'an old Simon would never hear of it anyway.'

'Nor would I. I was thinking more like one shilling and six pence a day. I would work hard for it.'

'I know you would, boy. You drive a hard bargain. One shilling and sixpence it is then and we will look at it again before you marry.'

Thomas was jubilant. At last his life had a purpose. He lay on his straw bed and looked at the stars through the tiny dirty window. He sought out the biggest and talked to it. 'You would like her, Ma. Our life together will be everything that yours was not. I promise you and I promise her.' He drifted off to sleep, his heart full of happiness.

***

It was Kerrin's wedding day and Thomas was glad to be included in the small group that witnessed the nuptials in Molly's father's garden. Kerrin did not seem the happiest of grooms but there was no denying that his bride, Molly, was very pretty.

'I hope it all works out for them. Kerrin is nice. He's just full of bluster. As long as Molly is strong and keeps him in his place they'll be alright,' Hannah said to Thomas.

'What place is that?' he asked impishly.

'You'll find out when you get married,' she replied. 'Let's go some place else for a bit. I'm sick of eating and drinking.' She watched the men getting stuck into the suckling pig on the spit and downing their ales and suddenly she was glad that Thomas was not like them. She could not imagine wanting to get close to any of them. She looked at Thomas and noted his clean complexion and hair. His clothes were a little worn but were also clean. She was happy that he wanted to be nice for her and working as a blacksmith did not make it easy for him. She stood up and held out her hand. 'Let's slip away quietly,' she whispered.

Nobody was watching them as they left the festivities and made their way down the lane behind the village to their favourite place by the river.

'We can get married soon,' he said. 'Kerrin will be gone so there might be a wee space for me.'

'What about a place of our own? I could work and help with the money.'

'Your father still needs you to take care of him. If he's happy to have us there, to start with anyway, it would help us. Just means I would have to travel five miles to work and five miles back. I'll cut across the paddocks and that'll save some time and money but I'll miss my chats with the pikeman. I can't wait to marry you, Hannah. My bed in the loft is getting more uncomfortable each night.'

She nestled into his arms. 'I can't wait either and my bed is very comfortable for one. I don't know about two though.'

'Then I'll make us a new bigger one. Nothing but the best for you, my love. A new bed for a new life.'

***

Thomas and Hannah were married six weeks after Kerrin and Molly. Thomas moved his meagre belongs to Simon's cottage and happily settled in with Hannah. The long ride to and from the smithy's each day was a small price that he was willing to pay for the pleasure of living with a family again and especially with Hannah. He had a wife. He could not believe it. Someone who wanted him as he was, with a not so-nice-history, with no money and no prospects of ever having any real wealth.

'I'll always love you, Hannah. You know that don't you? There'll never be anyone else for me,' he said as he snuggled into her in the new bed he had made.

'Nor for me either. Father wondered why I could never find a lad that I wanted to marry but I said that I would only marry for love. He couldn't argue with that because he loved my mother and never wanted anyone else after she died. So it looks like we're stuck with each other.'

'Suits me,' he answered closing his eyes and soon falling fast asleep.

***

'How are you enjoying being married to Tom?' Molly asked Hannah, who had walked the mile or so to the little cottage that she and Kerrin lived in. It was very spartan, but cosy, and Hannah got the impression that they were contented enough.

'Tom is very kind and considerate,' she answered with a big smile. 'What about our Kerrin? Is he looking after you? He'd better or I'll sort him out.'

140

'Actually Kerrin is far nicer married than he was before we were married. In fact, if it hadn't been for the baby I doubt if I would have married him. He always seemed a bit grumpy with a chip on his shoulder. But I didn't want to be an unmarried mother with all the nastiness and difficulties and snide remarks that go with that. Let alone the poverty. Anyway it took two of us to make the baby so I shouldn't have to look after it on my own.'

'Yes,' agreed Hannah. 'To have a child with no support would be really hard.'

'Pa was most unhappy about the baby and if Kerrin hadn't married me I would probably have been thrown out,' Molly confided. 'He and my ma had a dreadful row about it all. Pa I mean, not Kerrin, although he had some strong words to say to him too.'

'I'll bet he did. He had strong words with my father too. They all seem to have got over it now. Looks as though the baby is coming soon. Is there anything I can do?' Hannah liked Molly a lot and was willing to do whatever she could to help.

Molly sighed as she lowered herself into a chair. 'Not at the moment thanks. My back has been very sore today and I don't know if that means anything. Ma has gone to town for the day so I can't ask her. Just have to put up with it until something happens.'

They chatted on until it was time for Hannah to leave. As she stood up she suddenly became aware that Molly seemed to be in distress.

'What is it?' she cried rushing to her side. 'Is it the baby?'

'I think so,' she gasped.

Hannah grabbed her hand. 'It'll be alright,' she said as another spasm of pain passed through Molly's body. 'I'll go and get Kerrin to fetch the midwife. Don't you move.'

Molly gave a cheerless smile. 'Don't think I'll be going anywhere.'

Hannah ran out the door and headed for home where Kerrin still had his allotment.

She rushed up to him, shouting and waving and breathlessly told him to get Mother Marsham, the midwife. Kerrin started down the road and then turned back and headed for the barn. Mounting their one and only horse he whipped it into a gallop and tore down the road. 'Bet that horse won't get far at that pace,' Hannah said to her father. 'I won't be home for supper. Tell Tom what's happening and he can come and get me later. You could be a Grandpa before the day is out,' she laughed as she ran back to Molly.

'Wish there was some quicker way of getting around,' she said to herself. 'Maybe Tom could buy me a horse. That'd be fun.' She slowed to a quick walk and soon was entering Molly's home to find her reclining on the couch.

'Mother Marsham will be here soon. Now don't you worry. Let's get you into your bedroom. Come on.' Hannah took Molly's arm and pulled her into a sitting position. They waited until the next contraction was over and then, supporting Molly as best as she could, Hannah helped her to the bed.

'Don't know if that is more comfortable but it's a better place to have a baby, I think.' She held tightly to Hannah's hand.

'I think I want Kerrin,' whispered Molly.

'He won't be far away. But if the midwife gets here first, I don't think she'll let him in. It isn't seemly to have a man in the birthing room. Now rest a minute and I'll make sure there's some water boiling.'

She hurried from the room as Kerrin arrived breathlessly rushing through the door.

'She's in the bedroom,' Hannah told him. 'Go and sit with her. Where's Mother Marsham?'

'I couldn't get her on the horse so she's walking. She's huge, which scares me. Hope it doesn't scare Molly.' He paused. 'Thanks for being here.' He smiled and Hannah gave him a hug.

'All will be well. Now go and see her.' She gently pushed him towards the bedroom and set about trying to think what a midwife might need. She remembered when Davie had been born but she had been pushed into the background just as her father had been, so she did not know much of what was going on. She found a box that Molly had set aside with towels and linen and some tiny clothes for the baby and busied herself filling in the time while awaiting the midwife. She made a cup of tea and took it into Molly. Kerrin was sitting by the bed. He jumped up as Hannah appeared.

'Can't you do something, Hannah? That fat old woman will take forever to get here.'

'Babies come when they're ready to come and you can't hurry them up. Molly's doing well. Just rub her back when she has a contraction. That might help. Mrs Marsham won't be too far away.'

They sat and waited, all the time helping Molly through her pain as much as they could. After a little while there was a banging on the door. Hannah opened it to admit the largest woman she had ever seen. No wonder Kerrin couldn't get her on the horse.

'Right!' she said as she brushed past Hannah. 'Where's me patient?'

'In her bed. It's through here,' answered Hannah as she led the way to the bedroom. Mrs Marsham squeezed through the door, glared at Kerrin and as she approached the bed said, 'You'll 'ave to go out young man. Bad luck t' 'ave y' see all that goes on. 'Tis either you or me. I can't do nothin' 'til y' leave.'

'You don't believe that rubbish, do you?' he said scornfully.

'I don't wanna risk losin' yer missus or yer baby. Demons and evil spirits can enter in 'er if there's a man around. Now are y' goin' or am I? 'Twould be bad for me if she up 'an died wif you in 'ere. I'd get the blame.'

'Go Kerrin,' whispered Molly. 'I'm not going to die.'

Hannah followed him out of the room. 'Go and fetch her mother,' she suggested gently. 'She might be home now. I'll stay with Molly.'

'Let's 'ave a look at ya,' Mrs Marsham said to Molly when he had gone. She examined her and said, 'Not too far away, me thinks.' She issued instructions to Hannah and together they managed to get Molly out of her bed and onto a chair. She seemed to know what she was doing and Hannah relaxed a little.

'Have you delivered many babies?' she asked.

'Yes. Lost count, but this one makes about two hundred.' She looked sideways at Molly and whispered, 'Ain't all been successful. This one should be alright though. Nothing funny going on that I can tell. It don't look stuck or nuffin'.'

Molly's mother arrived and Hannah left them to sit with Kerrin. The noises coming from the bedroom unnerved him and he went outside. She followed him.

'It's a natural thing to have babies,' she said. 'It's just so painful. Midwives are licensed by the church and they believe that pain in childbirth is the Lord's punishment for Eve's sin. So midwives don't do overly much to help with the pain.'

'But not to let a man in with his missus if he wants to be, because of spirits is just dumb,' Kerrin said.

'I know how you feel and I think it's a lot of hocus pocus too but if she does the wrong things she could end up being tried as a witch. But she's done two hundred births so it should be alright.' She did not mention the 'unsuccessful' ones and thankfully Molly's was not to be one of them. She delivered a son

144

for Kerrin and herself and Mrs Marsham went off with seven shillings in her pocket for a hard day's work.

'I would love a son,' said Thomas as he escorted Hannah home.

'I would love to give you one, but after today and watching Molly, I hope I don't just yet,' she answered with a smile.

Chapter 14:
The Apothecary (1790)

Life was very happy for Thomas. He had everything that he wanted, except a son. Hannah loved him passionately, Simon treated him as his own, Kerrin had at last found some respect for him, the younger boys got on well with him, and Molly's baby, named Henry, was thriving. He had a new family. But he never forgot Sam and Jenny Crean.

'I'm going to take you south sometime, Hannah, to meet Sam and Jenny. They'll love you.'

'I'd like that. They're special to you and will be to me too. We can't leave here yet though.'

'Too cold for travelling anyway, but apart from that why can't we go? You're not...?'

She laughed. 'No I'm not. No, it's Papa.'

'But I haven't even mentioned it to him. How would he know?'

'Oh just listen, Tom. Father isn't well. It's a wonder you haven't noticed. He never says anything about it, but I've been watching him. This winter's been hard on him. He feels the cold and isn't as motivated as he used to be. Used to be we couldn't stop him from working hard but now everything seems an effort. It's no use my talking to him about it. He just says he's fine and stomps off. He's not telling me something, I'm sure. I've been giving him elderberry tea just in case he's in for a cold or the flu but it's been going on too long. I wish the town had a physician and not just that old quack. I don't trust him.'

'I could go and see him for you. Tell him what the symptoms are. Anyway, what about Mrs Marsham? Doesn't she know anything other than birthing babies?'

Hannah almost laughed. 'Maybe she does but I can't see Father baring his chest to her or anyone else for that matter. If we knew what was wrong we could get the right herbs and powders and treat him ourselves. Some of the women around here know more than any quack or physician for that matter. Alice down the road is very handy at curing simple complaints. Remedies get handed down from mothers to daughters but there are lots of things that can't be cured. We all know that. He doesn't have consumption or anything so serious as that. Or at least I haven't seen him coughing or spitting and he doesn't have a fever. He does seem to get quite tired though.'

'He's getting on a bit. We have to expect things to happen,' said Thomas.

'He's only fifty-five, Hannah objected. 'A lot of men live a lot longer than that. I don't want anything to happen to him.'

'Of course you don't. I don't either. I've only known him a few years but he's been very good to me.'

Hannah turned to him. 'I intend to make sure that he's with us for a very long time.'

'I'll help,' Thomas said but at the same time he realised that there was no way that Hannah would travel south with him unless her father made a full recovery from whatever was ailing him. He would have a talk with him and try and establish what the problem was.

***

Simon felt dreadful. His head ached badly. Up until now he had kept his pain from his family. But it was getting worse and he knew that he would have to seek help soon. He slowly straightened up and looked around for Andy. He couldn't see him.

Suddenly he realised that he couldn't see anything very well. With great difficulty he made his way to the edge of the field and sat down. Maybe if he rested a little the pain in his head would subside. He lay on his back and closed his eyes. Time passed. He did not know how long he lay there but he was suddenly aware of movement beside him.

'Come on Father, you can't laze about like that.' It was Andy.

Simon tried to speak to him but the words would not come. He tried to sit up and with Andy's help just managed to do so.

'Father! What is it?' Andy's face was full of consternation. Simon stared at him, panic appearing in his eyes. 'Can you stand?'

Simon shook his head. Andy tried to help him but Simon had no strength to assist. Andy looked around hoping that one of his brothers might be about but remembered that Davie had gone into the village with Hannah and Kerrin was attending to something elsewhere.

'Father I'll have to go home and get the wagon. Oh blow!' he exclaimed. 'Davie will have taken it. I don't want to leave you here. If I can get you up I might be able to carry you.'

Simon waved him away. The pain in his head was too bad for him to even think about being lumped over Andy's shoulder and carted home like a sack of potatoes. He would rather stay where he was. Even die where he was. He fell back down. Andy took off his jacket and covered him.

'I'll be back as fast as I can.' He raced off hurdling fences and gates in his rush and headed down the road to where his neighbour was chopping firewood.

'Whoa!' Hugh said, as Andy came to a standstill, his breath coming in huge gulps.

'I need your help,' he panted, 'and maybe your missus' help too for a few minutes.' He quickly explained the situation and asked to borrow his horse and wagon.

'Sounds pretty bad to me. I'd better come with you. Alice!' he called to his wife. A middle-aged woman appeared in the doorway. 'Old Simon is real poorly. I'm just going to help Andy here get him from the paddock. Hannah's away so maybe you should come too. Meet us at their cottage and bring some of your herbs and stuff,' he added as they started away. 'Don't think we'll need the wagon. T'would be more bumpy than us carrying him.'

'Yeah, maybe. But I don't think he can stand.'

'Don't worry, lad. We'll soon have him tucked up comfortably in his bed all safe and sound.'

'And still sick. I don't know what can be wrong with him,' ventured Andy.

'I think I do an' it ain't good. Alice might be able to help but she often doesn't know what to do for serious complaints.'

Alice watched them disappear round the side of the house and thought about what she might bring. She didn't know what was wrong with Simon so didn't know what illness to prepare for. In the finish she threw any herbs, poultices and powders that she had nearby into her basket and, gathering up her skirts, hurried as quickly as she could to Simon's house. Even so the men were not there when she arrived so she headed off to meet them. She saw them coming across the fields carrying Simon between them. She met them halfway and could tell at a glance that what was wrong with Simon was too serious for her meagre knowledge to cure. She cast a glance at Hugh and realised that he too knew that she would not be much help. However she would do her best.

It was difficult for the men to get Simon into bed. He was conscious, unable to speak and one side of his body did not work.

'We'll soon have you up and running the show again,' she said. 'Hugh, sit him up so I that can place these pillows behind his head. Have to keep it raised. Simon do you know what has happened to you?' she asked him gently. He nodded and immediately winced with pain. 'Can you see me?' she asked. He waved his good hand in a lazy fashion which she took to mean that he could but not very well. She rinsed some cloths in cold water and placed them on his head. She then rummaged through the supplies in her basket and found some mustard powder. She mixed this with a little oil and massaged it into his feet. When he was resting quietly she went out into the kitchen where Andy and Hugh were quietly discussing the recent turn of events.

'I'll wait until Hannah and Davie get back and then I'll go and tell Kerrin. Is he going to die, Alice?' Andy was tentative in his enquiry and anyway in his heart he already knew what the answer would be.

'He's very sick, Andy. Some would say that evil spirits have entered his brain but I say that something has gone wrong with his brain. I think it's apoplexy. I can't fix it. We'll talk about it when your sister and brothers get here but he really needs to see a physician. I know that there isn't one around here so maybe that 'quack' doctor in the town might be better than nothing.'

'Might not either. Hannah doesn't like him. Calls him a charlatan. I think Father would object too.'

'He's in no position to object too much,' said Hugh. 'He seems to be resting quietly now, but he doesn't look good.'

***

Simon did object as much as he was able and although Hannah was reluctant she was outnumbered by the boys and Thomas was despatched to the town as fast as possible.

Daylight was fading as he reached the building that housed Dr Venning and his apothecary shop. A low swinging sign with the words 'Dr Venning, Apothecarie' swung backwards and forwards on its chain. The dismal looking shop was almost in darkness as Thomas leapt from his horse and thumped on the door. He peered through the dirty window but could see no sign of movement. He rattled the door handle and then picking up a stout stick beat loudly upon it. Standing back he looked up at the grimy window above. He picked up a handful of gravel and threw it and stepped back as it rained back down on him. Desperately he looked around.

'Ya won't get much outa 'im now,' a voice shouted. 'Full o' the booze 'e'll be by now.'

Thomas turned and saw an old woman leaning against a door. 'I need his services,' said Thomas. 'How do I get to him?'

'Ye'd be better orf wiv this 'ere doorpost for all the use e'll bet 'ya.' she said hitting it with her fist. 'Ye could go up them there stairs down t'alleyway a bit. There's a door at the top.'

'Thank you,' said Thomas, racing down the alleyway and jumping to avoid the slush and puddles, he took the stairs two at a time. Hammering on the door he tried the handle. Surprisingly it was unlocked. He gingerly pushed it open and peered inside. It opened into a long hallway which was barely lit by a single candle placed in a recess in the wall part way along. There were two doors on each side and on a gamble he tried the first door on the left hoping that it led to the room above the apothecary's shop. He was right. It gently swung open to reveal a squalid interior with the minimum of furniture and devoid of all home comforts. In an old chair was a recumbent form. Beside this person, on a small table was an empty bottle. Thomas could smell the cheap booze that brought back memories that he preferred to leave undisturbed.

He shook the man by the shoulder. He felt repulsed. The man stank. Thomas had second thoughts and wondered if he should leave him where he was. He didn't think that Hannah would want him anywhere near her father. Maybe the old woman over the road was right. The door post might be better than this sot. He shook him again, this time more violently.

'Come on, you stupid old soak. We've got work to do.' He hauled the man to his feet and slapped him round the head.

'Nnnno,' Venning stammered. 'Don' do that. Take whatever you want.' He put his hands up to defend himself but Thomas had no intention of beating him up. He just wanted to make him sober enough to deal with Simon.

'Where's your horse? We need to take a little trip. You'll need your bag and some medicines too.' He had no idea what would be needed and looked about desperately for a medicine bag or something that Venning might normally take on his visits. Maybe it was down below. He dropped the man back in his seat where he sat wide eyed staring fearfully at Thomas.

'Now listen to me, you stupid old fool. I'm going down into your miserable little shop to look for your bag. You wait right where you are. If you leave I'll be after you like a shot and I think I can go faster than you. Old Simon Fenwick is ill and needs help and as you are the only one around you'll have to do it. Do you understand?' Thomas demanded.

Venning nodded feebly. 'Bag's in my shop,' he muttered and Thomas raced down the narrow stairs which led into the back of the shop. It was very dark. He found a lantern and lit it. Holding it high the flickering light revealed that the interior of the shop was just as dismal as the upstairs. There was a pungent smell which could have come from any of the large carboys which were filled with coloured liquid or from the high shelving which held jars, bottles and boxes, containing among other things dried roots, leaves, bone powder, dried blood, bird claws, animal teeth, dead rats and mice. Bottles contained aromatic waters, oils and many herbs and spices. On the wooden bench which ran down the side of the room were scales of various sizes, mortar and pestles, books and quills, phials and funnels. One clear jar contained leeches which crawled over each other in their search for an escape. Cages hung from the ceiling and birds squawked uncontrollably. A layer of dust covered everything. Instruments were laid out on a table in the centre of the room and Thomas, who was becoming increasingly queasy, could not look too closely at them. He saw a likely looking bag and grabbing it, he looked inside. It appeared to be what he wanted and he ran back up the stairs.

Venning was where he had left him and Thomas was gratified to see that he was still awake.

'Take a look and make sure that you have everything,' he instructed.

'How do I know what I need? Don't know what's wrong wiv 'im, do I? Won't know 'til I see him.'

Thomas grabbed him again. 'Take a look? You know the things you'd usually take when you go out on a call. Now hurry up.'

When he was satisfied that Venning had all that he thought was required, he pushed him out the door and followed him down the stairs. He noticed that he was carrying a bottle of booze but ignored the fact. As long as he got him to Simon the boys could take care of him.

'Where's your horse?' he asked as Venning took a swig from his bottle.

'Stables 'round the back,' he said wiping his mouth on his sleeve and preparing to take another swig of the booze. Thomas realised that if he didn't do something, Venning would never make it to the farm. He spotted a horse trough and in one quick movement grabbed the bottle and threw it in. At the same time he dunked his unfortunate companion head first into the trough in the hope that it might sober him up. He dragged him up coughing and spluttering and as he surfaced, Thomas yelled in his ear,

'There's no more of that. Unless you pull yourself together the Fenwick boys will sort you out an' that won't be much fun, for you I mean. I don't doubt they will get a kick out of it though. Now let's get moving.' The rough treatment seemed to work and after retrieving Venning's horse from the stable, Thomas escorted him back to the farm. Kerrin was outside.

'Well done, Thomas,' he remarked.

'You might not think so when you see this sot. I'm not sure that you will want him treating your father and Hannah sure as hell won't. Best sneak him in.'

'Can't do that. Hannah is sitting with him.'

'I'm alright now,' said Venning. 'I jist like a little noggin after a 'ard day. Treating folk ain't easy, y' know. Some things is pretty awful. I'm a good doctor though.'

'You ain't even a doctor so don't call yerself one,' said Kerrin. 'Just get in there and do what you can for my father.'

'What about a little drink first?' Venning pleaded.

'You're kidding. You're drunk enough now. I'm not gonna make you worse. Tell you what. I'll give you one when you've finished your work if you do it properly.' Thomas shook his head and followed them inside. Alice and Hugh were still there with Davie and Andy. Kerrin led the way into the bedroom. Simon was little changed from when Thomas had left.

'Hannah, you'd better leave us,' said Kerrin. 'Tom, would you take her out?'

Hannah looked at her father. 'I'm staying,' she said emphatically. 'This man is a charlatan and I'm staying to make sure he knows what he's doing.'

154

'Don't be silly Hannah! You don't know what's to be done so how would you know if he knows?' Thomas took her arm.

'Don't you call me silly,' she cried. Simon began to get distressed. He looked at Hannah and then moved his eyes in the direction of the door. She understood. 'I'll be just outside the door,' she whispered as she bent to kiss him. 'Kerrin, you stay and I'll get Alice.'

'No!' exclaimed Venning. 'Too many people. Not enough room. Just im.' He indicated Kerrin and waved his hand at the others. They quietly left and closed the door behind them.

Kerrin was fearful although he would not admit it. It might have been better if Alice had come in to assist but he couldn't suggest that now. He watched as Venning checked Simon. He looked into his eyes, down his throat, checked his pulse and enquired about his urine and motions.

'How would I know? I don't even live here. Does it all work, Pa?' he asked, looking into Simon's eyes. He didn't know if he would understand what he meant but Simon nodded painfully so he assumed that he did.

After checking his patient's arms and legs, Venning rummaged in his bag and removed a bowl and silver box containing a lancet. 'Something in his brain is getting his body out of balance. We need to bleed him.' Kerrin had heard of this but had never seen it done of course. 'Easier than cuttin' into yer 'ead, eh, Simon.' Fear showed in Simon's eyes and Kerrin took his hand.

'He won't do it while I'm here. I'd rather let you die,' he said.

'He probably would die anyway if I did do it. Not allowed to anyway. If I did an' he died I would be hanged for murder.'

'I knew you weren't a doctor,' said Kerrin. 'If you were you would be allowed to do it. You are a charlatan.'

'No I'm an apothecary and a good one.'

155

'A drunk one you mean. Now get on with it. Are you ready Pa?'

Chapter 15:
Bert and Mabel

It was two weeks since the onset of Simon's illness. He was no better and no worse. The blood-letting had made no difference. He lay on his bed and made no effort to move off it. Hannah and the boys did everything for him. His left leg was paralysed and his left arm partially so. He could not speak. Hannah made nourishing mutton broth which he managed to feed to himself but his appetite was poor.

'We've got to get him up or he'll die in his bed,' said Thomas. 'If he was up he could join in more with the family but he doesn't seem interested.' He thought for a moment. 'I'm going out for a bit. Back soon.' He kissed Hannah quickly and calling to Bouncer, who spent most of his time beside Simon's bed, he headed off down the road on foot, first calling into the barn to get some tools. He had gone half a mile or so before he spotted what he was looking for. In a blackthorn thicket by the roadside were some odd angled branches and shoots. He fossicked around for a while and soon found one that he thought would be suitable for Simon's needs. Taking his small axe he chopped the thick shoot together with a part of its main stem, fashioned an underarm support and trimmed the thorns. He smiled as he surveyed his handiwork and looked around for another suitable one. Soon he had two of similar size and shape and jubilantly headed for home with his handiwork.

'Let's try him on these,' he said as he burst through the door.

'Why didn't I think of doing something like that?' exclaimed Andy. 'C'mon, we won't take no for an answer. You and I should be able to get him up.'

'Wait until I wrap something around the tops,' said Hannah and soon the crutches were ready for trial.

Simon stared up at them and then looked away.

'No you don't, Pa. Tom made these for you and the least you can do is try them. C'mon Tom.' They pulled Simon into a sitting position and then swung him around until his feet touched the floor. Hannah watched from the doorway. Andy gently put his slippers on his feet and said, 'Easy does it. Stand on your good leg and don't worry about the other. We'll hold you up.' They managed to get him standing on one leg and put a crutch under his right armpit. He leaned on it.

'Too long,' said Thomas. 'I'll have to cut some off.'

'Wait until we measure the second one,' replied Andy.

Simon put his hand to his head and dropped back on the bed. They propped him up while Thomas went to cut a piece off the ends of the crutches.

'You've been lying down too long,' Hannah said to Simon. 'You have to make an effort to get up even if you just go and sit in the sun. I know you'd like to do more than that and that's probably why you're staying in bed. You don't want to see the others doing things that you feel you should be doing. Maybe when you are stronger you'll be able to do some work but you won't get stronger lying there all day and night.'

Thomas returned with the crutches and again they stood him upright. This time he was steadier. By standing on his good leg he managed to move the crutches forward although manoeuvring the left one with an arm that wouldn't work properly was difficult. However he persevered and stepping forward on his right leg he managed to drag his left one to meet it. It was painful progress to the door but he managed it. He was very weak and the effort tired him. Andy and Thomas carried him into the kitchen and placed him in his armchair. They felt that it was a good start and were determined not to let him waste away in his bed.

***

'Hannah, you're looking very tired,' Thomas said as he watched her getting undressed.

'I am,' she replied. 'I've all my chores to do and father takes up so much of my time. He's not demanding, but seems so lonely and miserable that I have to make time for him and talk to him even if he can't talk to me.'

'At least he's getting around a little bit, even if it's just around the house and yard. We can't expect too much of him.'

'I don't expect anything of him. I'm just happy to have him alive and still here with us. I just told you why I'm tired. There's possibly another reason too.'

'What might that be?' Thomas asked lazily.

'Maybe I'm having a baby,' she answered.

Thomas sat up quickly. 'Do you really think so? How do you know?'

'I just know. Anyway it's early days so we won't get our hopes up too high but I'll be very happy if I am. Will you?'

'I'll be the happiest man in the world. I'll look after you, I promise, and I'll be a really good father.'

***

The weeks passed and Hannah confirmed that she was pregnant. She also began to get very sick in the mornings and watching her, Simon managed a crooked smile. She guessed what he was thinking ... that it would pass in a few weeks and she would start to enjoy her condition.

'*Fat chance of that*,' she thought as she sicked up her breakfast. She remembered Molly and her cumbersome state and although she was happy with the prospect of having a son or daughter she was not happy thinking about the obvious changes that her body would go through. Some women got so big they could hardly move and they remained sick for nine months. It was particularly hard on women who already had small children. Hannah didn't know what she had done to deserve Thomas but he was very helpful. He made her brothers do more chores and he himself made sure that the tub was full of water each Monday morning and forbade her to empty it. But it was still heavy work lifting the wet washing out and rinsing it. Still the sickness continued.

'Hannah, I have an idea. Why don't we go south to Sam and Jenny? Now just listen to me,' Thomas said as Hannah raised her eyes in surprise. 'If we went down there we could stay with them. Jenny would help you and you wouldn't have to work as hard as you do here. Kerrin and Molly could move in here and take care of Simon. You might feel better then.'

'Tom, you know that I wouldn't leave Papa. How could I? Apart from that you said yourself that it was too cold to travel.'

'We'd manage that. We'd take a wagon with plenty of bedding and a tent. We'd plan it. Anyway we wouldn't be on the road all that long.'

'I won't do it,' Hannah said emphatically. 'What about highwaymen? I'm not as fit as I used to be. I couldn't run away.'

'It's fairly unlikely that we would see a highwayman, Hannah.'

'Well, I'm not going anywhere and that's that,' she retorted. 'How do you think I would feel if Papa died and I wasn't here? Now please don't mention it again.'

160

That was the nearest that Thomas and Hannah came to having a row. They loved each other very much and respected each other. Thomas knew how much she loved her father and didn't pursue the matter any further.

***

Thomas was annoyed. It was a cold wet day and he would have preferred to stay inside where the roaring furnace made the air in the smithy warm and cosy. But James had a mission for him.

'Does it have to be today, James? It's so cold and it's even snowing now. Tomorrow might be better. By then there might even be some sunshine,' he said hopefully.

'I promised that these hinges would be ready today and also said that we would deliver them to old Bert over at Wynchley. It ain't easy for him to get away what with his wife so ill and his son just having being killed by that runaway horse. Just do it Tom and don't argue.' James thrust the hinges into his hands and went back to his work.

'He won't be able to put them on in this weather anyway,' Thomas muttered to himself as he opened the door.

'I heard that, Tom and it shouldn't surprise you to know that some of the old timers are prepared to work in all weathers. Unlike many of the young ones today.'

Thomas ignored him and went round to the stable to get his horse.

'Be a miracle if you see the winter out, old girl. I ask too much of you. Maybe I'll look at getting another horse. Give you a spell. You'd like that, wouldn't you?'

The horse nuzzled into him as he put on the halter and led him into the yard.

Bert's house was not all that far away; about four miles in the opposite direction to the one Thomas took to go to his home. Conditions were miserable but he did not urge his horse on. He just let him have its head and he ambled along in the freezing cold at his own pace. The tree-lined country lane that he followed kept him protected somewhat from the wind but once out in the open it was bone-chilling and the snow fell heavily.

'James must be mad if he thinks Bert will be working out in this weather,' he thought. He kept his head down and eventually came to the track that lead to Bert's farm.

He knocked on the door. Bert opened it.

'Come on in, lad,' he invited as he ushered Thomas into the warm kitchen. Thomas handed him the hinges.

'I'd better get back,' he said. 'I'm dripping water on your floor.'

'Don't worry about that. What was James thinkin' abart sending y' out in a storm like this? The 'inges could 'ave waited.'

'That's what I said but he reckoned you'd be working and would need 'em for your gates.'

'Oi'd be pretty daft t' work on a day loik t'day. I ain't mad. This is me wife.' He indicated an elderly woman lying on a sofa. She struggled to sit up but Thomas put his hand on her shoulder.

'Stay there. I'm pleased to meet you and I'm sorry that you're ill. Is there anything you would like me to do for you?' he asked solicitously.

'No, nothin' ta. Bert 'ere. 'e looks out for me, don'tcha luv?' She gazed fondly towards her husband and Thomas instantly saw the deep affection they had for each other.

'Aye, I do me best. It's bin 'arder since young Leonard was killed. He were our only one and was a big 'elp to us. Gotta keep on going though. What wiv the farm and me wife sick, I don't get everything done that I want done. But it waits for me. Ain't no one else gonna do it.' Bert was very matter of fact.

'How did the accident happen?' Thomas asked.

'He was walkin' down the road when a 'orse that 'ad been spooked by a rabbit charged round the bend. It's rider couldna control it and it bowled Leonard over. Killed him straight orf. 'Twas awful.'

'I'm really sorry. My name's Tom Puckle and I'm married to Simon Fenwick's daughter. Old Simon's not too good either. If you want a hand with anything you just let me know. Send a message to James Butcher at the smithy and I'll see what I can do to help. Now I'd better head back. Nice to have met you both.' He struggled into his coat, wrapped a scarf around his neck and went out into the snow. Conditions hadn't improved very much and by the time he reached the village he was again frozen through.

'I'll probably catch my death thanks to you, James, and Bert didn't want them today. Too cold for him. He's a sensible man.' Thomas took some bread from his bag and using a long fork toasted it over the hot coals. The water was boiling on the trivet by the forge and he soon had a hot drink to go with it.

'Bert and his wife are a nice couple. I said I'd try and help them a bit if I could,' he said, taking a big bite of his toast.

'Thought you were busy enough what with Simon sick and your missus pregnant,' replied James.

'Yeah, I am but I felt I had to offer. Don't think Bert's the sort to ask for help though, so we'll see what happens.'

***

The winter continued to be very cold and Hannah was pleased that she had not agreed to go away with Thomas. Bert didn't ask for help as Thomas had anticipated but sometimes he rode over and gave a hand anyway. Hannah couldn't see the point considering that there was enough to do at the Fenwick Farm but she let him go all the same.

Simon was finding the winter very difficult. He was always cold despite the big fire in the kitchen and Hannah could see his health deteriorating.

The boys sat at the kitchen table eating their breakfast while Hannah made up a tray for her father and took it into him in his room.

'We just have to look after him as best we can. You do a marvellous job, Hannah,' said Andy when she returned, 'and I'm sure he appreciates it. Are you any better in the mornings?'

'No I'm not. I have my breakfast after you go and then I lose it all. I've seen Alice and she has given me a potion but it hasn't helped at all. I'll just have to put up with it.'

When her brothers left, Thomas lingered. 'I get so worried about you, Hannah. If anything happened to you I would die. I love you so much.' He took her in his arms and buried his face in her hair.

'I'll be alright, Tom. Women have babies all the time,' she answered.

'Yes but not all of them successfully,' he replied. 'I'll have to look after you with all my heart and keep you safe'

Chapter 16:
The hold-up

It had been a little while since Thomas had been to help Bert and his wife. He was so worried about Hannah that apart from going to work he did not let her out of his sight. However on this particular day as Molly had brought little Henry over for a visit he knew that she was in good hands. He decided to take the opportunity to go and see them.

There was not a lot that he could do for them but he did notice that their firewood heap was low, so, taking an axe, he went into the woods to cut some more. Bouncer followed but soon was on the scent of what he hoped would be a good meal and disappeared into the dense bush.

Thomas commenced his task and eventually had a large stack heaped on one side. He was breathing heavily. Hearing a noise, he looked up to see Bert leading the horse and cart.

'Can't let you do all the hard work, lad. You chop, I'll load.' They worked away steadily until they were happy with the load they had.

'Where's that dog!' exclaimed Thomas when they had filled the cart. ''E'll get himself into real trouble one day.'

'Don't worry, Tom. If 'e ain't back by the time you leave, we'll look after 'im and get 'im back to you.'

'Thanks Bert. I have to go. Hannah's still not well. Molly's with her but I must get home. I'll help you offload this and then I'll be off. Bouncer will come home at some stage.' He jumped on the back of the cart for a ride back and soon they were stacking the wood under the trees at the back of the house.

'See you soon Mrs Bert,' he called after he had finished, 'and you too Bert.'

'Ride safely, lad, and' ta for your 'elp,' Bert called as Thomas made his way down the lane to the road.

It was getting late.

'C'mon girl,' he said gently and urged the old nag into a slow trot. They rounded a bend in the road and Thomas suddenly pulled up. 'Whoa,' he whispered. Ahead was a carriage and pair but also a horseman mounted on a grey mare.

Thomas quietly dismounted and led his horse into the trees where he tied her up. 'You wait here,' he quietly urged. He made his way back to the road and carefully and silently crept towards the carriage. As he got closer his suspicions were confirmed. The man was a highwayman. *'Do you really want to get yourself into this?'* he thought. His mind flew to Hannah at home and he was of a mind to turn back when his conscience got the better of him and he proceeded cautiously towards the highwayman and his captive.

Thomas didn't really have a plan and he didn't like the look of the pistol being pointed towards the carriage. The driver was still sitting up in his seat with his hands on his head. Beside him, in a holder was a long horsewhip. His passenger sheltered out of sight inside the coach.

'This pistol is loaded, ma'am and I am happy to use it on your man unless you hand your valuables over to me. Unfortunately I don't have a lot of time and I would appreciate it if you could be quick about it.'

'Well at least you're polite,' a woman's voice answered from inside. 'But why should I give them to you?'

'Because I'm the one holding the pistol, so if you don't mind ma'am, I'll have your jewels.'

166

'I have absolutely no doubt that you'll be caught and we all know what happens to highwaymen. You'll suffer the same fate and I sincerely hope that I'm there to witness it.' As she leaned forward to hand her jewellery case out the window she spotted Thomas. His jaw dropped with recognition but she gave no sign of having seen him. She withdrew into the carriage, the jewellery still in her hand.

'Come on, come on. My patience is wearing a little thin, ma'am. I will count to ten,' he said waving the pistol in his impatience. 'Then your man will die.'

'I'm just checking something in the box,' she replied calmly.

Thomas steadied himself and with a tremendous leap, launched himself at the highwayman at the same time shouting 'Go!' Everything happened at once. The pistol went off with a huge report, the horses spooked and the carriage commenced a rollicking ride down the road.

Thomas's assault on the brigand caused them both to crash to the ground. They wrestled furiously, Thomas well aware of the pistol but knowing that as it had been fired once, the man would need to reload before he could fire again. Thomas also knew that unless he freed it from his grasp he could be hit with it. The man was strong. One minute Thomas was on top and the next they had rolled over and he felt the breath being squeezed out of him as the man sat on his chest. At last he managed to twist the pistol free and threw it with all his might deep into the undergrowth.

He felt a glancing blow to his head but managed to swing his right fist into the man's face. He fell to one side but swiftly recovered to hit Thomas a resounding punch on the nose. He felt blood running over his face and into his eyes.

'You villain,' he shouted and with a mighty effort he heaved the scoundrel off his body and leaped to his feet. They faced each other, fists raised.

'Come on you nogood blackguard! It's you or me and I've got too much to live for so it's going to have to be you.' They closed in and fought punching and kicking, matching each other in effort and strength. Thomas couldn't see very well but at last he managed to grasp the mask covering his opponent's face. He ripped it off and looked into the eyes of his foe. His guard down, the blow fell.

As his consciousness dimmed he said disbelievingly, 'Alfie???'

***

He came to his senses, his back leaning against a tree in a copse off the roadside. Night had fallen. His head pounded and his body ached. Then he remembered. 'Alfie,' he said as he looked around. He couldn't see anyone. Had he dreamed it all? Had he fallen from his horse and hit his head? He didn't think so. It seemed so real. Where was his horse? He must get home to Hannah. He tried to stand up but his head spun and he quickly sat down again. He couldn't see much in the dark. 'I'll wait a few more minutes,' he thought. He could hear the snorting of a horse and said, 'Is that you, old girl?'

'No, it's my horse,' said Alfie. 'You should have left well alone, Tom. This was my business.'

'Have you lost your mind, Alfie? I can't believe this is true. What in heaven's name do you think you're doing? A highwayman!! What in your life has lead you down this path? I thought you had everything when I left Athelney and here you are holding up innocent people at the point of a pistol and robbing them and heaven knows what else. Are you mad?'

'Sometimes the things that mean the most to you can be taken from you very quickly. You know that. Anyway I don't want to talk about it. That's past. What are we going to do now?'

'How would I know? I'm not the one who goes around holding people up with a firearm. I know what I'm going to do. I'm going home to my wife. You can do whatever you like. Charlotte was right. You'll be caught and hanged. Just like my mother was. Do you remember what that was like Alfie? I do. I still have nightmares about it. You were such a good friend to me then. My best friend, my only friend. And now this. You utter idiot. Why not go and hang yourself now and get it over with? The woman you held up in that carriage was Charlotte, daughter of Sir Edric Spicer. You've no doubt heard of him. Do you think he's going to let this 'little' incident die a natural death? He'll hunt you down and not rest until he gets you.'

'Athelney is a long way from here. I'll be long gone before he gets to hear of it.'

'Don't you believe it. He'll have friends in this area and he'll contact them. They could be getting a party up right now and coming to look for you. You'd better get going. I am.'

Thomas stood up slowly. He felt dizzy.

Alfie jumped up and hurried over. 'Where's your horse, Tom? I'd better accompany you to make sure you get there safely.'

'I'm not letting you anywhere near my family. You're a highwayman for God's sake. Do you want to put them all in danger?'

'That won't happen, Tom. I've only just arrived in this area and I've only been a highwayman for a little while. No one knows me and it was just my bad luck that you should decide to play the hero.'

'Yeah, my bad luck too. I've often thought of meeting up with you again but never dreamed it would be like this.'

'I thought you were dead. The posters at Athelney years ago said that you had drowned. Our family was very upset about it.' Alfie remembered the effect on his family as if it were yesterday.

'That's a long story but if a certain person had had his way I would have drowned. But I didn't and here I am.'

'We've no doubt both got a lot to talk about but I'd better get you home. Where's your horse,' Alfie asked again. 'I'll just drop you at your gate. I won't come in. I'll make sure you get home safely.'

Thomas's memory fled back to the times that they'd had together at Athelney where Alfie had always watched out for him. Alfie who seemed to have everything then and now lived by robbing others.

'Alfie you even look like a highwayman: your heavy black coat and your tricorn hat and leather boots. If anyone saw me with you they would immediately associate me with your nefarious activities. I certainly don't want that. I'm very happily married, my wife is with child and we live with her father and brothers. I can't shelter you.'

'I don't want you to. I don't want or need anyone's help. I look after myself.' It was the way he said it that made Thomas realise that perhaps Alfie was not as much in control of his life as he made out. Alfie had always been there to help Thomas in the old days; was this the time to return the help that he had always received? Not directly, but maybe something could be worked out that would be a help to Alfie without endangering the family.

'Have you got other clothes?' Thomas didn't know where or how highwaymen lived.

'I have a jacket. Why?' he answered.

170

'Then get rid of that greatcoat of yours and the hat too and come home with me. I'll make up some tale or other and hope that family doesn't see through it.'

'I don't need to, Tom. I'm alright. Really I am. I'll just see you to the gate.'

'Then if that's the case you can go on your way tomorrow,' Thomas decided. 'My horse is down the road a bit, I think.' He put his hand on the tree trunk to steady himself. He felt very woozy.

'One minute you don't want me, the next you do. Make up your mind.'

'You were always there for me Alfie, and you never hesitated to help me. Now it's my turn although I'm not sure what we're going to do. Come on. Let's get going.'

Alfie made the changes to his clothing and left his hat and coat hidden in the woods. They collected their horses and stiffly mounted them.

'Just as well we didn't kill each other,' said Alfie. 'Would you have killed me?'

'Only to save myself,' Thomas replied. 'Would you have me?'

'I probably would have. If it hadn't been you... I mean if someone else had attacked me.... he may well have lynched me anyway or given me to the magistrate to do so, so I thought I was really fighting for my life.'

'You might still have to someday if you carry on with this sort of life. At least your pistol is lost.'

'I think I know roughly where it is so I can retrieve it. It's too good to just forget it,' he smiled knowing exactly what Thomas was thinking. He remembered that Tom had always been a worrier although admittedly he had had a lot to worry about.

'Where did you get it?' asked Thomas.

Alfie laughed. At least he tried to. His face was very sore and had swelled up considerably. 'The first time I held up a traveller I didn't have a pistol. Just had a piece of stick under my jacket but he didn't know that. He had a pistol in a holster but didn't have time to get it out. I took it out for him and 'forgot' to give it back.'

They continued their journey home with Thomas wondering what he was going to say to Hannah.

***

Hannah was really worried about Thomas. She had expected him home a long time ago.

'He won't be far away,' Davie said to reassure her. 'Maybe Bert is sick or maybe his wife is and he stayed a little longer. Could be a number of reasons.'

'And maybe he's fallen from his horse and hit his head,' she retorted.

'He'd have to be drunk to fall off that old nag,' joked Andy.

'You could go and look for him instead of treating it as a joke,' she suggested.

Before he could answer there was a commotion at the door and Thomas and Alfie stumbled in. Hannah jumped up. 'Tom! What on earth has happened? Who is this?'

'I'll tell you later,' mumbled Thomas. Both their faces were beginning to swell up and their eyes starting to close. Davie started to laugh. Andy joined him and soon they were both rolling around unable to control themselves.

'You're gonna have some explaining to do, Tom! What's the other man look like?' Andy laughed. 'Maybe this is the other man,' he added roaring hilariously again.

'Stop it, you two. Maybe you could go and see to the horses. Do something useful. Now let's clean you two up and you can tell me what this is all about and who has done this to you?'

Simon watched and listened. He learned that this was Alfie, Thomas' friend. He knew that they knew each other from way back but didn't know what had caused their dishevelled state. And they weren't telling. They had certainly been in a fight though. Maybe tomorrow they would tell more.

***

Alfie lay on the floor wrapped in a blanket and tried to sleep. But sleep eluded him. There were a lot of thoughts racing round in his head and he could hear Hannah and Thomas talking in their room. Their voices were muffled and he wondered what Tom was saying. His body ached but a small smile creased his face as he thought of the improbable chance that had brought Thomas back into his life.

Life had not been kind to Alfie. The life that had promised so much had changed dramatically a few years after Thomas had left. He had continued working as a cobbler's apprentice and although he didn't enjoy it, he promised to stick at it for a few years to help his family out, after which he planned to venture out into the world just as Thomas had done. But then, disastrously, his father had been killed, set upon by a bunch of thugs as he walked home from work one night after dark. Some good people heard his shouts and came to his aid but it was too late and he died from his injuries.

It was a terrible blow to his family and although Alfie worked hard he could not make up his father's pay packet. His mother and brother Billy worked when and where they could but it was a hard struggle. As they could not keep up with the rent on their little home they were evicted. The dwelling they moved to was squalid although they did their best to keep it clean. Then Billy ran away, unable to cope with the misery that had engulfed his household. But it got worse. His two little sisters died of scrofula, undoubtedly due to the conditions that they were living

173

in. If their situation was bad it was nothing to what it became after his mother died.

Alfie had pleaded with his mother to leave the town with him and his one remaining sibling but she refused. Town living was all she knew and the thought of the unknown wide open country frightened her. Finally her misery overtook her and unable to put up a fight, she too died.

Alfie took his ten year old brother John and left the town. He was heartbroken but determined to make enough money so that he would not get in the same situation again. John was good company and together they roamed the countryside getting work where they could. Finally John was offered work and a place to stay and Alfie moved on alone. Earnings were small and everything he did earn was spent on keeping himself in food. He walked everywhere because he could not afford to buy a horse and he didn't know how to ride one anyway. He was bathing his feet in a stream one evening, having walked many miles and thinking that he could not keep up his present lifestyle forever, when he realised that what he needed to make the changeover was money. He couldn't seem to get enough of it by working and the thought suddenly came to him - what about stealing it? He had always been law-abiding and knew that his mother would be very disappointed if she knew that he was even thinking of it. However he would only steal enough to give himself a new beginning, then he would stop. He vowed also that he would never steal from the poor. He knew so well what it was like to be poor.

At the first opportunity he stole a horse. This was a hanging offence but he took a chance. It was a common looking horse, plain grey with no distinguishing marks. Alfie knew nothing about horses and this one appeared rather big but fortunately it was docile and did not throw him off the first time he mounted it.

In teaching himself to ride however, he had many spills but fortunately he didn't hurt himself. So with a stolen horse and a stick under his jacket he performed his first robbery and then high-tailed it out of the area. There was no turning back now.

***

Hannah and Tom lay quietly in their bed.

'Well, Tom. Are you going to tell me what happened and how you and Alfie met and then got so beaten up?'

'Oh Hannah, can't it wait? I'm so sore and tired. My head still aches. I need to get some sleep. I'll tell you tomorrow, I promise,' he muttered through swollen lips.

'Not good enough. I want to know now. If you've nothing to hide you can tell me briefly now. By tomorrow you'd have had time to dream up a good story.'

'I would never lie to you Hannah. You know that. That's why it's so difficult to explain this. You'll disapprove so much.' He closed his eyes.

'Now you really have my attention. Just tell me and I'll keep my questions until tomorrow, unless you had a fight over another woman and Alfie came to rescue you in which case I'll throw you out now.'

Thomas grimaced. 'Never. If you're not going to question me I'll tell you the bare facts now and then go to sleep. I was on my way home from Bert's house when I came across a highway robbery. I threw myself at the robber so that the carriage could get away and had to fight for my life. I got his mask off and just as I passed out I realised that the man was Alfie.' Hannah sat bolt upright. 'Those are the bare facts. Now goodnight!' He rolled over painfully. 'Oh, by the way it was Sir Edric Spicer's daughter that he held up.'

'And you brought him here!!!!' Hannah exclaimed.

'No questions, Hannah.'

175

'That's not a question. That's a statement of your stupidity.'

Thomas was silent. He knew that it had been a stupid thing to do but Alfie was his friend. He could have done nothing else. He drifted off to sleep leaving Hannah wide-awake to worry about this turn of events.

Chapter 17:
An unexpected windfall

Morning dawned and Hannah slipped quietly out of bed to commence her daily chores. Thomas was still asleep, as was Alfie. She ventured out to the long-drop toilet feeling as unwell as she had felt every morning. She was five months pregnant and had been sick all the while. Would it never end?

Back in the kitchen she stood looking at Alfie. He didn't look like a highwayman or a murderer. She shuddered. Was he a murderer? Had he killed or harmed any one? What would her father say? She resolved not to tell him. He would get too upset and maybe have another stroke, a fatal one this time. And her brothers? They would throw him out, maybe beat him up first but from the look of him Thomas had done a pretty good job of that.

Alfie opened his eyes and saw Hannah watching him. He struggled to sit up but his body was feeling very stiff. Hannah made no effort to help him.

'Tom must have told you,' he said flatly through swollen lips. 'I can see it in your eyes. I'll be away from here as soon as I can. I won't be any trouble.'

'You can go straight after your breakfast and you must go as far away as possible. Tom was silly to bring you here. You shouldn't have come.'

'I was going to come as far as your gate just to see that he got home safely. I felt bad about what I'd done to him.'

'What if he'd been someone else? Would you have killed him?' she asked quietly.

'I don't know. I haven't killed anyone yet.'

'Just robbed them and put them in fear for their lives,' she said. 'Tom said that it was Sir Edric Spicer's daughter that you held up yesterday. Tom worked on his estate when he was a boy. He'll be looking for you, Alfie.'

'I'll get well away from here. There'll be no danger for you all, I promise.'

'You can't make a promise like that and you mark my words, you'll be caught. In the woods there're a lot of corpses hanging by their necks from the trees. Bare bones a lot of them now. Country folk lynch any robbers they catch and ask questions later. They leave them there as a warning to other highwaymen and woe betide anyone who cuts 'em down.'

'I know all these things, Hannah, and Tom has already given me the message. I thought that if I was careful I'd get away with it until I wanted to stop. I would've too if Tom hadn't stuck his nose in.'

'You should be pleased that it was Tom. If someone else had come along you would be dead by now.'

'Maybe. But someone else didn't and I'm not,' Alfie swiftly responded.

Thomas appeared at the bedroom door. Hannah looked at them both angrily and went outside.

'I don't think she's happy with either of us, Tom. I'll leave after breakfast.'

***

Hannah sat on the tree stump near the barn. She felt very ill and was also exceedingly angry with both Thomas and Alfie. How dare they endanger her family! Alfie should have gone on his way and Thomas should not have got involved by helping him. Just quietly, she felt proud of Thomas for going to the aid of Charlotte but then initially, he hadn't known it was Charlotte and that Alfie was his adversary. It could equally have been a man who

178

could take care of himself more easily than Alfie had. The consequences did not bear thinking about. Thomas could have been killed. If only she did not feel so unwell. She stood up to walk back inside when she stopped suddenly and clutched her stomach. Gasping, she tried to call out to Thomas but no sound came. She staggered to the door and thumped on it. Thomas opened it and found Hannah collapsed in a heap on the step and looking up at him beseechingly.

'Hannah what is it? Is it the baby?'

She nodded and he carefully picked her up, his aches and pains forgotten and carried her into the bedroom.

'Alfie, wake Davie and sent him down the road for Alice,' he called frantically. 'She'll know what to do. Quickly now.' He placed her carefully on the bed and sat nervously beside her as they waited for Alice.

'I hope it's not my fault, Hannah. Maybe I upset you last night. I didn't mean to,' he fretted.

'Hush Tom. You did upset me but I've been unwell all this time. It's not your fault. It sometimes happens like this. I hope Alice can help.'

But Alice couldn't help. Andy raced away to fetch Mother Marsham but she was too late. She couldn't have done anything anyway. Hannah miscarried her baby and Thomas was devastated.

'Sleep now, Hannah. We'll talk about this later,' he said and left her tucked up in bed.

'You'll have to look after her Tom,' Alice instructed him as he sat with his head in his hands. 'She's very weak. No work for her for a while and no stress. She'll get well again but we must all help her. Now can I do anything for you two boys? You look as though you've been in a bit of a skirmish.'

Simon saw the look that passed between Thomas and Alfie. Nobody had had the time throughout the day to talk about what had happened the day before. Now it didn't seem to matter to Simon. Alfie hadn't left and he had made himself indispensable, fetching and carrying and even lending Andy a hand with the cooking.

'We'll be fine thanks Alice. Thank you for all you've done. Alfie, could you walk Alice home for me? It's just down the road a bit,' Thomas asked.

Alice gathered up her things. 'I just wish we'd been able to save the baby, Tom. I'll pop back later.' When they had left he sent Davie into the town to tell James that he could not come to work for a few days. At least his bruises and cuts might have faded a little by then.

It was a subdued household that sat down to a late supper prepared by Andy. They had all in their own way been looking forward to having a baby in the house and now that wasn't going to happen. Not now anyway.

There was no talk of Thomas and Alfie's situation that evening and Hannah was sleeping when Thomas went to bed. His heart was aching. He cuddled up to her. He was worried about her, was grieving for their baby and concerned about Alfie. By the time he fell asleep he had come up with a plan, albeit a temporary one.

***

'Alfie, you realise that you're going to have to stop your present 'employment' or you'll end up swingin' on the end of a rope. The people 'round here are very loyal but not all that forgiving and your chances of escaping their clutches forever aren't great.' Thomas and Alfie were sitting beside the little stream. It was the first opportunity that they had had to converse alone since Alfie had arrived. 'Maybe Charlotte has connections around this way. I don't know but if so, they'll be on her side, not yours. What started you down such a path?' he added.

Alfie hesitated. 'It isn't easy for me to tell you this, Tom. An' I ain't makin' excuses. I had a choice and I chose this way. I didn't mean to do it forever.'

'How long is forever, Alfie? 'Til you get caught or hanged? Forever is a very short time in a highwayman's life. But if by some chance you escaped hanging you could be deported. That could be a lot worse.'

'I know all those things. Knew 'em when I started out. But I still made the choice to do it,' he answered.

'Why though?'

'I was sick of being poor,' he said.

Thomas stared at him. 'We're all poor Alfie, but we're not all highwaymen! There are other ways.'

'Yeah, I know that but as I said it wasn't going to be forever. Just 'til I got some money behind me. Then I planned to stop.' He hesitated. 'I'd better tell you my story.' He proceeded to tell him all that had happened since Thomas left Athelney. It was a sad commentary and at the end of it they sat quietly, saying nothing.

Thomas finally spoke. 'I guess it's a reason Alfie, but not a very good one.'

'Best I can do, I'm afraid. My folks would be upset if they knew but they don't, so I'm the only one who has to worry about it,' he replied.

'I believe my mother knows almost everything I do and I wouldn't want her to be disappointed in me.' Thomas idly threw twigs into the stream and watched them float off down the river. He remembered mentally throwing his unhappy thoughts into the brook years ago and feeling much better for it.

Alfie interrupted his reverie. 'Tell me what led you here.'

'It's a long story, Alfie. After I left Athelney I walked...' and Thomas proceeded to tell him of the events that lead him to the Fenwick Farm and Penshurst Village. Alfie looked at him in astonishment.

'Wow!' he exclaimed. 'Is that fellow still after you?'

'I don't know. He could be but I try not to think about him. Life is for living and I'm very happy with Hannah. Losing the baby is a blow for us both but we'll have another one.' A shadow passed over his face and Alfie put his arm around his friend's shoulder. They sat there for a few moments.

'I'd better go and see Hannah,' he said finally. 'You wait here. I'll be back in a minute.'

He found her sleeping peacefully with Simon sitting by her bed.

'We're out by the stream if you want us.' he whispered. Simon nodded.

As Thomas turned to leave he heard a knocking at the door. He opened it and he found a well-dressed man standing on the doorstep.

'Are you Mr Tom Puckle?' he asked.

'Yes,' Thomas answered somewhat fearfully.

'I am the valet to Sir Francis Wentworth. He asked me to deliver this to you. He would have come himself but unfortunately he's very busy just now. He and most of his staff are out looking for the man who held up his coach. He gives his heartfelt thanks to you for coming to the rescue of his wife, Lady Charlotte Wentworth. You have earned his lifelong gratitude. Please be assured that he will never forget it and will not rest until the blackguard that you so valiantly fought off has been brought to justice.'

With that he handed a small pouch to Thomas, mounted his horse and rode off. Thomas stared after him. He looked at the pouch in his hand and tipped out the coins it contained.. There were ten gold sovereigns. Ten pounds. Half a year's salary for Thomas. He was astounded and clutched it in his hand. He could never save up that sort of money. What would Hannah say? He'd tell her later when she felt better. He pushed the little bag deep into his pocket and went back to Alfie.

'Just as well you kept out of sight. It would have looked suspicious if my visitor had seen two beaten up fellows,' he said as he sat down beside Alfie.

'Who was your visitor?' Alfie asked curiously.

'Valet to Sir Francis Wentworth whoever he is. Seems like Charlotte is married to him and he wanted to thank me for saving her from some blackguard who wanted to rob her.' For some reason he did not tell Alfie of the money. He didn't think for one minute that Alfie would rob him but it was such a treasure that Hannah was the only one he wanted to share the news with.

'Alfie, I have a plan,' he continued. 'I think it's far too dangerous for you to try to leave the area. For a few weeks anyway. You need to hide. Sir Francis says that he's not going to rest until you're caught and I know that Sir Edric will be feeling the same. You can't stay here. Hannah wouldn't allow it anyway. I know an old couple over Wynchley way. I help them out sometimes. They live in a quiet place on their own. Their son was accidentally killed a while ago and they struggle a bit.' He threw some more sticks into the water. 'How about I take you over there and you can hide away while you help them out? They don't get many visitors so if you keep your wits about you, you should be alright.'

'What if they tell someone about me?'

'They don't go out much. Bert's wife is unwell and he won't leave her on her own. Anyway it's only for a few weeks. Just until things quieten down. What do you say?'

'I think I'd rather be on my way. Hanging around waiting doesn't appeal to me.'

'That's an unfortunate expression to use but I know how you feel,' agreed Thomas. 'I felt the same way when I was stuck in William's loft. Couldn't see the point but it all worked out in the end. Anyway it's just a plan. You don't have to do it. It's your decision.'

'Why can't I skip away at night? No one would see me.'

'Sir Francis is scouring the countryside for you as we speak. You don't think he stops just because it gets dark, do you? The hold-up only happened yesterday even though with all that has happened it seems a lot longer. I can't keep you hidden in the barn. It will be hard enough hiding your horse somewhere for a few weeks. Anyway there is one other thing.' He hesitated. 'I'm really happy to have seen you after all this time and selfishly I don't want you to disappear again so soon.'

'Even with the risk of my getting caught! What about Hannah's brothers? They know I'm here.'

'We don't have to tell them where you've gone. Actually it might be best if I take you now before they get back. I'll just say that you've left. Simple. If you think about it the best place to hide something is under the noses of the people who are looking for it. They won't expect you to still be in this area. C'mon. I'll check on Hannah; you get the horses.'

***

It was two very relieved men who finally arrived at Bert's farm. It was almost dark and although they hadn't encountered any of the searchers, they had expected that they might. As they travelled along the road where the hold up had occurred. Thomas noticed Alfie peering into the bushes bordering the roadside.

'Don't think about it, Alfie. You don't want incriminating stuff anywhere near you.'

184

'Just thinking that it might be a good idea to have that coat. Guess I'll be sleeping in the barn and it's getting a mite cold at night.'

'If I know Bert and his wife, they'll sleep you in their cottage. Wait and see. If you need something I'll find you a cover.'

Bert and Mabel seemed to accept their explanation for Alfie's presence and obviously hadn't heard about the hold-up. They didn't enlighten them about it and Thomas explained that Alfie was travelling through the district and needed somewhere to stay for a little while. In return he would help them on the farm.

Thomas returned home to share his good fortune with Hannah. On the way he scouted for the gun that he had thrown into the bushes. After some time he found it and carefully thrust it into his bag. 'At least it's not around for Alfie to find,' he muttered to himself. He didn't know what he was going to do with it but in the meantime he would hide it away safely somewhere on the farm.

'Mmmmm,' Hannah murmured when he told her the news of the money. 'That's good, but I'd rather have had our baby.'

'It wasn't a choice, but I would too.' Thomas whispered as he held her close. 'There'll be another one some day, I promise.'

They were silent for a moment then Thomas added, 'Alfie has gone. He's no longer here. So you don't need to worry anymore.'

She was silent for a moment and then said,'Then why do I have this feeling that I do? Please be careful, Tom.'

Chapter 18:
Arrested and re-arrested

The days passed and life settled down at the Fenwick farmhouse. Hannah grew stronger but sadly Simon grew weaker. Hannah and the boys did their best for him and Alice plied him with a variety of pills and potions. Although at first he was reluctant to take any of them he finally gave in and tried all that was offered but they didn't make any difference.

'I don't know what else to do for him,' Hannah confided to Molly. 'I think he's slowly dying and there's nothing any of us can do. It's so hard to watch him going from being a fit strong man to someone who can't walk or talk or do anything. He's getting thinner by the day and more morose and moody.'

'You're doing a fine job, Hannah, but age catches up with all of us sooner or later. Could be that he's just wearing out and his life is ending. He's been a long while without his wife and probably wants to go to join her. You'll see. Maybe he's getting impatient.'

'Well he's my Dad and I don't want him to go anywhere,' Hannah replied vehemently.

'He's not going to get better, Hannah. You have to realise that. All you can do is make his last months as comfortable as possible.'

***

Thomas stayed away from Bert's farm for a little while but now realised that he would have to go and see how Alfie was getting on. He was his friend after all and Bert would be wondering why he hadn't called.

'This is madness, Tom,' Alfie greeted him. 'I need to get away from here. Bert does get the odd caller and I know that he's told some people that I'm here. I'm just wasting me time. OK, so I'm no longer a highwayman and I promise you that I'll never be one again but I can't hide away forever. Life's out there and I have to find it. I have some loot stashed away. I'll go and retrieve it and be on my way.'

'But you're being a big help to Bert and Mabel, Alfie. Think of it that way and it's helping me out as well. I don't have to come here as often.'

'You were doing it out of the goodness of your heart. God knows why I'm doing it. Just because you told me to? I'm me own man and I do what I like. I must've been mad to stay around. Well I've done me bit and now I'm off.'

Thomas sat down. He was silent. 'I've hardly seen you,' he finally remarked.

'I didn't come here to see you, Tom, but I am pleased to have met up with you again and to know that you are safe and happy. I just don't want to be 'ere any longer. I wouldn't be 'ere if all this 'adn't happened. So I must move on.'

'Give it another week Alfie. I haven't seen any searchers lately. I think they've decided that you won the fight and left. You'll be safe enough here. Maybe I could go and find your stash and then you could leave. Less risk that way.'

'Tom, much as I love and trust you I think I'll retrieve it myself. I'll probably have a hard enough job locating it anyway. Thanks all the same. I'll give it a couple of more days and then I'll be gone.'

'Yeah, well alright then. Has to happen sometime, I suppose. I'll see you before you go.' Thomas stood up and looked at Alfie. 'You're still my friend; more like a brother really and now we've met again and I know what you've been up to I'll probably worry more than I did before.'

'I've survived so far. I'm like you Tom. People like us survive. We do what we 'ave to do. I'll be fine and you've got Hannah. I hope one day that I find someone like Hannah,' Alfie remarked wistfully.

'You will, Alfie. Just keep out of trouble.'

***

As it was now several days since his conversation with Alfie, Thomas thought that he should call at Bert's place before going home and make his final farewell to him. He hadn't told him that he'd located the pistol. Alfie didn't have to know that but Thomas realised that he needed to dispose of it as soon as he could. To be honest, he'd had so much on his mind that he had forgotten all about it. As much as he didn't want Alfie to go he would be relieved when the threat that his presence posed was gone; he could then concentrate on looking after Hannah and Simon and get on with his life.

'You seem to have something on your mind, Tom,' said James as they worked together in the smithy.

'No more than usual James. Simon is always a worry with his health but Hannah seems to be getting well again. She's a bit sad at times but Alice said that if the baby had lived he would always have been sickly and would probably have had a very short life.'

'We lost quite a few babies over the years and feel lucky that we managed to keep two of them. You probably will also eventually.'

'Mmmm. Hope so. I need to get away a little earlier today, James. Is that alright? I want to go and check out Bert and Mabel.'

'As long as your work is finished I suppose that's alright,' replied James.

Thomas wandered over to the door to get a breath of fresh air. It was very hot in the smithy even though it was cold and raining outside. Perspiration poured from his brow and he took a mouthful of water from his bottle. Turning back from putting the bottle on the shelf he froze, unable to believe his eyes. Alfie was in the middle of the road trying to control his horse which appeared to have been spooked by a nippy dog. He was wearing his long black coat and of all the stupid things, his tricorn hat! He must have retrieved them from the woods after all! He looked just like a highwayman again.

'I'll be back in a minute, James,' he called as he rushed out the door and down the road towards Alfie. James watched him from the doorway.

'Alfie! What in God's name are you doing?' Thomas hissed grabbing the horse. 'Do you know what you look like? You utter idiot.'

'Cut it out, Tom. Bert needed me to do a message. What was I to do? Refuse him! It's bloody cold and I needed a coat. This one's a good one. I couldn't leave it in the bush.'

'That one's a highwayman's one and that's just what you look like. And take off that stupid hat. You'd better get out of here, fast.'

'I haven't done my message yet,' he answered as his horse spun around in another circle. Thomas clasped his head in frustration. People were looking at them.

'You're attracting attention. I can't believe this. I'll do the message. You just leave, please,' Thomas pleaded.

'You're the one attracting attention. It'll only take me a minute and then I'll be gone. I was planning on not going back to Bert's place so this is the last you'll see of me.'

'Maybe that's a good thing,' Thomas replied huffily.

Alfie managed to dismount and walked down the road to the drugstore to deliver his message. Thomas watched and finally trudged back to the blacksmith.

'I haven't seen that fellow before, Tom. Is he a friend of yours?' James queried.

'No. He just seemed to be having trouble with his horse. I didn't want him to fall off.' Tom brushed the rain off his clothes and stood by the fire to dry out a little. He didn't like lying to James and knew that it was a pretty lame reason. But it was all he could think of on the spur of the moment. It was best if no-one knew of the relationship he had with the horseman.

Venning was in his shop looking as dishevelled as he always did. Alfie delivered his message. 'It's Mabel,' he said rubbing his cold hands to restore some of the feeling. 'Bert needs you to see 'er.'

'Just a minute young man. I might have some stuff 'ere that could fix what ails 'er. If you wait a bit I'll look.' Dr Venning rummaged around in a cupboard at the back of the shop and finally produced a dirty dusty jar. 'This looks like it,' he said peering closely to try and discern the writing on the label. 'Yes, this should do the trick, don'tcha think?'

'How would I know? I don't even know what's wrong with 'er. I'm just the message boy. Anyway you don't know either. Maybe you should take a look at her before you give her some hocus pocus concoction.'

'It's 'armless stuff but it'll fix most things.' Venning handed it to him. 'Tell 'er to follow my directions carefully. Two spoonfuls each morning an' one at night.'

Alfie grabbed the bottle and turned towards the door.

'Hey, what about me money?' Venning came rushing out from behind the counter.

'You'll have to get it from Bert next time you see him.'

'But I hardly ever do see 'im.'

Alfie hesitated. 'How much is it?' he asked.

'One and sixpence,' Venning answered and held out his hand.

Alfie paid him and hurriedly left the store. It was a small price to pay for all Bert and Mabel had done for him. However he would now have to go back to the farm to deliver the medicine and give the instructions for its use. Being preoccupied with his own thoughts he didn't notice a man slip into the store behind him, but collected his horse and quickly headed in the direction of the farm.

'Who was the fellow who just left here? I ain't seen him before,' the man demanded of Dr Venning.

' 'An I ain't seen you neither, so what's it to ya?' Venning replied.

'Sir Francis Wentworth's me boss so's I reckon ya should tell me or you'll 'ave 'im to answer to. Now 'oo is 'e?'

'Dunno but 'e picked up some medicine for Bert Simmon's missus. They live over Wynchley way. Dunno what 'e is to them. Friend I s'pose. Now if you 'ave no further business I 'ave work t' do.'

The stranger left the store and rode back to where his companion was waiting just outside town.

'I think we mighta got ourselves an 'ighwayman. Old Francie boy will be very 'appy with us 'an there could be a nice bit o' money in it for us if we're careful.' He related his sighting of Alfie and his conversation with Venning.

'Doesn't mean 'e's an 'ighwayman though, does it? Lotsa men wear big dark coats. Even me bruvver does sometimes.'

'Yeah, but Venning didn't know who 'e was so 'e's a stranger. Why would 'e be 'anging around out at Wynchley? No, I gotta feelin' about this an' I'm gonna take a look. You comin or not?'

'Might as well but I 'ope you're right.'

They took the road to Wynchley and after asking some directions found themselves at the lane that led to Bert's farm.

'You wait 'ere. I'll go up and see if 'e's still there. If I ain't back in five minutes come on in an' give us a 'and. We'll try and take 'im back to Francie boy. Best not try to lynch 'im ourselves. Bert will be about an' I don't know if 'es young or old.'

'OK. How long's five minutes?' his not so bright companion asked.

'I dunno. Just guess it.' The man drew a pistol from under the long pocket inside his coat. 'Just as well the boss gave us this. Might be a tad 'andy.'

He trotted off down the lane to the cottage where he found Alfie's horse tethered to the rail by the door. *'Looks like 'e's still 'ere. This should be a piece of cake,'* he muttered dismounting and tying his horse to the same rail. All was quiet.

Knocking on the door he stood back as he waited for someone to open it. It was Alfie who did. Levelling his pistol, he pointed it at him saying, 'You'd better come with me, young fellow.'

'Why should I do that? Who the hell are you? You'd better put that pistol away before you shoot someone.' Alfie was determined not to show the fear that coursed through his body. Bert appeared by his side.

'What's goin' on 'ere?' he said eyeing the pistol. 'Get orf my property.'

'I could take you too Bert, for 'idin' an 'ighwayman. Move aside an' I'll say no more. But this is the man I want an' 'e's comin' with me.'

192

'Don't be so daft. 'E ain't no 'ighwayman. 'E works for me an' a good worker 'e is too. You've made a mistake. Now get orf or you'll be the one in trouble. Go inside Alfie.' Bert made to shut the door but the man swung the pistol round to point at him.

'I can shoot you just as easily, Bert. How long 'as this man bin with you an' was 'e livin' 'ere when Miss Charlotte got 'eld up?'

'I don't know nothin' about that an' he's been here since Thomas Puckle brought him to 'elp me. Nice lads both of 'em. You're barkin' up the wrong tree so bugger orf.' Bert was getting angry as Alfie eyed up their visitor and wondered if he could rush him and catch him off guard. The last thing he wanted was for Bert to get hurt. He was still weighing up his options when another man rode up to the house and said, 'Good work, Moe. I'll tie 'im up.'

'*If only Bert wasn't here,*' Alfie thought. '*I could take on these scoundrels. I'd rather be shot any day than hanged.*' He thought back to the day that Thomas's mother died and shuddered. He felt trapped. He couldn't do anything while Bert was so close.

'They don't want you, Bert. You go inside to Mabel. They won't shoot me. That would make them murderers and I don't think they are. Who sent you here?' he asked.

'Not that that's any business of yours but Sir Francis Wentworth 'as 'ad us lookin' for you. You know what you done an' you know the price you'll 'ave to pay. Now let's get movin'. We bin 'angin' around 'ere long enough.'

The other man laughed. 'Yeah but not as long as 'e will be.' Alfie's blood ran cold. How was he going to get out of this predicament? He knew that these men would get a good a reward from Sir Francis and therefore they would guard him very closely.

'Where're you gonna to take me?' he demanded.

'To Sir Francis. I'm sure 'e would wanna meet you afore 'angin' you from the highest tree. Tie 'im up, Harry, jist 'is 'ands behind 'is back. E's gotta ride. Jist remember if you try anything silly, I'll shoot you. Maybe not to kill but it sure as 'ell will 'urt.'

With difficulty, Alfie mounted his horse and turned to Bert. 'Don't worry Bert. I ain't done nothing wrong. Can you get a message to Tom? Tell 'im where I'm being taken.'

They rode slowly down the lane, Harry in front leading Alfie and his horse, and finally Moe, holding the pistol, bringing up the rear. Alfie was terrified but put on a show of bravado so that his captors wouldn't know how scared he was. He debated with himself whether of not he should try to escape or take his chances with Sir Francis. He might be a reasonable man.

***

Thomas was finishing his work a little early when Bert finally arrived at the smithy's. He was cold and exhausted and slowly clambered down from the dray as Thomas rushed to help him.

'Bert, what on earth has brought you out in conditions like this? You must be frozen. Come inside. At least it's warm in here. I was going to come and see you.' Thomas began to fuss around as James looked on with interest. 'Is it Mabel?'

'Nay, lad, nay she be foine, leastways she were when I left 'er. Nay, 'tis young Alfie.'

'Alfie?' responded a startled Thomas.

'Yeah, Alfie. Two men with a pistol came an' took 'im away. Said that 'e were a 'ighwayman. Been 'oldin' up people, so they reckoned. Absolute codswallop. 'E ain't no 'ighwayman. Alfie's a good lad.' He sat by the furnace, his face full of despondency. ' 'E said to get you an' to say that they're takin' 'im to Sir Francis Wentworth. He must think that you can help, seein' as you're 'is friend.'

Thomas felt the blood drain from his face. He turned away from Bert and found James looking at him with interest.

'James, I have to go. I'll make this up to you, really I will, but can you look after Bert and make sure he gets home safely? I'll need to borrow your horse too. It's faster than mine. Please, I promise to look after it.'

James looked at him. 'Tell me, Tom, is this so called friend of yours a highwayman or not?'

'He was, but not since I took him to you, Bert,' he answered turning to face him. 'Honestly. I don't have time to explain now. They could be hanging him. I have to get it stopped.' He remembered using those same words once before and he had not succeeded then. Please God, that he would this time. Buried thoughts came surging to the surface of his consciousness. His nightmare was starting all over again. Grabbing his coat he called out 'You keep Bouncer here,' as he rushed out the door and around the back to the stables.

***

Alfie's captors picked up the pace a little and with his hands tied, he had trouble keeping his balance and remaining astride the cantering horse. His eyes streamed from the cold as they glanced from side to side looking for a place of dense bush in the hope that he could jump from his horse and run into it before either of the two men had gathered their wits. But the pistol aimed at him was a good deterrent. It was a silly scheme anyway. The horses were travelling too fast for him to be able to land on his feet. He would be shot before his feet touched the ground.

But for once luck was on his side. After a short while Moe called out.

'Hey, 'Arry! Stop a minute. I need a leak.' Harry stopped. ''Ere. You better keep the pistol on 'im,' Moe added as he dismounted. Quick as a flash and whilst they were distracted, Alfie leapt off his horse on the opposite side and scarpered into the undergrowth as fast as he could. The two men banged into each other as they turned to give chase.

'Why didn't you keep an eye on 'im?' cursed Moe.

' 'An why didn't you?' Harry returned. 'C'mon it's no use arguing 'ere. We gotta get him back.'

They took off into the scrub in pursuit of Alfie. It was not easy. It was getting dark and there was no obvious track. Branches and brambles scratched their faces as they forced their way through the undergrowth. Harry tripped over a tree root and crashed to the ground.

'Owww!' he cursed picking himself up. 'This's 'opeless. We'll never see 'im in the dark. 'E could be 'idin' ahind any of these bushes or 'e could even double back an' pinch our 'orses. Then we'd be in a pickle.'

'Mmmm, p'raps you're right,' puffed Moe. 'Maybe you should go back and guard 'em just in case 'e does. I'll go on a bit further.'

'Yeah an' p'raps I should 'ave the pistol, jist in case.'

'Jist in case what, Harry? You don't think I'd let you loose with this, do you? If he does come back you'll 'ave to use your fists. 'E's unarmed an' tied up remember, so it shouldn't be too 'ard. Now get going!' Moe continued to force his way through the forest until eventually it thinned out and he came out onto a road. Carefully looking both ways he crossed it and then turned to study the bush from the other side. He couldn't discern any movement and couldn't make out any disturbance in the foliage where Alfie might have emerged. 'This is stupid,' he muttered. 'A good opportunity for some extra cash an' it's gone!'

He made his way back to where Harry was waiting patiently with the horses.

'There's a road on the far side of this 'ere bush. Don't know where it goes but if 'e made it through I doubt if 'e would carry on in the same direction that we're going. Probably go back the way we came or maybe keep orf the road altogether. Whaddya think?'

'Maybe we should go and get some 'elp. Leastways we knows 'e be 'round 'ere somewhere. I'll go and get Francie boy an' you go back down this road an' see if it meets t' other one.' Harry didn't want to go looking for Alfie on his own. Anyway Moe was the one with the gun. He could look after himself. They went their separate ways.

***

Thomas was not sure where Sir Francis lived but headed in the direction of the turnpike. His friend the pikeman would know.

'You need to go back the way ye come, lad. 'Bout half a mile back is a road leading to his estate. You'll know it when y' sees it. Huge place. Long way though. It's a wonder y' don't know it. But then he would 'ave 'is own blacksmith wouldn't 'e? Wouldn't 'ave no need of James Blackler, would 'e?'

'I can't stop to talk just now. I'm in a deuce of a hurry,' and with that Thomas wheeled his horse around and took off back the way he had come. He was wasting time. He should have thought to ask James. He came to the intersection and without losing stride galloped down the road as fast as he could.

Meanwhile Alfie had hidden until the two men had finished their cursory search and when the crashing in the undergrowth had ceased, he made up his mind to get as far away as possible. Scratched and bleeding, he emerged from the forest and took off down the road. It was difficult with his hands tied behind his back. Thomas, coming from the other direction rounded a bend and almost bowled him over. He reined in his horse and exclaimed, 'Alfie!'

' Hi, Tom. I can't run much further. Hows' about a lift?'

Thomas hauled him up behind him on the horse. 'Now what? Where the hell are we going to go?'

'Not that way anyway. That's the way to Sir Flamin' Francis. Turn 'round and get us outa here.'

Thomas did so and they sped away, Alfie desperately trying to keep his balance. Thomas had no idea where to take Alfie. The Fenwick farm was out of the question and they couldn't put Bert and Mabel in any more danger. He mulled ideas in his mind as they rode along and he was so preoccupied that he failed to notice a man standing in the middle of the road. But they certainly heard the shot that was fired over their heads and the jolt as their horse reared in the air and spilled them on to the ground.

'Well, what 'ave we 'ere? Two birds, eh! Get to y' feet or I'll shoot again. This time it won't be over ya 'eads.' Moe smiled gleefully.

Thomas shook his head to clear his senses. As he watched James's horse take off out of sight, the thought rushed through his mind, 'Oh God, I said that I'd look after it. I hope it goes home.'

Chapter 19:
A dire situation

'Come on Bert, I'll take you back to your wife. Maybe on the way you can tell me about this Alfie fellow. Tom seems to have been strangely quiet about him.' James gathered up his coat and after going around to the stables to collect Thomas' horse, led Bert and the dray home. Bouncer loped alongside. The talking was left until they arrived at the farmstead. It was warm in the kitchen and James made a hot drink for them all. Settling himself in a chair he said, 'Ok, Bert, tell me about this fellow.'

'Ain't much too tell, an' that's the truth. Tom brought 'im 'ere one night. They both looked as though they'd been in a fight but Tom said it was nothin' to worry about and asked could Alfie stay 'ere. 'E could 'elp out 'round the place if we could feed 'im, 'e said. Sounded alright to us, didn't it Mabel.'

Mabel nodded.'Tom said 'e was a good fellow and that was enough for us, weren't it Bert,' she said, adding, 'Been lonely 'round 'ere since Leonard died 'an Alfie was good to have about. 'E ain't no 'ighwayman.'

They both looked so upset that James felt he had to say, 'I'll see what I can do Bert. But I'm only a blacksmith. Sir Francis is pretty powerful. All them big blokes are. They gotta lot of say in the law.'

'Yeah but as I sees it, they still should be on the side of justice, don'tcha know. What proof 'ave they got 'gainst Alfie?'

'That I don't know, Bert. I'll try and find out. I'd better hurry though. I don't know how fast events are likely to move and Thomas might need some help. I'll let you know what 'appens as soon as I can. Will you take care of Bouncer for us? He might get in the way.'

***

Moe watched as Harry arrived with three other men to assist him in the apprehension of the dangerous criminal. 'Ha ha!' he laughed as he greeted Harry. 'I did it on me own, I did. Not only a 'ighwayman but 'is 'complice as well. Where's Old Francie?'

'He ain't at 'ome,' replied Harry. ' 'E's gorn t' Lunnen.'

'Well what you can do then, is take Bart and go to this fellow's 'ouse,' he said indicating Thomas, 'an' see if you can find anythin' incriminatin' so to speak'

'Who is he?' asked Harry.

'Dunno.' He walked over to Thomas who was sitting beside Alfie on the side of the road. 'What's yer name boy? Where do ya live?' he asked.

Thomas looked at him defiantly. 'Do you really think I'm going to tell you that. I'm not going to have you going upsetting my family. Get lost.'

'I know 'im.' One of the new men wandered over and said, ''E works with the 'smithy. Puckle's 'is name. Married old Fenwick's daughter. Think they live at 'is farm with 'im. I'll go. Come on Harry. See ya back at the big house, Moe.'

***

James was unsure of what to do. He felt that he should go and see Hannah. But if he did that he would be delayed in arriving to help Tom in the rescue of Alfie. He had nothing to say to her anyway except that Tom would be late and that knowledge was not going to help the situation. So he headed off to the Wentworth Estate, fearful of what he might find there.

Therefore he was not at the Fenwick farm when the two men arrived but Davie and Andy were.

200

'Can I help you fellows?' asked Andy strolling over to the men as they entered the yard.

'Dunno yet. Does a chap o' the name o' Puckle live here?' Harry enquired as he dismounted.

'Yeah but he ain't home yet. Can I help?' said Davie, joining his brother.

'Well it's like this,' Harry said. 'We need to 'ave a look around and see if we can find anythin' 'ere that'll confirm he's an accomplice of a 'ighwayman.'

The boys stared at him in disbelief.

'You must be mad to think that! What highwayman? What's his name? Anyway what gives you the right to think you can look around here? You'd better turn tail and get outa here real quick,' ordered Andy. He tried to sound more confident than he felt. This was a situation that he had never dealt with before.

Harry moved closer to him. 'His name's Alfie something. Dunno what, but he and Tom are both on their way to the Wentworth Estate right now and they are in a 'eap of trouble. So there! Now let's do our search.'

The door behind Andy opened and Hannah appeared. 'What's going on, Andy? I thought it was Tom. Who are these men?' she demanded.

'They have some crazy idea that Tom has been helping a highwayman. Alfie of all people. I've never heard anything so stupid. Now get out,' he ordered the men hoping against hope that they would just leave. But he knew they wouldn't. They seemed so sure of themselves and they did have Tom and Alfie captive... or were they just saying that? he wondered.

Hannah felt the colour drain from her face and feared that she would faint. She held on to the door frame to keep herself upright.

'Why Tom? Why Alfie for that matter?' she added. 'What have they done?'

'I don' 'ave to tell you nothin', missus. Sir Francis will sort 'em out. Now if you don' let us look we'll take it as bein' guilty but if we look and find nothin' 'e might jist get away wiv it. Waddya say?'

'Tom's got nothing to hide. Nor have we. Take a look around outside and in the sheds but not the house. I'm not having you upset our father.'

Hannah rushed inside and came back draping a cloak around her shoulders. Feeling sick to the core she followed her brothers as they accompanied the men on their search. She didn't know if they were looking for anything specific but was quite confident that they wouldn't find anything. However she felt very frightened. They searched the smaller sheds, the outhouse, the pig-pen and all the likely and unlikely places before heading for the barn. At least it was warmer in there. Hannah sat on a bale of hay and watched the activity, willing them to hurry up and get out of their lives. Her mind drifted from the search as she thought of Tom. She had always feared that his association with Alfie would get him into trouble. She loved him so much and couldn't bear the thought of life without him. There would be some sensible explanation as to why they had been taken. She didn't know that Alfie was even still in the area. Tom had told her that he had gone. She had thought that he meant 'gone away' but maybe he had meant just from their house.

Her reverie was interrupted by a wild shout from Harry.

'Well, what 'ave we 'ere,' he exclaimed. Hannah looked up to see him waving a pistol in the air. She jumped up. How on earth had it got into their barn, she wondered and who did it belong to anyway? She looked askance at her brothers but they looked just as mystified as she felt.

She sat down heavily. What did it mean? Was it Alfie's, or worse, was it Tom's? Had she misjudged him all along? Had he always been a highwayman? Impossible! She did not believe that for one moment. She loved him. He was kind and considerate and he would never do anything to harm others, of that she was very sure. But how could she convince these men?

'But it's not Tom's,' she implored grabbing hold of Harry's arm. He shook her loose.

'It ain't up t' me to decide that, missus. Sir Francis now, 'e's the one who'll need t' do that. Ta all for your help,' he replied as he turned to go.

'Just a minute,' said Andy. 'Where are you going? I'm coming too. You can't just expect us to do nothing.'

'Andy's right,' agreed Davie. 'I'm coming as well.'

'We can't all go. We can't leave father. Davie, you'll have to stay and look after him. I'll go with Andy,' Hannah insisted. 'Tom's my husband. I need to be there.'

'We can't wait Missus. We need to get back with this 'ere evidence,' Moe said impatiently.

'But that's not evidence of anything,' Hannah protested. 'It could belong to anyone.'

'It was in your barn and that needs explaining. Your men can explain to Sir Francis. Now unless you've got a fast 'orse you won't be comin' wiv us. C'mon,' he said to his companion as they retrieved their horses and took off.

'He's right,' exclaimed Hannah. 'We've only got old 'Cobbler'. He won't get us there very fast pulling us on the dray. Do you think he could carry you and me on his back, Andy?'

'We have to give him a try, Hannah. See to Father and I'll get him.' Andy ran to the stable to prepare the horse while Davie looked beseechingly at Hannah.

'You can't go Hannah. You don't know what you'll find. There might be a fight, they might have already hung them or anything. It won't be a place for you.'

'I know you mean well, Davie, but Tom is my husband. Of course it's a place for me. He needs me and I have to be there whatever happens. I have to try my hardest to save him or I'll never forgive myself.'

'I understand that, Hannah, I really do. But I still don't think you should go. It could be very upsetting and you mightn't be able to cope with it.'

Hannah stared at him. 'You mean well, Davie. I know that. But it seems that you don't know me very well. I'm going to save Tom, and Alfie as well if I can. I know more about this than you think. Trust me. Now look after Father. We must be gone.'

Davie watched them as they headed off down the road. What did she mean by that remark, '*I know more about this than you think.*' He went back inside the house where Simon was alone. He still could not speak but Davie knew that he would want to know all that had transpired outside. He related it in as few words as possible and Simon's eyes grew large with frustration. He tried to get up but fell back.

'It's alright, Father, Davie soothed. 'Hannah and Andy will have him back here in a wink. Don't know about Alfie though. We still don't know anything about him, 'cepting that he's Tom's friend. I wish I was with them.'

***

Tom and Alfie lay on the floor of the shed at the back of the barn. With both hands and feet securely tied they realised that any attempt to escape would be futile. There were two men on guard outside the locked door and the walls lacked any windows.

'I remember the last time you and I spent the night in a shed, Tom. There wasn't a good outcome then,' Alfie sighed. 'I hope this one will be better.'

'You can hope all you like Alfie but I don't think it'll do much good.' He was silent for a minute. 'God, how did I get into this mess? I know how you did, Alfie, but I should've let you leave. I was stupid to think that keeping you in the neighbourhood was a good idea. Good for you at the time maybe but certainly not good for me. Why didn't you just go when you wanted to? I couldn't have stopped you. You could be well away and I could be home with Hannah. Instead we're probably both going to be hanged tomorrow.'

'I really didn't want to go, Tom,' said Alfie quietly. 'You know that having nobody in your life is lonely. Everyone needs someone. You were lucky to have Sam and Jenny and then Hannah and the Fenwicks. Who have I got? No one! Then I found you again.'

'Pity,' grunted Tom bitterly.

'I know it's all my fault,' admitted Alfie. 'I'd make it up to you if I could but at this point I can't think how. Here we are trussed up like chooks for the pot and can't move a muscle. Anyway it might not come to hanging. What evidence have they? Just a fellow who happens to have a dark coat and a fancy hat.'

'And a woman who no doubt can give a reasonably good description of you and your horse. And the coach driver too of course. Anyway there's something I haven't told you.' Thomas lowered his voice. 'I have your pistol,' he whispered.

'You what?' exclaimed Alfie. 'And you called me stupid?' He looked at Thomas in astonishment. 'You do realise that that links you with me, don't you?'

'Of course I do, and you being a highwayman leaves me with no chance,'Thomas exploded.

'I thought you would be alright. They can't hang a man just because he knows someone! But this puts a whole different light on the situation. I can now see us both swinging from that tree.' He groaned as he shuffled himself around and lay facing Thomas. He sensed the fear that Thomas was feeling although in the darkness he could not see his face. He too was full of fear but then he was guilty; Thomas wasn't and to be hanged for something you didn't do somehow seemed a lot worse than hanging for a crime that you had actually committed. He wished that he hadn't made the comment about swinging from the tree. None of this was Thomas's fault.

'Don't say that, Alfie. It terrifies me. I'd rather be shot if I have to die at all.'

'Me, too,' replied Alfie. 'We must remember that. We could make a break for it once our feet are free and then it would all be over. Anyway, why have you got that pistol anyway?'

'I didn't think I could trust you. I thought that you might go back for it. I'm sorry about that,' said Thomas contritely.

'Don't be. You were right. I did go back but couldn't find it. I just thought I must be looking in the wrong place. I never thought for one minute that you would've taken it. But why did you keep it?'

'I wasn't going to, but I haven't really had the chance to get rid of it. That's no excuse though. I should have made a chance.' He paused and then added, 'Between us we've made a bit of a muck up of everything, I reckon.'

'They might not find it,' Alfie said hopefully.

Tom was silent and then spoke quietly. 'I didn't hide it very well. I think they will.'

***

Hannah was right to worry about Clobber. He had given faithful service all his life but a fast gallop through the dark after a

206

hard days toil with two fully grown people on his back was a gallop too far and asking too much of him. He became very breathless and slowed to a halt. The two riders slid off his back and led him to the side of the road.

'What are we going to do, now?' asked Hannah. She became very agitated. 'We must move on quickly.'

'Calm down Hannah. We can't ride him or he'll die. Look at him,' he said as Clobber's legs buckled under him and he sank to the ground. Hannah dropped down beside him and stroked his head. Clobber heaved a big sigh and Hannah knew that it was his last. She wept as she rested her head on his neck.

'We'll come back and get you,' she whispered. 'I promise but just now we have to get on. Come on Andy.' She jumped up and ran on. Andy followed and finally caught her.

'Slow down, Hannah. We've a long way to go and you'll run out of puff. I will anyway,' he said grabbing her by the arm.

She slowed down but still walked very quickly. 'Andy, there's something I should tell you before we get there. It'll help you to understand. Alfie is, I mean was, a highwayman. I thought he had left the area. It seems I was wrong.' She related the whole story to an astonished Andy. 'I know Tom isn't a highwayman. His mother was hanged many years ago and Tom would never run the risk of suffering the same fate. It was too horrifying for him and he still has nightmares from seeing her die. Anyway, he's too kind and gentle. He wouldn't do it.'

Andy stopped in his tracks. 'I was right. They did do it to each other.' He started to smile at the incongruity of it but soon changed his expression when he remembered the seriousness of the situation.

'So who are we going to try to save?' he asked.

'It'll be a miracle if we can save either of them.' Hannah answered gruffly and they quickly walked on in silence.

After a short distance Andy stopped. 'Listen,' he said. 'I can hear a horse. We might get a ride if we're lucky.'

They waited and were surprised when James Blackler rounded the bend on Tom's horse. He quickly pulled up.

'Hello, you two. Are we all going to the same place?' he queried.

'Possibly,' Hannah answered quickly. 'James, I need the horse. Please. Andy, tell him what I've told you. I have to save Tom.' Hannah mounted Tom's horse and balancing as best she could in her long shirt took off as fast as the poor old horse would go.

Chapter 20:
Lady Charlotte

Lady Charlotte Wentworth sat quietly in the drawing-room. She finished her supper and rang for the butler. He picked up her supper tray and asked, 'Will that be all, madam?'

'Yes, thankyou, Summers. I don't think I will require anything further tonight. Would you please send my maid to me at nine thirty? Thank you. I'm going up to my sitting-room now,' she added. 'You may extinguish the lamps.' She gathered up her handwork and put it in her basket. The lamps on the wall lighted her way up the stairs and down the long passage to her sitting-room. She was glad that Francis would be back tomorrow. It was very lonely without him and he was good company. She enjoyed going around the estate with him and she knew that he would want to do that tomorrow soon after his return.

The fire was blazing in the grate and the sitting room looked warm and inviting. She picked up her book and settled herself in the big comfortable chair beside the hearth. She soon became engrossed in the story and not for the first time wondered where writers got all their ideas from.

There was a knock at the door disturbing her reading. She put her book down as Summers entered.

'What is it, Summers?'

'A woman is asking for you, my lady. I have put her in the drawing room. She looks a little dishevelled and very agitated, if I might be so bold to say,' he replied.

'Does this woman have a name?' Charlotte asked.

'Apparently it is Puckle, ma'am. She says that she has to speak with you immediately.'

'Does she indeed? It's very late, is it not?'

'Yes, ma'am. Shall I send her away?' Summers asked.

'There can't be too many Puckles in the area. I had better see her. Bring her up and please remain with me whilst I talk with her.'

Hannah felt very nervous as she climbed the staircase behind the butler. He knocked on the sitting room door and entered in response to Lady Charlotte's reply.

Charlotte was standing by the hearth and looked very beautiful in the firelight. Summers lit a few more lamps and the room lightened to reveal Hannah looking very travel-weary. Her boots and the hem of her skirt were very muddy, her cloak was dirty and her hair dishevelled. She felt very embarrassed when she saw Charlotte looking so dignified and composed.

'Ma'am, thank you for receiving me. I'm sorry for the lateness of the hour and my disreputable appearance, but this couldn't wait. I'm Hannah Puckle. Tom is my husband and there has been a dreadful misunderstanding and his life and that of his friend are in jeopardy.' The words rushed from Hannah's mouth as Charlotte held up her hand.

'Summers, I think we will have some tea, please, and a sandwich for Mrs Puckle. Now Mrs Puckle,' Charlotte said when the butler had left, 'tell me, what has brought you here at this time of the night.'

Hannah took a deep breath and as quickly as possible related the events of the day and what had led her to come to plead for their lives.

Charlotte was silent and then spoke calmly. 'Tell me, Mrs Puckle, is your Tom the same Tom who worked on my father's estate? I thought that he had drowned.'

210

'He should have, ma'am but was lucky in that he was rescued by a couple who looked after him and thought it best that he did not go back to your father's manor. Mr Cotter told your father all about it.'

'And is he the same Tom Puckle who rescued me from the highwayman?'

'Yes, ma'am,' she answered.

'I thought he was a good man. But now you are telling me that it was his friend who tried to rob me. I would not have thought that he would keep such bad company.'

'He'd not seen Alfie since he was twelve years old. I'll explain quickly from the beginning.' Hannah related Thomas's history, as far as it was relevant, from the time of his mother's death when he left Athelney, until tonight. She also told as much as she knew of Alfie.

'I thought that Alfie had left the area but obviously I was wrong,' she said when she had finished her explanation. 'I'm sure that he's not held up any more people. I'd like to think that Tom has been a good influence over him.'

'I'm sure you would,' Charlotte answered with a smile. 'Do you think that it is possible that together they thought up the idea of the hold-up as a scheme for getting money out of my husband?'

'Oh no Ma'am! I'm sure that's not the case at all. Initially they did not realise who they were fighting and they were both beaten up dreadfully as though they were fighting for their lives. I'm certain they would not have done that if it was all make-believe,' Hannah protested.

A knock on the door interrupted them. Summers entered with the tea tray.

'Excuse me Ma'am,' he said as he placed it on the round table. 'There are two gentlemen downstairs who say that they are associated with Mrs Puckle. They would also like to speak with you.'

'My word, I am popular tonight. Bring them up, please. Oh, and Summers, it would appear that Mrs Puckle's husband and his friend are being detained on the estate somewhere. I'd like you to ascertain their whereabouts and well-being and indicate to whoever is guarding them that nothing is to happen to them before Sir Francis returns. Nothing at all.'

'Very well, ma'am. I'll see to it,' he said 'Will that be all?'

'Yes, thank you. That is all just now.'

'Please, ma'am, may I see them?' Hannah pleaded.

'I think not. Summers, please tell Mr Puckle that his wife is here and is being taken care of. Now let's see these new visitors.'

***

Andy and James stood awkwardly inside the door of the sitting-room.

'Please come in further so I can see you clearly,' commanded Charlotte.

'Lady Wentworth, this is my brother Andy and this is Tom's employer, James Blackler. They've come to help me plead for the lives of Tom and Alfie,' Hannah's voice was almost breaking but she was determined to appear strong in front of this commanding woman.

'I can understand your concern for them. However it is my husband who will examine all the facts, not me therefore I cannot do anything about it,' Charlotte explained. 'Sir Frances will make that decision. He is a magistrate and also the offended party. However I will talk to him when he returns home tomorrow and will tell him all you have told me.' She turned to James and asked, 'Is Mr Puckle a reliable worker?'

'He's very good at his work, ma'am, and I would trust him with my life,' James answered.

'Mmm. That is not what I asked, but I take the point you make.' She turned to Andy. 'Do you live with Mr and Mr Puckle?'

'Yes, my lady, I do,' he answered nervously.

'Is he a good husband?' Charlotte enquired.

'You would have to ask Hannah that. He appears to be very good to her and to my father, who is quite ill. We didn't like him at first but now we do.' Andy nervously shifted from one foot to the other and wished that he hadn't said that when Charlotte asked,

'Why did you not like him?'

Andy hesitated. He would rather not have answered that question but this was a lady of some importance and Tom's life might depend on what he had to say.

'He just arrived in the middle of the night and we thought that he might be a burglar.' Andy explained about Thomas' unexpected arrival and the events of the night that he arrived. 'We got into a fight with him but it turned out he wasn't gonna rob us and now we know 'im better, we all like 'im.'

'I see. It's seems very fortunate for him that he met your family. Now if that is all... By the way, how did you all travel here?'

Hannah explained about the horses and Clobber's passing. They now only had one horse between the three of them.

Without hesitation Charlotte offered assistance. 'I will arrange for a coach to take you home. Tomorrow your dead horse will be removed and returned to you for burial. Is that a satisfactory arrangement?'

'Oh yes! Thank you ma'am.' It was Andy who spoke. 'We really appreciate that. I didn't know how we were going to move poor old Clobber.'

'Tomorrow after Sir Francis returns I will send the coach for you, Mrs Puckle. In case things do not go as you would wish

213

perhaps you may come here as well, Mr Fenwick, to support your sister.'

Charlotte rose and rang the bell. After a few minutes the footman appeared. 'Please arrange for a coach to take these people home,' she ordered. 'Meanwhile would you take them to the drawing room to wait.' She turned to Hannah and the men and said, 'Thank you for telling me of your concerns and although it may be difficult, try not to worry. Good evening to you all.'

When they had left she rang the bell again and this time her maid appeared. 'Fetch me my cloak, Hettie. I'm going outside when Summers returns. Send him to me.' She fidgeted about the room and as soon as Summers appeared, she rushed him down the backstairs to avoid the visitors.

'Take me to our prisoners, Summers. Do we know who apprehended them?' she asked.

'Seems it was Moe Smith and Harry Plumber, ma'am. They had a bit of luck to get the two of them. Sir Frances will be pleased.'

'Mmmm maybe. I think they got one wrong, but we shall see. Now where are they?'

'In a shed behind the barn. Mind you don't trip, m' lady.' Summers hesitated and then took her arm as he held the lantern high so that the pathway was more visible. As they rounded the end of the barn a voice called out, 'Who is it?'

'It's Her Ladyship. She'd like to see the prisoners,' Summers answered.

The man guarding the door stood up. 'Are you sure that's wise, ma'am? They might try to escape and then I'd have to shoot them.'

'I don't think they'll do that. Just open the door and stand guard. You can come in with me, Summers.' Charlotte followed the guard into the shed. It was dark and the one lamp they had

214

cast flickering shadows over the walls. Thomas and Alfie were sitting on the floor and as Charlotte entered they struggled to stand up.

Charlotte turned to the guard. 'Please untie them,' she ordered.

The guard was uneasy. He had his orders from Moe who did not like being disobeyed.

'Moe said that they should be tied up,' he mumbled.

'And I am saying that they should not. If Moe has a problem with that, tell him to see me in the morning,' Charlotte spoke firmly. The guard capitulated and soon Thomas and Alfie had their hands free.

'Now Thomas,' Charlotte said. 'Do you remember me?

'Yes Ma'am,' Thomas replied quietly.

'Do I have your word that you will not try to escape?'

'Yes Ma'am.'

'Alfie, what about you? Do I have your word?'

'Yes ma'am,' Alfie answered after some silent deliberation.

'Good. I'm trusting you both. If you do try you will no doubt be shot immediately. Now Thomas, please tell me everything from when you first saw the highwayman until Moe apprehended you.' Thomas took his time and did not leave anything out. He told her about not wanting Alfie to leave and getting him to work for Bert Simmons. He even explained about the pistol being in the Fenwick's barn. He also said that he felt sure that Alfie would not re-offend.

'Now it's your turn Alfie,' she invited.

Alfie was just as honest and when he had finished Charlotte thanked them both and said that she would see them the next day. As she made her way back to the house she asked Summers to provide them with some food and a blanket each, to make their night, if not worry free, at least a little more comfortable.

***

Since Sir Francis had married Charlotte he always loved coming home. She made his house a home. It was a magnificent house on three levels with eighteen bedrooms, a huge library, music room, dining-room, drawing-room, breakfast room, a ballroom, numerous sitting rooms, two studies, bathrooms, servants' quarters and utility rooms. There were fifteen inside staff and an equal number of outside workers. It was surrounded by one thousand acres of land, eight hundred acres of which were farmed by his tenant farmers and two hundred acres in beautiful park-like gardens with lakes and ponds.

As his carriage swept up the driveway he felt a great sense of pride. He was the eldest of three sons and he was the lucky one who had inherited such a treasure.

He raced up the steps of the front portico and calling for Charlotte, he hurried through the large entrance hall. Summers appeared and helped him out of his cloak.

'Welcome home, sir. Lady Charlotte is in the drawing-room.' he informed him.

'Thank you Summers. All is well here I take it?'

'Yes sir. Lady Charlotte will bring you up to date, sir. There have been some happenings but she will tell you I'm sure.'

Sir Francis entered the drawing-room and Charlotte jumped up and ran into his arms. 'Oh I have missed you Francis. I'm so glad you're home,' she whispered.

'I promise I'll take you with me next time,' he murmured as he kissed her. 'London is wonderful and you would enjoy it so much. Now what has been happening here? Summers said that you would bring me up to date.' He led her to the settee and made himself comfortable.

'We shall have some tea first,' she said. 'Then I'll tell you. It can wait a little bit. Now tell me about London.'

He told her about all he had seen and done, how his meetings had gone and about the business he had conducted. She told him how lonely she had been and that she was thinking of getting a companion to ease her loneliness while he was away.

'I think that is a good idea, Charlotte. Do you have any one in mind?' he asked.

'Not yet but I am sure it won't be difficult. Just someone who can stay while you are away. I wouldn't want her here when you are home. I couldn't give you my undivided attention then could I?' she answered coyly.

Sir Francis laughed. 'Now what's this news I have to hear? Tell me now and then we'll go around the estate and ensure all is well.' He sat back on the settee and waited.

Charlotte took a deep breath and started to explain.'Your highwayman has been captured. He's in the shed behind the barn. He has a companion with him as well. Now wait,' she restrained him as he jumped up. 'I want to tell you the story first. All of it. It could take some time and they are not going anywhere. I also need to send the carriage to pick someone up. But first the story.' She rang for some tea and then as clearly and quickly as she could she related the events of the previous night. She talked about Thomas and Alfie, all that Hannah had told her and what they themselves had said. She talked of Thomas's life at her father's home and of Marty Dewson's attempts on his life: how, when he had met Alfie again in such dreadful circumstances he could not desert him.

She talked of Hannah and Thomas' marriage and also of her belief that Alfie was not really a rogue and would hurt nobody.

'How do you know?' her husband demanded. 'You don't even know the man.'

'They promised me last night after Hannah and the men left.'

'You went into the shed last night?' he asked in disbelief.

'I had Summers with me and the guard was there with his gun. There wasn't any danger and having talked to Hannah Puckle about them I was sure that it would be safe.'

'Ah yes, Hannah Puckle. Of course she would stick up for her husband and come to plead his innocence. To think I gave the man ten pounds and he was hiding the villain all the time!'

'That's not a hanging offence though. Tom's mother was hanged and he witnessed it. Hannah said that he would never put himself in a situation where he might suffer the same fate. Anyway he did save me, you have to acknowledge that.'

'That's true, my darling. Maybe we can save your Tom. Perhaps he was in the wrong place at the wrong time for his own welfare but the right place for yours.' He paused. 'I suppose it's Hannah that you're sending the coach to collect. You must have been certain of my response,' Sir Francis said as she nodded her head. He pulled the bell-rope and when Summers appeared, asked him to send the coach to pick up Hannah.

'We also need a dray to pick up their dead horse from the roadside and take it to the Fenwick's farm. I promised them that we would,' Charlotte said. Raising his eyebrows, Sir Francis added that to his orders for Summers.

'Now what about Alfie? He's a different kettle of fish. The law takes highwaymanship very seriously and the sentence is either hanging or deportation. If I was him I would prefer hanging. I'm told that deportation is pretty grim. Anyway there's no doubt that young Alfie is a thief. We don't really know how many people he has held up. If the lynch mob had got him he would be dead by now. I don't know if he's lucky that it was us who got him or not. The result might be the same. I'm going to have to send him to the Royal Court. They deal with all serious crimes, including treason and murder and robbery. He'll have to take his chances there. Now let's go and see these prisoners.'

'Just a minute Francis. You can't do that. Send him to Court, I mean. You're a magistrate. Why can't you deal with it? I am happy that you are saving Thomas, but Alfie isn't a real robber. I don't think he was even very good at it,' Charlotte implored.

'He is a robber all the same, Charlotte. He's shown that and he admits it. I can deal with local people and make sure they obey the rules set down by the landowners. But this is a life or death case. It's outside my jurisdiction.'

'But you know what the verdict will be if you send him to London,' she pleaded.

'Whatever it is, it will be the right one. Anyway, I don't know where I'll send him yet. I'll have to give it some thought. When I decide, I'll send a statement explaining a few things but I can't do much more than that. These fellows have to be taught a lesson.'

'Shouldn't I be at his trial? After all I was the one who was held up?'

'His trial is the last place I would let you go. There will be many others on trial that day for all manner of offences. There usually are. Anyway, we'll hear about the verdict on young Alfie in due course.'

***

Thomas was distraught all the way home. He would never forget the look on Alfie's face when Sir Francis delivered the news that Thomas was free to return home but Alfie would be sent to prison to await trial. Saying goodbye to him this time was harder than the time he left Athelney. They both knew all too well that the outcome would be either hanging or deportation.

Hannah held his arm firmly as Sir Francis's carriage took them home.

'We did our best to save you both, Thomas, and I'm so happy to be taking you home with me. I wish that we had Alfie with us too but, hard as it may be, we have to forget about him and get on with our lives. I have a feeling that Alfie is a survivor and he'll not hang. He's young, so deportation might not be such a bad thing. When he's done his time he can start a new life in a new country.'

'Hannah you are so naïve. What do you know of prisons and deportation and such things?' Thomas said miserably. He ran his hand over his face to brush away the tears. 'The prisons are overcrowded, disease-ridden, rat-infested holes. It's because they're so overcrowded that many of those not hanged are housed on old warship hulks on the Thames River until they can be transported. Many die there. Either way, Alfie's in for a tough time.' he fell silent for a while as the carriage jolted over the rough road. 'I think when I know where he's being sent, I'll go to support him.'

'Thomas you can't be serious. Look where your support of him landed you this time. If you love me you won't put yourself in such a stupid situation again.' Hannah was horrified at the thought. 'If the court knows that you hid him they could charge you as well, despite what Sir Francis says. Don't be so silly. You've done your best. Now let it go.'

But Thomas knew that he couldn't just put Alfie to the back of his mind and forget all about him.

***

The news they all received about Alfie was not what they expected. The guards transporting him to Newgate Prison took their eyes off him once too often. He escaped and vanished into thin air. No one except his fellow prisoners on the wagon saw him go and they wouldn't say anything. Sir Francis was furious and sacked the men who were supposed to be guarding him. Lady Charlotte was secretly pleased that such a pleasant young man, as she now deemed him to be, had escaped a horrible punishment. Hannah had not wanted him to die either but now fervently hoped that having made his escape he would stay well away from them. As for Thomas, it brought a smile to his unhappy features and as he gazed at his mother's star, he whispered, 'Watch out for him, Ma, please.'

Part 4:
1792

Chapter 21:
Peggy (1792)

Alfie lay back in the bed thinking about the last year. The threat of his hanging or deportation was a distant memory but often came to the fore in his moments of melancholy. He could not believe that he had escaped so easily. There had been two armed men guarding four prisoners on the way to Newgate. The other three had seemed resigned to their fate but Alfie had made up his mind that he would escape or die in the attempt. Better to be dead with a bullet through the back than suffer the indignities of hanging as Mrs Puckle had done. And if he wasn't to be hanged, the conditions of the prison or the hulks would probably finish him off anyway.

The wagon had been uncovered and the guards as well as the captives had been exposed to the elements. Cold and wet as he was, Alfie had maintained his alertness whilst the other three had given in to the wintry conditions and drifted into semi-consciousness. The guards were in not much better condition and struggled to keep their concentration.

'Do ya think we oughta lay up somewhere 'til this passes?' one had said to the other as they huddled together whispering, so that the convicts couldn't hear them. 'We could shelter under the wagon.'

While they were preoccupied with their deliberations, Alfie had surreptitiously wriggled to the end of his seat which was a little difficult with his hands restrained but at least they had been tied in front this time. The guards had continued their quiet discussion and hadn't noticed Alfie's movements. He saw that one of the other prisoners had opened his eyes and was silently looking at him. He had made a silent 'sssshhhh' with his mouth and suddenly dropped off the back of the wagon.

He had landed in the road with a wallop that jarred the wind out of him for a second and then, not waiting to find out if he had injured himself, had taken off into the scrub. He was stiff from the cold and from sitting so long but felt his body loosen up as he ran as fast as he could, crashing through the bushes and scrub until he had no breath left in him. He stopped, leaning against a tree and gasping, all the time listening for the pursuit. He had expected to hear the sound of the guards behind him but apart from the wind in the trees and the patter of raindrops on the leaves there was no indication that his pursuers, if any, were close behind. His breath had become more even and his thoughts more coherent. With lightened spirits he realised that maybe the guards had not chased him. One convict was gone but there were still three others to watch more carefully than ever. They could not afford to let any more escape. They would be in a heap of trouble as it was.

He had continued on his way, blindly pushing through the undergrowth, not knowing or caring in what direction he was travelling just as long as he put as much distance as possible between himself and the prison wagon. When darkness fell he had stopped for the night in a small thicket. He had no food or water, nor anything to protect him from the cold and had spent all the night shivering as he had tried to sever the cord that bound his hands together. After many hours of rubbing the cord on a sharp rock he had succeeded and for the first time had felt really free.

At first light he had continued his journey, tossing the rope into a stream at the first opportunity and he was cheered that the rain had stopped and the sun was shining brightly. His clothes had steamed in the warmth and he had felt much better. All he needed now was food and water. The latter was easy enough with many little streams and brooks frequently crossing his path but food had eluded him. He was very conscious of the trouble his presence had made for Thomas and had been reluctant to make contact with any of the country folk who might live nearby. He had not seen anyone but kept himself concealed as much as possible, just in case. He had travelled parallel to a cart track but resisted the temptation to walk along it. He did not want to be seen until he had worked out a plan, but what that plan would be he had no idea. He had realised how Thomas must have felt when he started on his journey all those years ago, not knowing where he was going. But at least Thomas wasn't a fugitive as he was although he may have thought of himself as one. He vowed to remember that. He mustn't look like a fugitive. He would have to get some respectable clothes from somewhere. Then he would work out what to do.

***

Finding clothes had proved easier than he had thought it would. He had approached a small town and found a tavern on the outskirts. He watched it for a while and the making up his mind he approached the back door and knocked on it. It was opened by a maid who was just as surprised to see him as he was to see her. They stared at each other.

'Alfie, is that really you under all that hair?' she asked enquiringly with a smile in her voice.

Alfie could not believe his luck. 'Peggy! How did you get here? Is this ever my lucky day?'

'Don't count your chickens before they're hatched, my lad. You look as though you could do with some luck, though. What on earth has happened to you?'

Suddenly Alfie had felt exhausted. The colour drained from his face and he sagged against the door jamb. 'You'd better come in quickly,' Peggy had said, 'I'll see what I can do.'

***

That day had indeed been his lucky one. Peggy had taken him into the kitchen, explained to the cook that he was an old friend who obviously needed some help, found him some food and when he had eaten his fill, took him home to her little old cottage not far from the tavern. There he had had a hot bath in front of a roaring fire and Peggy had washed his hair and scrubbed his back. It had felt like heaven. He had then wrapped himself up in a blanket and one by one had thrown his dirty, ripped clothes into the fire. His worn out boots had followed.

'There we are, Peggy. I only have the suit I was born in.' He stared moodily into the flames that were rapidly consuming his entire possessions. 'I haven't made much of my life, have I? You've done a damn sight better, I must say.'

She had not commented nor asked questions and he had appreciated that.

'You can't go about like that, Alfie.' she answered instead. 'You'll get arrested. You'll have to stay here until I can find you some clothes. I'll ask Mr Miller, at the inn tomorrow. He might be able to help. Meanwhile pop into my bed and have a sleep while I cook you some food.'

He had fallen asleep immediately and woke sometime later to find Peggy sitting on the edge of the bed. He had said nothing but put his arms around her and pulled her to him. 'Your dinner is ready,' she whispered.

'Later,' he murmured. 'This can't wait.'

She had slipped out of her clothes and crawled into the bed with him. 'It's been a long time since we did this, Alfie.'

He had laughed at that. 'Have you forgotten how?'

226

'I'm sure you'll remind me,' she had said tenderly as she stroked his face. His touch was just as she had remembered it as she closed her eyes as she submitted to his passion.

***

Not only had Mr Miller found some clothes for Alfie, but he had also offered him a job. Not a great one but Alfie knew that beggars couldn't be choosers and he had been very close to being a beggar.

***

Alfie watched Peggy as she lay sleeping. It would be hard for him to leave her. She had saved his life after all and he felt that he owed her something. He had not told her anything of his life since he left her in Athelney and she'd not asked. It didn't matter to her. She gave him shelter and love but they both knew that it wouldn't last. Their affection for each other was not deep enough for that. They had used each other before and then parted amicably. It would happen again.

Peggy opened her eyes as if she sensed that he was watching her. She smiled.

'When are you going, Alfie?' she asked giving voice to his thoughts.

'I hope you can't always read my mind, Peg,' he smiled, 'and anyway what makes you think I am going anywhere?'

'That seems to be your style. That's what you did last time, anyway. Remember,' she reminded him.

'Peggy, I was just a kid. Things were tough. Did you mind too much?'

'I decided after one day that I would live. I don't suppose this time will be any different.'

'You have kept me here a lot longer than I intended and as much as I care for you, I don't want to spend the rest of my life rolling barrels of ale around and sweeping the yard. I've appreciated all you and Mr Miller have done for me but it's time to move on.'

'I knew you were starting to get restless. I will miss you though, Alfie. Where do you think you'll go?'

'I thought I would have a plan by now but I haven't. I have some money. I'll work it out as I go along. Better to be flexible. I might go to London or I might go to Bristol or even Plymouth and become a sailor. Often thought of doing that. See the world and all that.'

'What do you know of the world?' Peggy asked as she snuggled up to him.

'Absolutely nothing. I know that the English have settled America so I could go there. Work my way across on a sailing ship.'

Peggy laughed. 'No you won't.'

'No, probably not, but I might go and find brother John and see if he's all right. It's a long time since I saw him. He could be anywhere by now. See if he's done better than I have. He wouldn't have had to do very well to be better off than me.'

He was quiet for a while. Was he making a big mistake in leaving Peggy? He often wished that he had someone to make his life as happy as Hannah had made Thomas but he knew in his heart that Peggy was not the one. He would marry for love just as Tom had done if he ever found someone who wanted him.

Chapter 22:
Leaving Penshurst (1795)

Several years had passed since Alfie had disappeared from Thomas and Hannah's lives. Simon continued to exist. His life was such that an existence was all that it could be called. Hannah, sadly, suffered several more miscarriages and Thomas was resigning himself to the fact that they would probably never have a child or, if they did, it might be sickly. Kerrin and Molly had three little ones and he felt really envious of them. Andy was engaged to be married and this event was also causing Thomas some concern.

'Hannah, when Andy and Kate get married I think they should live here and we should go south. Andy is Simon's son and a farmer as well and I'm neither. We can't all live here, and especially not if we do have babies and they do as well. It would be hopeless.' He knew what her answer would be before she even opened her mouth.

'I've always said that as long as Father needed me I would be here for him.'

'But Hannah, he has lived far longer than we thought he would. That's thanks to you and Alice. Kate could care for him now.'

'No she couldn't. I'm his daughter and she isn't. She wouldn't love him as much as I do and that makes a difference.' Emotion swept over her face.

'Anyway,' she added, ' to be frank, I don't think he'll last much longer. I think this winter will be hard on him, if he lasts that long.' She was silent as she sadly watched the brook rippling by.

She remembered the time Thomas had proposed to her and then they had both fallen in. 'I'll make you a promise, Tom. We'll go after he dies and I think that will be soon.'

Thomas gathered her to him and held her close. He did not know what to think. He did not want Simon to die but he did want to take Hannah home to Jenny and Sam at Gunnislake.

***

Hannah was right. The winter was a harsh one and despite Hannah's ministrations old Simon died. She felt bereft. She wept as Alice helped her to prepare his body for burial.

'E's at peace now, 'Annah luv. 'E couldn'ta wished for a better family and despite 'is wife dyin' youn', 'e's 'ad a good loife.' Alice tried to comfort her.

'I know all that, Alice,' Hannah concurred. 'But it doesn't make it any easier for us.'

'Emotionally, probably not, but your loife'll be so much easier now. 'E was a burden and 'e knew it. Ye all managed 'im well, but now that 'e's gorn, y' can all get on with what you want to do.'

'Alice, you don't know what that is. I've promised Tom that I'll go away with him. I don't think that I want to, but he's been very good staying here when he wanted to move on. He was on his way to London when we met, but now he wants to take me back to Gunnislake and meet some people dear to him. I don't think I want to go, but a promise made is not to be broken, so I'll go. This is my home, though, and I'll miss it dearly. The boys too. Oh Alice, is it the right thing to do?'

'I don't know, luvvy. Where is this Gunnislake place? It's a funny name. Don't worry about leaving. You go with him. There'll be a changing of the guard on this farm, but I'm sure that there'll always be a place for you and Tom around here somewhere. And any little ones that you have,' she added. She turned back to the bed. 'Look at Simon. He does look peaceful doesn't he? The creases have gone from his face and he looks just like a baby.'

***

Hannah busied herself preparing for the funeral. She wanted to do it right but there wasn't much money. After discussions with her brothers they settled for a modest affair, one that she knew her father would be comfortable with. He was not a man for wasting the little money he did have and certainly not to have it buried in the ground in the form of a posh box. Funerals could cost as much as twenty eight pounds, but admittedly for that huge amount you would get a lot. Hannah read slowly from the card the undertaker had left them:

> 'A hearse and four horses.
> Two mourning coaches and four horses with feathers.
> Velvet covering and cloths for the hearse and horses.
> A lid with feathers.
> An outer elm case covered in fine black cloth finished three rows all round with best black nails.
> A brass plate inscription, handles and other achievements.
> A wool mattress.
> Burial dress, winding sheet and a pillow.
> Two mutes in silk dresses.
> An attender with silk hat-band and gloves.
> Men to bear the corpse and attend as pages with hat-bands, gloves, truncheons and wands.
> Use of best silk, velvet, pall, crepe hat-bands, hoods and scarves for twelve mourners.'

'That's all very well for the posh Wentworths but Father rarely got the chance to travel in a coach and I'm damn sure he wouldn't want to go to his own funeral in one.' Kerrin was having his say. 'The dray was always good enough for him and that's the way he can go to his funeral. We can clean it up and put flowers on it. And we certainly don't want mutes. The day will be sad enough for us anyway without having a couple of black-dressed, gloomy-faced individuals that we don't even know, wandering about.'

'I agree. The undertaker's card has a cheaper version though,' Hannah countered. She read,

'A strong elm coffin, covered in black and finished neat.
Plate inscription.
Handles etc.
Mattress, pillow and sheet,.
Use of pall.
Dresses for six mourners.
Patent carriage and pair of horses to convey body and mourners.
Men to carry corpse.
Fittings for coachmen and attenders.'

'We'll make the coffin. That's no problem,' said Andy. 'We only need one horse to pull the dray and ours'll do that. There'll be plenty of mourners with all his friends there and we can carry him. Anyway there's three of us and Tom. We can do it. He was ours and we'll look after him until the end. Don't need none of that flash stuff. An' we certainly don't need to pay for dresses for you women to wear.'

'Well said, Andy. You're right. We don't need no engraved plate on the coffin either. We know he'll be in there and it ain't as if we're gonna dig him up again. We could paint his name on it anyway. We can even do his headstone. We'll do it right. What do you think, Hannah?' asked Kerrin.

232

Hannah sat on the couch close to Thomas. She loved all these men dearly. 'I think that'll be fine. There's too many people making money out of funerals. Funerals are very personal and you're right, Andy, he was ours and we'll do it our way. I'll leave the preparation of his coffin and dray to you boys. I need to think about the favours we'll give out for the mourners to wear and also the food.'

'Molly and Kate will help you. Don't worry too much,' said Kerrin.

***

The funeral went off as planned and as the mourners sat around reminiscing about their association with Simon, Hannah watched her brothers interacting with them. She felt remote. Her thoughts dwelt on the past, the present and the future. She had to let the first two go and concentrate on her future; their future, hers and Thomas's. She noticed Thomas watching her. Going over to him, she put her arm around his shoulders whispered, 'It's our time now, Tom.'

He smiled up at her. 'Thank you,' he answered. 'All will be well. I'll tell James that I'll be leaving.'

***

'We'll be back, Molly,' Hannah promised as they made their farewells to their family. They would be travelling light. Hannah had taken a few small mementoes but knew that if she needed or wanted anything else her brothers would let her have it and send it to her. They had Alfie's horse and Thomas's old nag which Hannah would ride. Thomas had bought a replacement for Clobber which he would leave at the farm. He had felt that as Clobber had died because of him, he should make some recompense. Hannah found riding the horse in her long skirts and petticoats very difficult. She tried to ride side-saddle as the fashionable ladies did, but not having the side-saddle to support her made it very hard for her to maintain her balance.

'You'll have to get me my own side-saddle, Tom. I can't ride astride like you because of my skirt and I can't ride aside because I am likely to fall off''.

'We can't afford one, Hannah. We have to take some money with us and I've used up quite a lot already with the farm horse and the tent and all the necessaries we need for the journey. I suppose I could sell Alfie's saddle and get you one, but when we get to where we're going you probably won't do much riding and I might, so that could be a silly thing to do.' Thomas though more about it. 'Tell you what. We'll share mine. Not together, silly. We'll swap it over every now and again.'

'That won't help with my skirts. Are you suggesting that I share your trousers too?' she asked.

Thomas whooped with laughter. 'That'll be the day.'

'Then I'll have to make my own,' she retorted as she stormed off into the house. She'd had to visit Molly several times for guidance on her sewing, and on the day of departure was resplendently dressed in what looked like a long skirt but which was in fact, a skirt split into two legs. Thomas was impressed and declared them suitable as they didn't show any ankle or leg. Therefore he felt that she had maintained her respectability. Hannah didn't care if he approved or not.

So here they were: ready to go. Everyone had made the effort to come and farewell them, even Alice and Hugh. Hannah tried to put on a brave face but unbidden tears rolled down her cheeks. 'I love you all,' she said as she quickly turned her horse and headed out the gate. Thomas followed, waving as he went. They continued down the lane to the road, not saying anything, but alone with their thoughts. Bouncer bounded ahead, every now and again stopping to sniff the hidden odours in the long grass. But he never allowed Thomas and Hannah out of his sight and kept returning to check that they were alright.

'That dog does pretty well for an old fella,' said Thomas. 'He must be eleven or twelve by now.'

'Mmm,' Hannah replied absently.

'Do you realise that this is the first time that we've been alone, I mean really alone, since we met? That was eight years ago. I hope you like being alone with me, Hannah' he asked.

'Of course I do. And we'll be travelling further than I've ever been from home. I've not seen all the things that you have, Tom. Nor met all the people. It will be nice to meet Sam and Jenny and William and Joan.'

'William and Joan might not remember me. They might not even be there still. It doesn't matter. Sam and Jenny are the important ones. They'll love you. There's just one person from the past that I don't want to meet and that's Marty.' He was silent for a moment. 'Maybe he's dead. I hope so.'

'That's not very nice, Tom,' rebuked Hannah.

'Well he wasn't nice to me and I'll never feel nice towards him. Anyway, with the sort of life he led, he'd be lucky to still be alive. He must've made a lot of enemies in his time.'

'Well let's not think of him now. I think I need a wee spell. Let's walk a bit.' She pulled her horse to a halt and dismounted. Bouncer came racing up as Thomas also dismounted. They all walked quietly along the road until they came to a bridge over a small stream. Bouncer jumped around in the water while Thomas threw him sticks and Hannah laid out their lunch.

'This is the life, Hannah.' Thomas lay back in the shade of a willow tree and watched as the long tendrils of branches swept the surface of the water. 'I think I'll become a gypsy. I'll build you a wagon and we can just roam the countryside working when we have to.'

'You were going to build me a wagon the very first time you asked me to go south. Remember?'

'We only had one horse then,' he recalled. 'Now we have one each.'

Hannah lay down beside him and closed her eyes. She felt unbelievably tired. The last few weeks culminating in her father's death and funeral had left her feeling drained of energy and the preparation and parting from her family had made her sorrowful. Thomas stroked her face and kissed her gently.

'We don't have to hurry. It doesn't matter how long it takes us to get there. We have our tent, so if we get caught between towns which is quite likely, we'll camp out. Let's just rest here a while.'

They both fell asleep and awakened with a start. It was getting cold. The winter was not yet over and the later afternoons laid their chilly dampness quite early.

'Goodness, Hannah. We must get moving if we're to make any more progress today. I know I said that we weren't in a hurry, but we'd better find a more sheltered spot if we have to pitch the tent.'

He helped her on to her horse and they then cantered down the road. Night fell quickly and early at this time of the year, and they were overtaken by the darkness before they found a suitable place. Thomas stopped and lit the lantern. Holding it high, they rode silently along the road looking left and right into the bushes, seeking a camp-site.

'I'm sorry, Hannah. I shouldn't have fallen asleep. Maybe we should have stayed where we were.'

Hannah pulled her cloak closely around her. 'Maybe we should have,' she agreed. 'But we didn't, so the sooner we find somewhere the better. I'm cold and hungry. This is not a very good start to our trip, Tom. We'll have to take more care in the future. There's still plenty of wintertime left, and we might even get snow at times. We don't want to be caught out in that.'

Thomas stopped. 'Is that a light I can see through those bushes?' he asked. Hannah looked and could see the flickering of lanterns at a distance off the road.

'There must be a track in there somewhere,' said Tom. 'You stay here and I'll take a look.'

'No, Tom. Wait. We don't know who they are. They might be highwaymen or outlaws or any one.'

'Be reasonable, Hannah. Highwaymen usually operate alone and certainly don't travel around and camp out in groups. These people are more likely to be gypsies.'

'Well I'm coming with you,' she answered. 'C'mon, Bouncer.'

They made their way along the road and soon came to a track leading off towards the lights. Bouncer trotted ahead, they followed.

Chapter 23:
The Gypsies

The track had been churned up by many feet and wagon wheels and was rough and muddy.

'Who's that?' a voice called out of the darkness. Bouncer growled.

'Come here, Bouncer,' ordered Thomas. He dismounted and held up his lantern as two men carrying long sticks emerged from the darkness. They were dressed in dark woollen tunics laced up their chests and had bright scarves tied around their necks. Their legs were clad in long baggy trousers and colourful rugs were thrown around their shoulders to keep out the cold damp evening chill.

'We were looking for a spot to set up camp when we saw your lanterns,' said Thomas. 'Do you mind if we make our camp here? We'll keep out of your way.'

The first man asked, 'Are there just the two of you?'

'Yes, this is my wife,' Thomas answered drawing Hannah's horse forward.

'Come with me,' the man ordered. 'Better tie the dog up over there. We have dogs as well as some other animals here, and we don't want yours to start a fight, do we?'

Hannah dismounted and the second man led their horses to a tree where he tied them up. Thomas, having also restrained Bouncer, took Hannah's hand as they followed the man through the camp-site to a large bender tent erected on the far side. The bender tent was made from hazel rods pushed into the ground and covered with a large sail-cloth. Looking about him, Thomas noticed that there were quite a few light wagons and tents. Hannah had seen gypsies at the Penshurst fair and although their appearance was a little rough, she felt comfortable in their presence.

Many people thought of the gypsies as vagrants, vagabonds or tramps, but she knew that this was not always the case. Many were hard workers and had known no life other than the one they were leading now. She didn't know what these people did for money, but many of the larger bands included men who were very skilled in all forms of metal work including tin, copper, silver and gold. They could make almost anything; pots and pans, kettles, jewellery and charms. They were similarly astute buyers and sellers of a great array of things including horses. Their womenfolk were also very versatile. They were the ones who sold much of what the men made and took care of the money. They also told fortunes for they were very good at communicating with the populace and gleaning all sorts of information that could help with their advising or healing and above all, their predictions.

Their escort spoke to the man sitting outside the large tent.

'These two want to share our camp-site tonight. I think that would be orright, wouldn't it? There's just the two of them.'

The man who was obviously their leader looked at Thomas and Hannah carefully, and then, nodding assent, indicated some cushions and bade them to sit. He did not speak but finished his meal after which he slowly stood up and went into the wagon beside the tent. Hannah and Thomas looked at each other nervously and wondered if they should move on. Before they could leave however, a woman appeared carrying two plates of food which she placed before them.

'We're happy to have you here,' she said. 'I hope you enjoy this food.'

'Thank you very much,' replied Hannah. 'My name is Hannah and my husband is Tom. It is very kind of you to allow to stay. We do have food but just needed a safe place to camp.'

'I'm pleased that you think us safe. Unfortunately, many people don't, but we're just a family who have followed the way of life that our forebears led. My name is Aisha. My husband is Mander; he's the head of the family.' Just as she spoke, Mander reappeared. He called something to a young man who immediately ambled across to the central fire and fed it a small log. A myriad of sparks flew heavenward to join the stars in the dark sky. Hannah was strangely comforted by it.

'When you've finished your meal, we'll sit around the fire. We usually have a musical time together and a few drinks before we retire,' explained Mander.

'Thank you, Mander, but we should put up our tent first and get our sleeping spaces ready,' answered Thomas.

'You're welcome to doss down in this tent. We sleep in the wagon. You'll be cosy in here. You'll find it quite warm. Just bring your bedding over.'

They understood why it was warm when they entered. They hadn't noticed any smoke but now saw that there was a central fire, and, with a hole in the centre of the roof, the smoke could easily escape. There was no furniture to speak of and Thomas wondered why they had gone to the trouble of erecting it when their wagon was so handy. However, they thankfully laid out their blankets and once organised, they ambled over to the wagon. This wagon was a very cosy living space for Aisha and Mander. It had a raised area at one end upon which a double bed had been made with coloured blankets and cushions. There were plenty of cupboards and a small stove stood just inside the door.

The whole of the interior was colourfully decorated as was the exterior. Obviously Mander and Aisha took great pride in the wagon and their own artwork contributed to much of the decor.

'I told Hannah I would build her a wagon but this looks pretty much beyond my skills. It's beautiful. I assume you have horses to pull it,' said Thomas.

'Yes. We only need one for each wagon. We call these wagons vardos. If the way is particularly hilly, we hitch two up and then it's no effort for them. We are used to the wandering life. We have an old gypsy saying...

'We are all wanderers on this earth
Our hearts are full of wonder,
Our souls are deep with dreams.'

Thomas smiled. 'We may not be the wanderers that you people are but we too have our dreams.'

'That's good. Dreams are often what keep us going. If we don't dream, we die. Now it looks like the family is gathering,' Mander said as he looked out at the fire. 'Come and meet them.'

He led the way to the group and once he had made all the introductions he settled himself comfortably on a rug covered with cushions. Aisha sat beside him.

'You're a very lucky man to have such a large family. I'll never remember all these names,' Thomas commented.

'Don't worry about that 'cos I don't remember them either. I know the adults but there are too many little ones to recall all their names. As long as they know who I am, that's all that matters,' laughed Mander. A small girl came and sat on his knee. 'I know this little one, though,' he added. 'She's called Maya and the spitting image of her lovely mother, my daughter in law.'

The child was beautiful, with a fair complexion and blonde curly hair. She was different from the other children who all seemed to have brown or black hair. But it was her big round brown eyes that tore at Thomas' heart. *'Oh to have a daughter like that,'* he thought. He glanced at Hannah who was watching one of the women feeding her baby and knew immediately what she was thinking. *'One day,'* he mused to himself. *'One day we will.'*

'Isn't it a little late in the year for you to be travelling, Mander? It must be difficult on these muddy roads with the horses and vardos,' he asked, attempting to take his mind off babies.

'You're right. We are later than we'd like to be. We would've liked to be well settled in our winter encampment by now but we had a few setbacks. The axle on Jonno's vardo broke and that took a while to fix. Then Stefan's horse went lame and couldn't pull his vardo and finally little Luca got sick. We had to wait until he was better. Usually when anyone gets sick we can carry on. Not this time though. The rough journey would have been too much for him. He is still not well but much better than he was.'

'I'm glad to hear that,' said Hannah. 'Is one of your family a healer?' she asked turning to Aisha.

'We all know a little bit about healing,' she replied, 'but Jonno's wife Nadja knows the most. She looks after us very well. Sadly, though, she doesn't know everything and two of our family died last winter.'

'My father has recently passed on too,' commented Hannah.

'I thought I saw sadness in your eyes. I think you have a good man here though,' she said looking at Thomas. 'He'll look after you.'

'I don't need looking after,' replied Hannah.

'Don't you? I think you do,' answered Aisha. 'It's not always easy to lose someone you love and now you're on the

242

move away from familiar people, it will be hard for you. Where are you going?'

While Thomas talked with Mander, Hannah briefly told Aisha of their life at Penshurst, the circumstances of her father's illness and death and their decision to journey south to visit Jenny and Sam.

'And what of your illnesses?' Aisha enquired.

'I haven't had illnesses. I'm fine. I've had a lot to worry about recently but now we're on our journey I can relax a bit and enjoy it.'

'Do you mind coming into my vardo for a moment? We can talk privately in there.' Aisha stood up and held out her hand. 'We'll be back in a few moments,' she said to Mander. 'Then we can have a sing-song and dance.'

Hannah began to feel uncomfortable. Aisha was a lovely woman but Hannah knew of the gypsies fortune-telling and healing powers. The healing she could accept to a degree but the concept of foretelling the future was something she found difficult to comprehend.

'Sit down, Hannah,' said Aisha indicating the couch in the vardo while she seated herself on the chair opposite.

'How old are you, Hannah?'

'Nearly twenty-eight.'

'How long have you and Tom been married?'

'Seven years,' Hannah answered.

Aisha took her hand. 'Do you know anything about foretelling?'

Hannah shook her head and tried to pull her hand away.

'Don't be afraid. Palm reading is the first method of foretelling that we are taught as little girls. I still think it's the best. It's all here.' Aisha picked up Hannah's left hand and studied the palm. 'Just as your eyes are a mirror into your soul, your hands chart your life. Your left hand reveals the life you are born with and the right what you have made of that life. You've had much sadness in your life but also much happiness. Your happiness began when Tom came along. Am I right?'

'Yes, I had never fallen in love with anyone before Tom. My father couldn't understand why I didn't want to get married. I'd had some young men who wanted to marry me but I told my father that I would only marry for love as he and my mother had done. They had been very happy.'

'I see too that you have had much sadness... illnesses and deaths. Little deaths too. Babies?'

Hannah clenched her hands but Aisha gently stroked them until they opened. She was silent.

After a few minutes, it was Hannah who spoke.

'Will I have more babies?' she whispered.

Aisha hesitated. 'It might be best if you don't,' she answered quietly.

'Why ever not?' Hannah exclaimed. 'Tom and I love each other passionately. We know that we can make babies and one day we'll have a baby that I can carry until it is born.' Tears spilled down her cheeks. 'I don't want to talk about it. It has nothing to do with you, anyway. Just Tom and me and we will have babies,' she said emphatically.'

'Hannah, I know how difficult it is for you understand that we can tell from the lines on your palms much of what the future holds.'

'No you can't. You're just guessing... making it up.'

'You didn't ask me to read your future, so I won't. But if I tell you that I already know that you are a country girl; someone close to you, probably your mother, died about twelve years ago; your father suffered a long illness of the brain before he died; you

244

have lost three babies and you have been ill after each of those... shall I go on?' Aisha stopped talking and waited.

'I told you most of that. I'm determined that Tom and I will have a baby, even if I die in the process,' Hannah retorted. 'Anyway I don't know how not to have a baby but I surely know how to get with child. And I'm not going to stop making love to Tom.'

'Very well,' said Aisha. She shook her head sadly. 'Hannah, I see that each time you lose a baby you get really ill. This weakens your body. If you want me to, I can give you some medicine that may stop you becoming with child and also some that might help you not to miscarry it if you do.'

'I've just told you that I want a baby. Why would I want to take stuff to stop me?' she protested.

'You should talk to Tom. It's his decision too,' Aisha reasoned.

Hannah began to get angry, She had not ask for this. It was none of Aisha's concern. Just hers and Tom's. She stood up.

'I don't want to argue with you Aisha. You have been very kind to us. Thank you for your concern but if you don't mind I'll go back to Tom now.'

Aisha stood up and gave her a hug. 'Then just let me give you something, please,' she suggested. She went to the back of the vardo and returned carrying a small drawstring bag. It was made of leather and beautifully decorated with beads and embroidery.

'This is called a putsi. You can wear it around your neck or hang it from your belt.' She handed it to Hannah. 'It's for you to keep, but I have something that I want you to put in it. This is called a bloodstone,' she said, handing Hannah a chip of a green stone with red jasper spotted through it. 'It not only helps prevent miscarriages, it also eases childbirth. Keep it with you at all times.'

'I'm sorry. I've been very rude to you and you have been so kind. I don't know what the future holds for us and I don't want to. I'll keep this putsi and the stone. If it does nothing else it'll remind me of you. Thankyou.' Hannah put the putsi around her neck and tucked it out of sight inside her blouse.

***

Most of the children had gone to bed by the time they returned to the fireside. Some of the men were drinking ale; others were supping cider. Some women were dancing to the music of the fiddlers; some were clapping and singing. It was a very merry group but Hannah felt dejected after her conversation with Aisha.

'Is something wrong?' Thomas whispered to her.

'No, I just feel really tired. Do you think they would mind if I go to bed?'

'They might,' Thomas replied. 'Stay a little while and then we'll make our excuses together. I've been watching some of the others and now I know why the bender tent was put up. Some of the younger men have been carrying their bedding into it so it looks as though we'll have company tonight. I don't think that there'll be much sleep for any of us.'

He was wrong. Exhaustion meant that they were oblivious to the snores issuing from their sleeping companions and they awoke in the morning refreshed and ready to recommence their travels.

***

Hannah lay quietly in her wire bed at the inn listening to the even breathing of Thomas as he slept beside her. It was not the most comfortable of beds with its sagging wire and lumpy mattress but she was grateful for it and the shelter the inn offered from the storm raging outside. It was four days since they had left the gypsy encampment and had meandered contentedly along

246

the rough roads and lanes on their way to Gunnislake. They hadn't been in a hurry and they had enjoyed their time together, content to pitch their tent as soon as they found a suitable spot. They hadn't wanted to be caught out by the darkness again.

But the wet weather had come and they had gratefully sought the shelter of the inn. Now, with her sleep disturbed by Thomas's heavy breathing, the uncomfortable bed and the wet tree branches slapping on the bedroom window, Hannah recalled her conversation with Thomas earlier that night. 'Hannah you know I want a baby but I don't want one if it means I might lose you. If Aisha has the powers that she said she has, she must believe that it is dangerous for you. Maybe our lives are meant to be just you and me.'

Hannah fingered the putsi around her neck, and then put her arms around Thomas.

'She might believe it, but I don't and you mustn't either. I love you, and I love what you do to me and the way you make me feel. I don't want you to stop doing it. Forget about Aisha and her silly forebodings.'

'Why have you kept the putsi, then?' he asked.

'Healing is different from foretelling and this might help when I do get pregnant again. It's harmless anyway. Just a pretty stone in a bag.'

In a strange sort of way the little bag gave her comfort, and she clutched it in her hands as she finally fell asleep.

***

Three more days passed before they arrived at Gunnislake in the Tamar Valley. It was still as beautiful as it had been when Thomas had left eight years previously. Jenny and Sam were very happy to see them and more than pleased to make Hannah's acquaintance.

'You look very tired after your long journey, Hannah. Are you sure that you are lookin' after this child, Tom? She's very thin. I'll have to fatten 'er up a weeny bit for you,' she remarked.

'I'm fine, Mrs Crean. A good night sleep will help me.' Hannah did not want to divulge all her health problems just now but thought that this motherly looking woman might be just what she needed.

'Call me Jenny, Hannah. Tom does. Oh, it's so good to see you both. Come on in. I know you'll have lots to tell me.'

Thomas felt sure that he had done the right thing in bringing Hannah to Jenny. He hoped that her common-sense approach to all matters could benefit Hannah.

Chapter 24:
The return of Marty

The sailing ship Tempest was tied up at the dock in Plymouth. Its battered condition gave credence to the arduous conditions that its passengers and crew had endured on the journey from Sydney. The cargo had moved constantly and this combined with a hull that had sprung many leaks put the ship in serious danger of sinking during one of the many storms it had encountered. It had taken the constant pumping of the bilges to prevent a disaster. Fortunately, Tempest was mainly a cargo ship and therefore carried few passengers.

'You won't see me on another bloody ship,' grizzled one weather-beaten sailor.

'Now, now Toby. Ya know well you'll be the first to sign on when we's ready to sail again. What about you, Marty?' the Second Officer asked another of the Ordinary Seamen. 'Are you gonna come back?'

'Not on your life,' Marty Dewson replied. 'I only worked me way back 'cos I didn't have no money for a ticket. I ain't no sailor an' never will be. Soon's I gets me leave from ya, I'm off outa 'ere an' ya won't see me again.'

'You're a grumpy old bugger, Dewson. We'll be pleased to see the back end of you too. Good riddance, I say!'

Marty made to cuff the man who spoke but one glare from the officer made him withhold his fist. He had no desire to spend any more time in the brig. Too many times he had ended up in there when his temper got the better of him and he lashed out at someone or something. 'Yeah, an you too,' he spat out instead and stalked off to finish his duties and collect his pay.

***

Marty swaggered down the gangplank with his kit over his shoulder and headed for the nearest beerhouse. *'Land at last. Thank God!'* he thought. He ordered a tankard of ale and flopped down in a corner and began to drink. Ah! That tasted so good. He hadn't had ale since he left Sydney twelve weeks before. The crew had been given grog on the ship, a watered down rum but that was rubbish compared to the rum he had smuggled in the old days. Still, it was better than nothing and he had managed to pilfer extra rations from the hold. The Captain knew that it was being stolen but the wily Marty had avoided being caught. The penalties for stealing anywhere were severe but shipboard thefts were viewed even more seriously. However, Marty considered it worth the risk. If caught he might have been flogged or 'keel-hauled' or tied to a rope and swung overboard. But he hadn't been caught and here he was back after more than nine years to get even with that little bastard Puckle. He'd still be smuggling it if it wasn't for him. It had to have been Puckle who had betrayed him, and it had happened just after that episode with Puckle at Polperro. That was too much of a coincidence.

He swirled the beer around in the mug and contemplated his next move. So completely lost in his thoughts was he that he didn't notice another man approaching until his shadow spilled over him.

'Well if it ain't Marty. Thought ya would'a died out there in that convict place.' Robbie smiled his toothless grin as Marty slid over to let him sit in the booth.

'Y' still look as ugly as ever, Robbie. I fair near did die lotsa times. But I got me wits, y' see,' he said, tapping his forehead. 'They kept me alive. Gotta 'ave y' wits.' Marty drank deeply from his tankard and called loudly for another one.

'Gonna tell me about it?' Robbie leaned closer to him.

'Nope, I ain't. I'll jist tell ya if ya ever have the choice 'tween transportation and 'anging, choose 'anging. 'Tis only short term sufferin'. Not like that place I just come from. There the agony goes on forever.'

'Where ya gonna be stayin', Marty?' Robbie enquired, his scarred mouth appearing to give him a sneering look.

'Dunno yet. Find a doss house somewhere 'sppose. Meanwhile I'll just have another ale and stay where I am. By the way, you ain't seen that traitor Puckle have you?'

'Puckle? Waddya want him for?' Robbie answered with a strange look on his face.

'You don't need to know why. I just do, that's why. Ain't nothin' to concern ya. I owe him somethin' that's all.'

'William'll know. He said that Tom visits him sometimes. He's got hisself a nice wife, I hear. William has too.'

'Now that's really interestin'.' Marty's face took on a contemptuous look that made Robbie think twice about giving any more information.

It was dark when they left the beerhouse together and having spent all their money on booze, wandered around seeking a suitable bench or doorway to sleep in. Both were exceedingly drunk and could only negotiate the dirty, stinking streets by holding each other up. There were many people about but most were in the same condition as Marty and Robbie or worse.

Marty tripped over a body lying prostrate in a sea of rubbish. He fell, dragging Robbie with him. He cursed and swore as he picked himself out of the muck and kicked viciously at the man lying at his feet, oblivious to the crunching of bones as his boot crashed against the man's skull.

'C'mon, Marty. Let's get outa 'ere.' Robbie dragged at his arm. 'Ye'll bloody kill 'im.' He pulled at Marty's jacket and eventually Marty gave up the assault and staggered off, with

Robbie following. They drifted down an alleyway, not knowing where they were or where they were going. It was pitch dark and the stench from the open drains was nauseating.

'Do y' wanna comfit fo' t'night?' a voice penetrated the blackness and they stopped quickly. The woman appeared from a doorway and beckoned to them.

'Slut,' murmured Robbie but she heard him.

'It's whatcha used t', ain't it?' she replied flouncing about, her dirty red skirt dragging in the filth of the street.

'Shut up, Robbie. This is just what I need. I've bin at sea remember. Ain't much to get ya goin' there. Come if y' wanna or git goin'. Well wench, where to?'

She took him by the hand and drew him inside. Robbie followed. They climbed the narrow winding stairway up to a third floor attic room. Inside was a dirty narrow bed but Marty was unaware of that. Neither did he notice the clothes strewn everywhere, the dirty wooden table covered in decaying food, nor the pots and pans sitting in a bowl of dirty water. The woman opened her arms invitingly and Marty walked into them. His hands travelled roughly over her body and he threw her onto the bed. Robbie sat down to watch, his head spinning and aching with the alcohol he had drunk. The tiny candle threw shadows all over the walls and lulled him into drowsiness. He forgot about Marty and his lustful activity as he fell asleep.

When he awoke it was still dark. Apart from the noises rising up from the street below all was quiet. There was no movement from the bed. He looked carefully. Was Marty still there? Suddenly the bed clothes erupted into life and Marty sat up. Grunting, he heaved himself upright and looked around.

'Where is she?' he demanded.

'Dunno. I was asleep. She's probably 'ad enough of the likes of an animal like you an' gone to find 'erself someone more genteel-like.'

'Shut up y' pervert,' he glared, fossicking around in the bed for his britches. He pulled them on and patted himself all over. 'Where is it?' he muttered looking around wildly, his eyes beginning to smoulder. 'If she's taken it I'll find 'er an' kill 'er.'

'What're yer on about?' Robbie hated Marty when he was like this and thought that he would get away from him as soon as he could. Marty's company was better than no company to Robbie at the moment but he knew that he would have to be wary of him, unpredictable as he was.

'Me money bag, y' big oaf. Did y' see 'er take it.' Marty grabbed Robbie by the jacket and began to shake him.

'Course I didn't. I was sleepin'. Ain't my job to watch ya money. Ya din't 'ave any in it anyways, so ya said. Leggo o' me.' Robbie struggled to free himself from Marty's vice-like grip.

'When ya with me ya watch me back. Ya know that,' he hissed.

'Maybe in the old days, Marty, but times 'ave changed an' I don't 'ave to do anything ya say. I owe ya nuthin'.'

'Y' don't don'tcha? What 'appened to loyalty, I ask ya? After all I did for you blokes y' owe me summat.'

'Nope. Nothin'. We worked 'ard an' risked a lot for ya. You were the one oo got rich, not us. Ye've probably got a stash some place. We'll go an' get that. Now let me go.'

He tried to free himself but Marty drew back his arm and smashed his fist into the unfortunate Robbie's face. He dropped like a stone and lay on the floor, not moving. Marty breathed slowly and heavily and looked around. He stripped the ragged coverings from the bed, tipped up the lumpy old mattress and searched frantically. By the time he had finished the room had been ransacked. There was no money bag. Fury surged through him as he rushed out the door kicking at the incumbent Robbie as he did so.

It was still dark when he stumbled out onto the street. Lanterns had been lit in some of the doorways but their dim beam did not do much to light his way. His anger exhausted him and after a while he sank into a doorway and fell asleep.

It was daylight when he awoke, cold and stiff. The mist swirled around him as he struggled to his feet. He remembered the theft of his money with anger. His wits had let him down that time. He now had no more than two pence in his pocket. There was no stash of money as Robbie had suggested. He would have to get some more from somewhere and then he would start looking for Thomas Puckle. He did not give Robbie a passing thought and had no concern for his fate.

Chapter 25:
A gathering of friends (1798)

Robbie staggered to his feet, holding his head in his hands. He felt sick. He didn't know how much time had passed since Marty had knocked him out, but light was showing through the grimy windows so he knew that he had been unconscious for some time. *'That Marty,'* he thought. *'I'll kill 'im when I see 'im. I don't owe 'im nothin'.'* He stumbled down the stairs and out into the squalid streets. What a place! Who'd want to live here among the dogs and pigs that roamed everywhere and where you could be healthy one day and dead the next from a variety of virulent diseases. Far better to be in a village like Polperro, with its fresh sea breeze and tidy little cottages. That's where he would go now, he decided; back among the friendly people who looked out for each other. He would see William and John and tell them that Marty was back and just as bad-tempered and more vicious than ever.

He felt very muddle headed as he wandered along. Something niggled at the back of his brain and he couldn't bring it to the fore. But somehow he knew that it was important.

He thrust his hands deeply into the pockets of his coat and his fingers wrapped around an object. A farthing! He suddenly felt rich and very hungry. He bought a plain bun and continued on his way all the time wondering what it was that he was trying to remember. He also wondered where Marty had got to. He didn't know if he wanted to run into him or not.

***

Marty replaced some of his lost cash by picking pockets but it wasn't only money he purloined. Even he could not believe his luck when his hand encountered a pistol in an unsuspecting victim's pocket. He quickly and gently extracted it and was gone before the man knew that he had been robbed. He made a speedy exit from the town and headed for Polperro, twenty-seven miles away. Even if he hurried it would take him two or three days journeying over the rough countryside but he wasn't in a hurry. He just wanted information as to Puckle's whereabouts. Once he had that he would seek him out and deal with him.

He was tired when he reached Polperro and although he would have liked to rested up in the hotel, the fewer people who knew of his presence the better. He had had time on his long walk to decide how to approach his quest. He knew that William didn't like him and would surmise that his intentions towards Tom would not be beneficial. He decided to wait until William was away from his house and then he would approach his wife.

He hid himself in the hills behind the town but kept William's cottage in his view. He saw William and his son leave and waited thirty minutes to make sure that they didn't return.

Sarah answered the door to his knocking. 'Mornin', Missus. Is William at 'ome? I'm an old friend of 'is and am just passin' through,' he explained in a friendly voice. 'Thought I'd look 'im up.'

Sarah looked at him curiously and noted his grimy appearance. 'He's down at his boat. What did you want?'

'Jist wanted to see 'ow 'e's gettin' on an' that. I bin away an' jist wanted t' know about our mutual friend Tom Puckle an' if he had seen 'im lately. I owe him something an' want to give it to 'im. My, that's a pretty baby you have there,' he said in a smarmy tone.

Sarah held her baby closer. 'Tom and Hannah were here but have returned to Gunnislake. Now if you don't mind, I'm busy,' she said as she closed the door, breathing uneasily as she waited for him to leave. There was something about the man that she didn't like. She heard him walking down the path and peeking through the curtains was pleased to see him turn up the road leading towards the outskirts of the town.

'Mmmm,' she wondered. 'Strange that he didn't go down to the beach if he wanted to see William.' She soon put the visit to the back of her mind as she continued with her chores.

***

Robbie was exhausted when he reached William's house. He bashed heavily on the door and when William opened it he fell inside.

'Robbie, what on earth happened to you?' William asked as he helped him to his feet. 'Sarah, some brandy. Quickly.'

When Robbie had recovered a little he grabbed William by the arm and gasped. 'William, I've remembered. We gotta help 'im.'

'What are you talking about and what happened to your face? I've seen worse when we've had bare knuckle fights in the Square.' William smiled but became serious when Robbie gingerly putting his hand to his face and answered, 'Marty Dewson done it.'

'What! Is that scumbag back?' William looked at Robbie in horror. 'You're not saying we have to help him, surely.'

'No, course I ain't. It's Tom we have to help.'

'Tom? Robbie you'd better start at the beginning,' said William, filling up Robbie's glass again as well as one for himself.

'When I remembered what I'd forgotten, I ran all the way 'ere. That's why I'm so tuckered out. Marty wanted to know where Tom was an' I said that you would know. That's what I forgot an' then I remembered.'

'Robbie, start at the beginning,' implored William.

So Robbie told him of his meeting with Marty in the pub, the night Marty had with the wench who robbed him and the furious mood that Marty was in when he beat Robbie up.

'Robbie what's this got to do with Tom? You haven't told me yet.'

'I'm a bit muddled. Sorry. 'E 'it me hard. Knocked me senseless. 'E wanted to know where Tom was 'cos 'e 'ad somethin' to give 'im. We were in the pub at the time, friendly-like. I thought nothin' of it and just said that you'd know 'cos 'e visited you at times. Was only when I was walkin' 'ere that I remembered that Marty tried to kill 'im before so I ran to tell you not to tell 'im.'

'Well, he hasn't been here yet an' I wouldn't tell him anyways. He hasn't been here has he, Sarah?' he asked as an afterthought.

'A man did come looking for you yesterday. He asked if we'd seen Tom. I didn't like him and I didn't like the way he looked at the baby so I got rid of him quickly. I was relieved when I saw him take the road out of town.'

'Was he short and fat?' William asked quickly.

'He's a bit skinnier now, William. Remember he's been in a convict place for nine years an' they don't get much tucker there.' Robbie rubbed his sore head thoughtfully. 'What do we do now?'

'I didn't know who he was, William. I certainly didn't know that he was a convict. Oh! what have I done,' Sarah wailed.

'It's a long story, Sarah and I'll tell you sometime. Now what did you tell him? Did he talk about Tom?'

'He wanted to know if we had seen him lately. I said that he and Hannah had been here but had left and gone back to Gunnislake.'

258

'So he now knows where they live and he headed out of town without anyone else seein' him. I would say that was the only reason he came here....to get information about Tom. We're gonna have to go after him, Robbie.'

'What do we do when we find him?'

'Dunno. Depends what he's doing. You get some rest. I'll nip out and borrow a horse. We can both ride it. Sarah, can you put a bit of food together. We'll leave at daylight. I doubt if even Marty would find his business urgent enough to warrant travelling in the dark.'

Robbie groaned. 'I just thought of summat else. He called Tom a traitor. Must think that he's the one who ratted on 'im.'

'That's rubbish. Tom was nowhere about. Marty had a lot of enemies although he never ever thought that he did. Too arrogant for that. He treated lots of people badly. It could have been anyone. But if he thinks it's Tom, he won't show him no mercy.'

***

Alfie didn't have a plan when he left Peggy but he did go to try to find John. He was unsuccessful in his search but he learned that John had left his job with the intention of working his way on a ship to America. He remembered his conversation with Peggy and thought that maybe he could follow him there. He still had not found the woman that he wanted to spend the rest of his life with and he was getting sick of roaming aimlessly. He had kept his word to Thomas and did not rob any more people even though his funds were often very short.

He made up his mind. He would head south to Plymouth, sell his horse and sign on to the first ship that would take him to America.

***

After many days travelling he came to a town called Okehampton. It was situated on the northern edge of Dartmoor and he wasn't keen to ride across the moors on his own. Not much frightened Alfie but he had heard so many stories about the place from all sorts of travellers that he thought it best to talk with the locals and get their opinion.

'Don't go there, lad. There's all sorts o' things on the moors that'll getcha.'

'Yeh! My friend went out there wiv 'is dog. Dog came back but 'e didn't. Dog was a right mess and almost outa its mind.

'Yeah! Them there piskies musta sent that mist down an' 'e got lost. Maybe fell inta a bog else 'is dog woulda got 'im 'ome.'

'Ain't just the mist. There's huge wild animals and dogs out there too. Their howl is the dreariest, most awful sound. Freeze the blood in yer veins, it would.'

'Anyone who dies on the moor, well their soul don't get off. Stays their forever, wandering about an' scaring good folk who are just going about their business. No lad, don't risk it.'

'What a load of old cobblers,' another one countered. 'The Moors is beautiful. If you believe them stories you're as daft as they are.'

Alfie listened to these stories. He suspected that they were just stories but he also knew that the mist was real and could descend at anytime. It was about 50 miles across the moor and he would have to spend one night at least on it. His lantern wouldn't light the way much and anyway he didn't know the way. If he got off the track he could be in trouble.

'Thankyou gentlemen. I'll take your advice and go the long way round. Now which way is it best to go? Round to the left or round to the right?'

Having established that the 'round to the right' was the shortest route to Plymouth, he set off early in the morning and by late afternoon had reached Tavistock. This was a small village, smaller that Oakhampton, but what made Alfie stop on the outskirts was a signpost that said 'Gunnislake'. Could it be the same town? Tom was always talking about Gunnislake and he remembered the name because it was so unusual. Sam and Jenny lived there, or had done. Were they still there? They might know something of Thomas and Hannah. Without hesitation, he turned his horse and headed off down the narrow winding road.

It didn't take him long but it was getting dark when he arrived. He was feeling very tired but made some enquiries and was directed to number 4 Pembroke Lane. It sounded so nice and cosy that Alfie began to imagine a warm fire, slippers at the hearth and a stew-pot hanging from its hook.

He wasn't disappointed for when Jenny opened the door to him, that is exactly what he found.

'I'm Alfie Pike, a friend of Tom's. We grew up in Athelney together. I was passing and thought you might have some news of him,' Alfie explained.

'Come in, come in,' Jenny urged. 'A friend of Tom's is very welcome. We know of you. Tom has told us many good things about you.'

Alfie wondered if he had also told them the bad things but said nothing.

They talked long into the night and he was amazed and excited to learn that Tom and Hannah now lived in Gunnislake and should be on their way home from Polperro.

'Maybe I'll go and meet them in the morning. I'm not in a hurry and I'd love to see them. Maybe I could take Bouncer with me,' he offered.

'Bouncer doesn't go very far these days. Too old an' he gets sore in his joints. He just sleeps all day,' Sam told him. 'Better leave 'im 'ere or you might end up havin' to carry 'im.'

***

Hannah had enjoyed the break away at Polperro but she was feeling tired and wanted to get home. Because of her condition, Jenny had been against them going in the first place, but Hannah felt that she was well enough to make the journey. The weather was good and all told it had been a happy visit. Now they were on their way back.

'Can we stop for a wee break, Tom? I need to stretch my legs.' She was wrapped up on the small cart and propped up with cushions. Thomas reined in the horse and lifted Hannah to the ground.

'We could have a little picnic here, if you like. It's quite a pretty place.' Without waiting for an answer, he fetched the basket and laid out a rug on the grass. He was feeling very happy. Hannah was six months pregnant and seemed to be in good health. Around her neck was the putsi that Aysha had given her along with the bloodstone. Maybe it did help and this baby would be the one that would survive.

***

Marty was feeling very pleased with himself when he left Sarah and took the road to Gunnislake. He had travelled quite a distance and sitting down to rest his weary legs he suddenly he spotted a horse standing alone in a paddock. Glancing around and not seeing anyone he took a chance and stole it. Soon he was cantering down the road albeit a little awkwardly with no saddle and no bridle. But he clung on grimly. The miles sped by under the horse's hooves and suddenly, rounding a corner, he spotted his quarry sitting quietly in a clearing. He threw himself off the horse which continued cantering down the road past a startled Thomas and Hannah.

Thomas sat up quickly and looked down the road from where the horse had come. He could not see any movement.

262

'Wonder where the rider is?' he said thoughtfully.

'As it doesn't have a saddle or nothing I suppose it doesn't have a rider either. Maybe it just ran away,' suggested Hannah.

'Maybe it did,' replied Thomas.

Marty watched from a distance. He lay flat on his stomach weighing up his options. The gun in his pocket dug deeply into his hip but he didn't move. He shifted his eyes from side to side, assessing his next action. The road was bounded on one side by tall trees with thick bush rising up the steep hills behind. The other, where the two people were having their picnic, was sparsely vegetated and revealed a steep descent to a meandering rocky stream fifty feet below.

Marty wriggled his body back into the undergrowth and once well off the road, silently crept closer to his quarry.

'We should get going, Tom,' Hannah suggested. 'Home before dark. Sounds good to me.'

'Mmmmm,' grunted Thomas. 'It's nice here too.' He paused. 'I think can hear another horse. Listen.'

The familiar sound of hoofbeats resounded down the road even before the horse appeared round the corner. Marty ducked down as Tom stood up.

'Hey, Tom,' shouted William.

'William! What are you doing here? And Robbie too? Well bless me. What on earth do you lads want?'

'You, Tom. Thank goodness you're alright. You too, Hannah,' William slid down from the horse and gave her a big hug. 'We had to make sure so we came along after you.'

'Why? What's happened?' she asked nervously.

William turned to Tom. 'Marty Dewson's back and he's after you.'

'Me!' Tom felt panic in the pit of his stomach. He still didn't know what it was about him that Marty disliked so much, but he would never forget the previous occasions when he had tried to kill him. Was there to be another one?

'It's a long story Tom, but he's already around somewhere. He left before us and we didn't see him on the way so he's gotta be close by somewhere,' William reasoned as he looked around.

'Well, we haven't seen him either obviously but I'm glad that you two are here now that I know he's about. We'd better get along home and work out what we're going to do.' Tom began to gather up their picnic and quickly threw it onto the cart.

'We'll come with you,' offered William. 'At least we can watch your back until you get there.'

Thomas shivered and looked at Hannah. She was very pale. 'I'm sorry I got you into this mess, Hannah. All of you. I suppose this is something that I have to sort out with Marty one way or the other.'

Marty watched from his hiding place across the road. He silently cursed William and Robbie for turning up. The pistol was still in his pocket and if he took it out now they would see the movement. He hoped that it was already loaded because he didn't have any gunpowder and anyway, surely the owner wouldn't have it in his pocket for self-protection if it wasn't pre-loaded, or so he hoped. He would be dead before he extracted the ramrod and pushed the powder down the barrel. He would have needed it to be ready. Marty cursed himself for not checking. *'Me mind must be slippin','* he thought.

He saw them start down the road with Tom, Hannah and William on the dray and Robbie on the horse. *'What a cosy bunch,'* he thought. He sat back in the bushes and began to formulate another plan. He hated Thomas. He always had done. He didn't know why. Some people you like, some people you don't and Tom was one who had got right up his nose from the start. Marty remembered how he had given him cheek when he first discovered him in the thicket. Of course he'd been poaching then but he'd got around Mr Cotter and it was Marty who had been made to look stupid while Tom got a job out of it. Then there was the time when they were sawing wood in the pit. He shouldn't have taken on Ethan but he really thought that he could beat him. They laughed at him over that, the scum.

They all seemed to like Tom and nobody liked him. The poaching ring he had led got caught and he only just made his escape. That was probably Tom's doing too and so was the trap that he got caught in with his smuggling. His hatred of Tom had eaten into his mind all the time he was in the convict settlement and he wasn't going to let the likes of William and Robbie stop him from getting his own back. A new plan came into his mind and he smiled to himself at the thought of it.

Chapter 26:
An unfortunate decision

It was a sombre party that made its way back to Gunnislake. There was no sign of Marty and they didn't expect there to be but neither did they expect to meet up with Alfie. Tom's spirits lightened considerably when he saw him but Hannah didn't know what to make of his sudden reappearance.

'You don't seem happy to see me, Hannah. I promise you I'm a changed man,' he said as he rode beside them. 'I've never been in trouble again. Kept me nose clean, so to speak.'

'Alfie, you're the least of her problems at the moment,' said Tom and he quickly explained the current predicament.

'Surely there's enough of us to take him on,' he answered. 'You can't just let him appear and shoot you or do whatever he's planning to do.'

'Of course I don't intend to just let him do what he ever he wants. But the first thing we have to do is get Hannah home where she'll be safe. Then we can work out a plan.'

They called at Sam and Jenny's cottage to collect Bouncer and to tell them of the latest events.

'You must stay here tonight,' implored Jenny.

'We'll be safe enough tonight, Jenny. We have Alfie, William and Robbie to look after us. I don't think Marty would be stupid enough to try anything tonight but tomorrow is a different story. We'll have to think about what we are going to do then.'

***

After a light supper during which they tried to come up with ideas of how to get rid of Marty without actually killing him,

Hannah ventured to say, 'We're the ones who'll have to disappear, Tom.'

'No, Hannah. We're not leaving. I'm not going to creep away in the dark and leave Marty to track us down again. Now we know he's determined to get me, I'll always be looking over my shoulder.' Thomas paced up and down the room. 'We'll never have any peace in our lives if Marty is around. It's obvious that he wants to kill me. Sometime I'm going to have to face up to him if we want any sort of happiness. I think I should do that now.'

'But Tom, he could kill you. That's what he wants to do, though heaven knows why. You're no good to me dead. The baby and I need you. I can't bear the thought of living without you.'

'Hannah, I'm not likely to be the one to die. Marty and I are hunting each other now that I know he is around so the odds are evened up.' He paused. 'William, you should go home tomorrow. I know how it is with you and you need to get back to your family and your fishing. You go too, Robbie.'

'I could stay a bit,' responded Robbie. 'I owe Marty something for beating me up.'

'No, thanks all the same. You go. Alfie might stay a few days and help out.' Thomas looked askance at Alfie who nodded. 'I think tomorrow morning I'll take Hannah to Jenny and Sam and then Alfie and I will go hunting for him.'

'And what will you do when you find him? Kill him? You know you couldn't do that in cold blood?' Hannah questioned.

'I could if he was about to kill me. Alfie and I had a conversation about that subject once, didn't we Alfie? If it meant preserving my own life, or yours, I could do it.' Thomas took her hand. The lamp flickered on the table and cast moving shadows over his solemn face. 'I'd be very careful, Hannah. I have too much to lose if I fail. I'm looking forward to a long life of happiness with you and the baby and I won't have that if I get killed.'

She kissed him. 'You have to go to the smithy tomorrow. Jack won't want you to be away another day.'

'I'll nip over first thing in the morning and tell him what has happened. I'll make it up to him. Alfie will be here to watch out for you and then we'll take you to Jenny.'

***

Marty was cold and irritable when he awoke from his fitful sleep under the stone bridge over the Tamar River. He was very hungry and that didn't improve his mood at all. Mist was all around him and he shivered in the dampness. The sooner this job was over the sooner he could get away, he thought. He would have to come back one day and rid himself of Thomas but he would let him suffer first. This was the best way. He thought about his plan. It was simple. His enquiries the night before had told him where Tom had his house so all he had to do was wait for William and Robbie to leave, Tom to go to his work and he would have Hannah all to himself. His unkempt appearance did not raise any questions in the minds of his informants. Vagrants often passed through the town on their way to somewhere.

He brushed the grass out of his old jacket and was about to climb the bank to the road when he heard a horse coming towards the bridge. He ducked back under and peered out as William and Robbie passed by and cantered up the road and out of sight. He rubbed his hands in glee. The first part of his plan had worked even though he hadn't known that they would go home at dawn. But he had thought that William wouldn't leave his fishing for too long. He clambered up the bank and made his way to 8 Orchard Lane, Tom's cottage, and hid himself behind a tree directly opposite it. He waited, shivering in the cold morning air. After a while his patience was rewarded. Thomas hurried from the rear of his house and quickly made his way down the road towards the town. Quick as a flash, Marty dashed across the lane

268

and around to the back of the cottage. He checked that his pistol was cocked and the safety catch off. Slowly he opened the wooden door and crept into the kitchen. Hannah was stirring the porridge in the pot over the fire.

'You must be Tom's wife,' Marty said quietly.

Hannah jumped and spun around. She gasped and then froze as she saw the pistol pointed at her. She couldn't call out to Alfie. All her senses were suspended.

'Thought I'd kill you first and Tom another day. That way he will suffer twice.' Marty looked at her condition. 'Three times 'cos I guess the baby will die too.' He smiled his ugly smile.

He glanced at Bouncer who was asleep by the hearth.

'Still got your stupid dog, I see. 'Ain't much of a watch dog. Pity I ain't got a shot for him too.'

Hannah's brain began to work but she was still immobilised by the threat of the pistol. Bouncers presence annoyed Marty and he kicked out at him. He awoke from his slumber with a growl. Standing up sluggishly he ambled over to Hannah. Something was wrong. He could sense Hannah's fear and this man disturbed him. He sniffed and it came to him—a long recessed memory of a man who had ill-treated him. Nobody else had ever hurt him but this man had. And now his mistress was afraid of him. He bared his teeth and growled.

'Shaddup dog, or you might get the shot instead and your lovely mistress get something else.'

Hannah saw the back door opening silently but Marty was too preoccupied to notice. Alfie stood there with his finger to his lips. Marty kicked out again and suddenly, with a throaty growl, Bouncer launched himself at him. They both tumbled to the floor as the pistol went off with a thunderous explosion. Marty screamed as he felt Bouncer's jaws wrap around his throat. He fought to get a grip on Bouncer but the dog tightened his hold and shook his head vigorously. Marty's arms waved feebly as blood gushed from his throat and pooled on the floor. Then he lay still. It was all over in a matter of seconds.

Alfie leapt across them both as an ashen-faced Hannah slumped to the floor in a faint. He put his arms gently around her.

'Hannah, wake up, please wake up.' He looked her over desperately praying that she had not been shot. He could not see any blood. Bouncer nosed his way between them making Alfie feel sick when he saw his blood-covered muzzle.

'Outside, Bouncer,' he commanded and Bouncer reluctantly left Hannah and obeyed Alfie. 'Hannah, wake up,' he implored. Where was Tom? he wondered frantically. He didn't have far to go. And why hadn't someone heard the shot? It had been so loud his own ears were still ringing. Hannah stirred in his arms. 'It's alright,' he murmured. 'Tom will be here soon and then I'll go and get help.'

She slowly opened her eyes and looked at him. As he was about to speak a spasm of pain gripped her. She winced. 'Don't talk. It's over now. Marty's dead. He can't harm you or Tom.' Alfie kept comforting her and suddenly Thomas was there with a look of horror on his face.

'She's not dead, is she? Oh Hannah, why did I leave you? Hannah, say something.' He knelt down beside her and took her hand.

'Tom, I think she'll be alright. Marty fired a shot but I don't think it hit her. She's in pain though. I need to go and get help but don't know where to go.'

Thomas pulled himself together. 'Go to Jenny. She'll know where to get Mrs Barnaby. She's the midwife. She'll know what to do. Hannah, have you been shot? Where does it hurt?'

Hannah opened her eyes. She shook her head feebly and put her hand on her stomach.

Without another word Alfie ran out, leapt on his horse and raced off to get Jenny.

Thomas comforted Hannah as best he could but his eyes kept straying to Marty. What on earth could have happened here, he wondered. Had Alfie cut his throat?

As if she had read his thoughts Hannah whispered faintly. 'Bouncer did it. He was protecting me. Marty was going to shoot me.' She closed her eyes again. Thomas gently picked her up and carried her to the bedroom. He laid her on the bed and carefully covered her with the bedclothes.

'My putsi,' she muttered feebly. 'Where is it?'

Thomas groped around in her dress pocket and found it. He gently put it in her grasp and whispered, 'I'll be back in one minute. I promise. I have something to do.'

He returned to the kitchen and, without looking at him, took Marty by the feet and dragged him out of the house. He could not bear the thought of him being in his home any longer. He threw an old sack over his head and was about to return to Hannah when Bouncer woke up and whined at him. His muzzle was still covered in blood.

'Oh, Bouncer,' Thomas said tearfully. 'But for you, Hannah could be dead.' He filled a bucket with water and grabbing a cloth from the shed washed Bouncer's face, all the time listening out for Hannah. He then tied him up and rushed back into the house. Hannah was awake.

'I've just had another pain, Tom. I think the baby is coming,' she said, faintly gripping the putsi tightly. She held out her hand and he took it tenderly. 'We have to be ready for the worst because isn't time yet.'

Thomas didn't speak for a few minutes. Thoughts ran through his head. If only he had not encouraged William and Robbie to go early. If only he had not gone to tell Jack that he would not be at work. If only he had let Hannah stay with Jenny and Sam last night. If only Marty hadn't come back. If only...

'This is all Marty's doing. If he wasn't already dead I'd kill him,' he said savagely.

'Well, he is and he can no longer bother us. We won't have to wonder where he is any more.'

'I didn't before he came back,' returned Thomas. 'William told me ages ago that he'd been transported for his smuggling. I never thought that he'd come back. He must have hated me very much and now I'll never know why.'

He held her hand as another spasm passed through her body. 'Where were Jenny and Mrs Barnaby?' he wondered.

'I think Marty was jealous of you right from the beginning,' Hannah answered slowly. 'You were all the things that he wasn't. People have always liked you because you are kind and thoughtful. Marty was the opposite and so he had no one. He was not nice looking, he was rude and uncouth. He was a liar and a cheat and a bully and didn't care who he hurt and so no one liked him.'

'Then he found out that I had you,' Thomas said tearfully. 'Someone to love and cherish all my life. So he tried to take you away from me.'

'He said that. He was evil. He knew the baby would die if I died. He was going to come back and kill you later. He wanted you to suffer first. But you won't. We'll live through this,' she murmured as she closed her eyes.

Chapter 27:
Confessions and forgiveness

Thomas knew little of the events of the next few days. Things happened around him that did not penetrate the outer shield of his emotions. The local magistrate had been to view the scene, Marty's body had been removed and the cottage had been cleaned up. People came and went, arrangements were made, condolences given. But even with all this activity he was still unable to fully comprehend that the baby was dead. It was not as Hannah had said it would be. The baby had not lived. Through the skill of the midwife Hannah was still with him, albeit very ill, but their precious boy was not. He had attended his funeral, his defences telling him that this was for another baby and it was not his little one in that box. He thanked people for their kindness and then went home to Hannah.

She was very ill but there was no local hospital that she could go to. Thomas and Jenny were in constant attendance but progress was slow.

Thomas began to lose hope.

'Do you think she will ever recover, Jenny,' he asked pitifully.

Jenny did not know what to say. 'I don't know, Tom. Give it time. She's very weak and unless we can get her to take some broth and build up her strength I can't say. She's just not interested in anyone or anything.'

***

Alfie was never far from Tom's side. He could hardly look at him, such was his remorse. He felt so responsible. Hannah had been left in his care for such a short time and he had failed her. Failed them both. Failed everyone. Thomas had never said anything to him about it but Alfie felt sure that he would when his thinking processes had recovered. Alfie had not been aware that Marty had entered the cottage that fateful morning. He had been in the privy and had known nothing of Marty's presence until he heard voices coming from the kitchen.

He helped Tom as best he could. He coerced him into eating food although he had no appetite, made him sleep in a bed beside Hannah where he rested more comfortably than in a chair, and talked to him incessantly in the hope that he could break through his shield. He took him for walks, often against his will, and horse rides in the countryside. Mostly these activities were accomplished in silence or with Alfie conducting a one way conversation.

'I don't know what to do with him,' he confessed to Jenny one day. 'It's as if he isn't there anymore. Just a body with no mind or brain.'

'He has a lot to think about, Alfie. Mrs Barnaby told him that Hannah can never have more babies and he has to come to terms with that as well.'

'But it's as if he's not even thinking of Hannah. He's just wrapped up in his own little world. I'll do whatever I can but I think also that maybe I should move on. I am part of the memory of that awful day. I failed him and he'll remember that when he comes to his senses. He'll blame me for not watching out for her. It's my fault.'

'Stay a while longer, Alfie. He'll need all of us when he comes to his senses. He'll blame himself, Alfie. Not you. He made the decision to go and tell Jack what he was about to do that day. He also made the decision to send William and Robbie home. If he hadn't done those things, Marty wouldn't have had a chance. If it's anyone's fault though, it's Marty's. No one could know that he'd changed his plan and would harm Hannah instead of Tom.'

'Yes I suppose it is. Can't change any of those things now. Even so I can't help feeling guilty. I was the last stop so to speak.'

'Marty was wicked to plan what he did and he deserved what he got,' reasoned Jenny. 'His was a horrible death though but I certainly don't wish him back. The world will be a better place without him.'

***

Thomas did not notice Sam as he entered the cottage. He sat in his chair staring into space and didn't acknowledge his presence at all, even when Sam spoke to him.

'Come on lad. It's time you took hold of yourself.' He shook him by the shoulder and Thomas started from his reverie. His face relaxed a little when he saw Sam.

'Oh, Sam, it's you. I was in another world. I didn't hear you come in. Sit down,' he said flatly. He motioned him to a chair but Sam didn't sit down. He stood over Thomas who looked away from his serious face.

'Tom, look at me. Look at me, I say,' he insisted. 'You have to make an effort, lad. I know you've suffered a severe loss, but you must try to rally yourself or you're going to get sick. You can't look after Hannah when you are in this state. She needs you fit and well. You won't be much use to her if you get sick too. People are worried about you. Alfie has done his best to rouse you but doesn't know what to do next.'

'Alfie should just go away and leave us alone,' Thomas responded unexpectedly. 'We were always just fine until he came along.'

'Why should he do that?' exclaimed Sam. 'He's your very good friend. And Jenny is so worried about you, too.' Sam stopped suddenly as Thomas stood up quickly.

'Let me be, Sam. I failed Hannah and I failed our son. If I'd been here Marty wouldn't have frightened her and the baby wouldn't have come early. She'll never forgive me for that.'

'Don't be so stupid, Tom,' said Sam vehemently. 'Forget blaming yourself. Marty was to blame for all that Marty did. He chose the course he was going to take. He was evil and now he's dead. He'll be in that awful place, Hell, where he deserves to be.'

Thomas slumped back into his chair.

'There are many people who love you both and want to help you,' continued Sam. 'You must stop thinking of just yourself. Think of Hannah. When she realises just what she has lost she will need you healthy in body and mind. Jenny and I have been like parents to you and love you as we loved Will. Remember him?'

''Course I do, but he has nothing to do with this.' retorted Thomas.

'We lost one son, Tom. We know what it's like and we don't want to lose another. We'll help you but can't do much unless you help yourself. We're here for you both and Alfie is as well.

***

Alfie hesitated as he was about to enter the cottage. He had once loved the warm atmosphere created by Hannah but now found that the despondency that had settled over the place since Marty's intrusion and violence was affecting his cheerful and optimistic nature. He had done his best for Thomas. Nothing had worked. Now it was time for him to leave.

He imagined what would happen. If Tom continued like this he would lose his job; would not be able to pay his rent on the cottage and they would be thrown out. They would be penniless and who would want to employ Tom in his present state.

Alfie shivered at the thought. He would make one last try. He would make Thomas angry and jolt him out of his misery.

He found Thomas in his usual chair.

'Hello, Tom,' he said cheerfully. Thomas grunted in acknowledgement. Alfie sat opposite him. 'Tom, I'm leaving. I can't stand seeing you wallow in such self-pity. You don't need my help to do that anyway. You are managing quite well on your own.'

Thomas did not reply.

'It's no wonder Hannah's not gettin' better with you 'round lookin' like that. You look scraggy and unkempt. Not at all like the boy she married. She probably wouldn't even have looked at you then if you'd appeared like this.'

'Shut up, Alfie. If you're leaving, go now. Go on. Get out. No one asked you to stay.'

'Somebody did. It was you, Tom. You did the night before it all happened.' Alfie led the conversation down the channel he had been dreading. 'Conveniently put it out of your mind eh! You wanted my help then, didn't you? Wanted to make use of me when you thought I could help protect you both. Well I mucked up, didn't I?'

'Yes, you did!' Thomas jumped up and confronted him. 'In a big way. I thought I could trust you or I would never have left. You mucked up alright and I'll never forgive you, Alfie. Never!'

'Who else mucked up, Tom? It wasn't just me, was it? What about you? Who sent the boys home? Yeah, you did. Who went to tell Jack you wouldn't be in for work? Yeah, you did that too. How important was that?'

Tom shouted,' I didn't know that Marty was after Hannah. I would never have left her if I had. But you were here. You should have stopped him.'

'Well I didn't know that he was coming for Hannah either, else I wouldn'ta gone to the privy now would I?' Alfie shouted back.

'You were having a piss?' yelled Thomas incredulously.

'Yes I was. Pathetic isn't it?'

Thomas lunged at him and they both fell to the floor.

'Cripes,' thought Alfie. '*I wanted to make him angry but not this angry.*' They scrabbled around on the floor desperately trying to get the best of one another.

'Cut it out you two idiots.' It was Jack, the blacksmith. He waded into the melee and hauled the two combatants to their feet. 'Look at you both. I thought you were friends?'

Alfie's breath came in gasps. Blood poured from his nose and one eye was beginning to swell up. Thomas was in a similar condition. He stood with his hands on his knees trying to catch his breath.

'What's up with you two?' Jack asked, concern showing on his face. 'Are you mad. Hannah's in the next room. She needs peace and quiet not two oafs having a fight in her living room!'

'Don't worry about it, Jack,' Alfie puffed. 'I'm leaving. I just thought I might be able to get through to him before I went but he flew at me. Maybe he's best left in his own little world. He's not even thinking of Hannah, just of himself. Goodbye, Tom.'

'No! Wait! I....' and with that Thomas collapsed in a heap on the floor. His loud sobs almost broke Alfie's heart. Jack stopped him as he started towards him.

'Let him be, Alfie. Just let him get it all out and then, hopefully he'll talk about it. I'll come back later.'

When they were alone and Thomas had quietened down a little, Alfie said, 'I'm still going Tom. My being here will always upset you. You blame me and that's fair enough. I'll get out of your sight and you'll never see me again.'

278

'Alfie I don't want you to go. I'm hurting so much I have to blame someone. You were the only one here.'

'I know I was. But what Jenny said was true. If you think about it Marty was to blame. He was the one who set out to do that awful thing. Neither you nor I knew that he was coming for Hannah. If we had we would have planned things differently, don't you think?' Alfie reasoned.

'Sam said the same thing about it being Marty's fault. He was wicked. Wickedness is hard to fight.'

'Wicked! That's an understatement. He was evil. At least he's not around to bother you anymore.'

'Alfie,' Thomas looked at him with tears in his eyes. 'You look a mess. I'm sorry I blamed you. Hannah will hate me for blaming you. And you were right. She won't like me like this. I want her to love me always so I'd better clean myself up.'

Alfie smiled and held out his hand. 'Friends again?'

'You've always been my friend even when you were a highwayman, Alfie. I just haven't always shown it.'

***

Later that evening Thomas went outside. He sat quietly on the old rustic seat beside the back door. Bouncer nuzzled up to him.

'Whaddya reckon, old boy,' he said. Looking up at the star studded sky he picked out his favourite star, the largest one. Then for the first time he noticed a smaller star next to it and he smiled.' Look after him for me Ma.'

***

Hannah's eyes followed Thomas around the bedroom as he prepared for bed.

'I heard raised voices,' she whispered. 'Is everything alright?' Thomas turned and approached the bed. 'You've been fighting again,' she said as he knelt down and took her hands in

279

his. He kissed them gently. 'Alfie and I had a disagreement but it's alright now.' he murmured. 'I'm going to devote all my time to getting you well again, I promise. I have been so selfish. I didn't know how to help you and ended up just thinking about myself. Can you forgive me?'

'Oh Tom. We've lost so much but we still have each other.' She stroked his hair. 'We'll get through this, I know. Who knows what the future might hold for us?'

Later that night as they cuddled in bed Hannah said, 'Tom, do you think that Aisha could foretell that this was going to happen?'

'I don't think so. She couldn't have known about Marty and things were going well with the baby until then.' He looked over at the dresser where the putsi and its contents lay. 'Do you want me to get rid of it.'

'No. It is pretty and she was a nice person. I don't mind being reminded of her but I want you to promise that we'll never speak of Marty again...ever.'

'I promise,' Thomas replied and closed his eyes.

Made in the USA
Columbia, SC
15 July 2021